Innocence Derailed

Based on a True Story

Book 1 of The Spirit Quest Series

W0008354

Jane Catherine Rozek

Paperback ISBN: **978-0-9919917-4-7**
Cover images: Royalty Free @Kindle Direct Publishing

The poem 'The Hoods' was written by Yevtushenko, Yevgeny, a courageous political Soviet Russian poet who passed away in 2017. Permission for its use in the first edition of this book was given to the author on Nov. 19, 2021, by his widow Maria Novikova through correspondence with Zhenya Yevtushenko, son of Yevgeny Yevtushenko.

Scripture quotations marked (NIV) are taken from the Holy Bible, New International Version, NIV. Copyright 1973, 1978, 1984, and 2011 by Biblica Inc. used by permission of Zondervan. All right reserved worldwide. (www.zonderman.com) The NIV and New International Version are trademarks registered in the United States Patent and Trademark Office by Biblica Inc.

Author's Bio photograph: Sean Pegg

Published in Canada
Books of Life Publishing House
630 Almandine Court, Kelowna, BC, V1W 4Z5, Canada
www.booksoflifepublishinghouse.com

DISCLAIMER

Based on my true-life story, the names in this novel are changed to protect the privacy of individuals. The events themselves are represented as faithfully as possible from my perspective.

Music is an integral part of our memoires, and major influences in our lives. Certain song titles in the chapters are footnoted with YouTube links at the back of the book. For copyright reasons, the lyrics are not quoted, but by listening to this collection, you are sure to experience what I felt and be transported back in time!

ACKNOWLEDGMEMTS

My heartfelt appreciation goes to my professional editor Rebekah Antkow for her enthusiasm and support,
and to my beta-readers:
Sean Pegg, Cheryl Meier, Marianna Boda, Marilyn Kriete and Suzanne McDougal for their valuable suggestions.

FORWARD BY MARIA TRAUTMAN

Author of *After All*, Amazon #1 Best Seller for Memoir/Inner Child Category

"I have long admired Ms. Rozek's ability to write books that can keep you reading till you lose track of time. I read and immensely enjoyed The Celestial Proposal where she takes us on a spiritual adventure like no other and now, I find myself loving Innocence Derailed.

...To start, we get to know innocent Kate who is experiencing love for the first time. When Kate and Mark get together, they bring the reader back to the magic of youth. But the magic doesn't last forever, and Kate is soon disillusioned and hurt by Mark's betrayal. That takes her on a journey of discovery, and she soon gets entangled in more serious pursuits.

...Kate wonders about God. Is He guiding her and if so, how should she deal with it? Sometimes she thinks she hears God's voice in her head, advising and protecting her... Kate's faith is pure and strong, and the author portrays that faith beautifully. The story brought me to tears a couple of times, but its message is clear. Sometimes all it takes is a glimpse of goodness to make us whole."

From READER VIEWS

Kicking off the Spirit Quest series, Innocence Derailed, is a standalone coming-of-age novel based on the author's personal experiences. The story begins with fifteen-year-old Kate living in Oregon in 1968. It was at this time she felt Spirit connecting with her through brief messages. Shortly after, Kate falls in love for the first time and experiences life fully through this relationship. And while there is a great deal of joy, there are some painful, life altering experiences...

Kate launches herself out into the world on some grand adventures, journeys down into Mexico to help a friend and ends up fully immersing herself in what life has to offer there. Spirit continues reaching out to Kate with messages to help her understand the meaning behind some of the events.

Jane Catherine Rozek tells her story so vividly and heartfelt. Her friendships were so meaningful, and heartbreaks so devastating. Watching her begin to embrace her connection to spirit was wonderful.

I had similar experiences like this, and I suspect others will also relate (and) feel connected with this book on a level that goes beyond just enjoying an exceptionally written story, which this book is.

This book will be an excellent choice to share with women's readers groups, friends, and sisters. The conversations that will develop from discussing this will be amazing! I look forward to the next book in the Spirit Quest series. --Paige Lovitt for Reader Views

From *SELFPUBLISHING REVIEWS*

Young love and history mingle together in Innocence Derailed...with the Vietnam war raging on and American culture seemingly changing by the minute, young love has its own joys and sorrows. The book's basis on a true story gives the narrative a feeling of authenticity, unfolding like a rich work of fiction, rather than an embellished memoir.

Rozek's deft crafting of characters' emotions and dialogue brings the era to life, while the historical setting gives the story an enduring sense of tension for the characters, felt equally by readers.
–Editor, Self-Publishing Review

PRAISE AND REVIEWS

"With the Vietnam war raging on and American culture seemingly changing by the minute, young love has its own joys and sorrows. Rozek's deft crafting of characters' emotions and dialogue brings the era to life, while the historical setting gives tension for the characters, felt equally by readers."
Self-Publishing Review

"A lovely exploration of traveling to new countries and uncovering spirituality. I enjoyed the way you blended Kate's real-world travel alongside the journey she takes within her own heart." Allie Foxen

"This book is a delightful read. The emotion, the historical backdrop, and the ultimate journey of the main character are all designed to captivate the reader. Kate's search for love is interspersed with a depth of political history and the intrigue of a courageously lived life and makes an interesting radical story that is highly readable. Definitely recommended!"
Leigh McFarlane, The Lakeland & The Peachland Passions Series.

"*The raw beauty of this book reminds us that life is messy but exquisitely breath-taking when Spirit whispers to our soul."* J. Antkow, Books of Life

"The writing style was so captivating it brought me right into the story. I kept wanting to know what happened next." S. Pegg

DEDICATION

This book is dedicated to Rebekah, Ben, Kris,
Charlie and Keaton
who know they don't have to be perfect to be
loved,

and to Sean, who understands me so well and
loves me anyway,

and in loving memory of
MaryJo Chrisman, Mary Smith, and Krystyna
Bellamy.

*The Spirit Quest Series is also written for readers of my narrative nonfiction book, The Celestial Proposal, who want to know how in heaven I came to write the depth of it!

TABLE OF CONTENTS

Chapter   Page

INTRO

When did it all start, her search for truth, for a faith she could use as a source of power? Kate's mind skimmed back in time, the parts she endured, the parts she treasured, all so different, but all important in the quest.

There was the first day, back in 1968, when Spirit began to manifest its presence into her being. And after that came a love so strong, she still carries the embers in the back of her heart. It was the beginning of the immeasurable expanse of intensity for what was to come....

Jane Catherine Rozek

***

Chapter 1

FIRST CRAVING OF THE HEART

Kate meandered down the streets of Portland's inner city, where shabby second-hand shops elbowed each other, and old gum dotted the sidewalks. Her steel-blue eyes followed the vertical lines of the towering buildings that reached up to pierce the sky.

What would my life be like if I lived here one day? She imagined being on a rooftop, a young fledgling at the edge of the nest, poised for take-off.

Kate was fifteen and her years of living in a small eastern town in Oregon were in sharp contrast to that dingy part of the big city landscape. She meandered off alone, leaving her mom and big sister leisurely shopping for college clothes a few blocks away. She looked around and adjusted the strap on her purse, but her mousy blonde hair and faded bell-bottoms jeans melded right in with the flow of other pedestrians.

A sign propped up in a grimy window read, "Office of the Salvation Army." *Ha! That's ironic. Armies don't save people. The soldiers drafted to fight in Vietnam are trained to kill.*

That thought bothered Kate because after all it was 1966 and the war had been escalating for years. Then she stopped dead in her tracks as the weathered door of the office flew open and a strange young woman burst out onto the sidewalk. She glowed with poise and glided past with an oh-so-buoyant smile.

Kate absorbed the joy and the powerful aura radiating from the woman but where did it all come from? The young woman had on a simple T-shirt, dark jeans, and scuffed boots but worn with such artistic flair. No timidity in her presence, just bold in spirit, like she walked the earth on a glorious mission.

Her strangeness intrigued Kate in a tingling awareness. *Where does she get that boldness and confidence? Because what this girl has—is what I want.*

As if in response to her thoughts, clear and simple words whispered into Kate's conscience as the young woman disappeared down the street.

~~AN~~INVITATION~~
~~EXTENDS~~TO~~YOU~~

Kate stood on the sidewalk and looked around. No one else was nearby, so who had spoken? Had the woman issued an invitation to her…subliminally? It had seemed so real. She shook her head to clear the strange thoughts but then had to backtrack fast to the dress shop where she'd left her mom and sister.

"For heaven's sake, where did you disappear to?" Her mother was paying the clerk at the cash register for the college clothes her sister Anna had picked out.

"Didn't you find anything you liked at the store?" Anna asked.

Kate shook her head. Bourgeois fashion wasn't her thing, and she'd been bored out of her mind. Besides, the hand-me-downs from her two older sisters were what she wore, anyway. Anna was leaving home for good this September, and that would make two older sisters who left to escape their parents' constant bickering.

Kate forgot the minor scolding for her disappearance as they left the big city for the hour-long drive back up the Columbia gorge to her hometown of Hood River. She pondered the strange invitation she had received, so vivid and real, and not one that she'd ever forget. Something significant had happened. A mysterious presence of power communicated something valuable to her. But what was it? And to what was she being invited?

...

Three weeks later, on a Friday night, Kate and her two girlfriends stood on a hillside watching their school's football team play against the other high school's team in town. In the chilly autumn air, the decaying leaves of the oak trees gave off a pungent aroma.

Kate stood a little apart from her friends and admired the shimmering rainbow colors in the misty rain radiating from the fluorescent lights on the football field below. Her long hair blew around in the gusty wind. Despite being dressed in her favorite warm clothes, powerful shivers crept up her spine.

She watched the opposing teams line up again, hike the ball, and slam into each other again. Her school's team gained only a few yards toward the goalpost. She imagined the waves of movement as invisible forces of light and darkness battling against each other in the world.

Tonight, it's beginning. Kate didn't understand how she knew that, or even what it was, but then her girlfriend's animated chatter broke the spell.

"Look at those older guys over there watching the game," Leah said, nodding her head in their direction. "Aren't they dreamy?" Leah, a small, popular brunette, just became a cheerleader for the junior team. Kate's ego had been squashed when she wasn't chosen, even though she did a forward flip for the try-outs.

"Where? Oh, I see them," Joey giggled. "I want the dark-haired one, cause he's the cutest." Joey, daring and outspoken, wasn't afraid of anything. Her dark hair flowed almost to her waist. Despite the differences between her two best friends, Kate was close to them both.

"Hey, you guys, they're totally checking us out," Leah whispered. She flung her dark hair back from her wet cheeks as the wind blew their miniskirts against the black tights they wore for the cold.

"I doubt it. Those guys are probably in the senior class and too old to be interested in us." Kate was logical and more serious than her flirtatious girlfriends, but she dared to glance at the tallest guy a few yards away.

With perfect millisecond timing, he captured her gaze, pinning her for a dozen seconds. The rain, a catalyst to their instant attraction, choose to pelt down hard then. It swirled in angry gusts, whipping Kate's blonde hair across her face as the wet, noisy squall threw her back. Still, the older boy stared, locked in on Kate's face.

"Hey," Joey tugged her arm, her dark hair glistening, tangled in the wind. "Let's get out of here before we get soaked." She pointed to the nearest shelter at the school's back entrance and dashed off with Leah.

But Kate hesitated, reluctant to break the magnetic pull she felt. The guy disappeared then, behind some other spectators, moving for cover. She felt the loss, until half a minute later, he was right beside her.

"Would you like to share my umbrella?" he said, his face less than a foot away.

Kate had to take a half-step back. When she did, she noticed the tanned square set of his jaw and the warmth in his eyes. She could smell his male scent, even in the rain. Maybe it was his aftershave.

His black umbrella sheltered them from the sheets of rain and muffled the cheering fans. The football teams continued to block and tackle each other on the field below, yet Kate's reality shifted in the heat of the strange intimacy. Dusty Springfield's new song "The Look of Love" played out in her mind as if she'd turned a radio on.

"I haven't seen you around school before," he said, staring at her.

"Probably because I don't go to your high school in town here. I attend the one out in the valley." Kate struggled for composure.

"Ah, you're one of those country girls." He grinned.

She nodded and couldn't help but smile a little. "Thanks for saving me from the rain."

"It's my pleasure." He tugged at the collar on his jacket and leaned toward her to introduce himself. A cheer rang out from the crowd, and they checked to see who scored.

"Are you a sophomore or junior in school?" Mark asked after the noise quieted down.

"No, I'm a freshman," she said.

"Oh, little miss innocent," he teased. "I've got this year and one more year to go." The conversation became comfortable after that, and they cheered their rival teams on the field.

The angular planes of his face fit together in perfect proportion. His lower lip looked soft, and she drew closer to the warmth coming from his body. By the time the game had ended, most of the fans had already taken refuge from the storm, but she and Mark still stood alone, shivering from the cold.

"I'd better go find my ride." Kate drew away, but Mark was quick to take her arm. His dark eyes penetrated hers, forcing her to take a deep breath.

"When can I see you again?" he asked.

"I'm going to the teen dance tomorrow night at the Community Center." Kate was going to meet up with her friends, including Ron, who played defense on their football team. She had watched his stocky form earlier on the field, but now her interest in him had undergone a substantial change.

"You've got a date already?" he asked.

"It's not really a date." Kate had never dated anyone before.

"If I show up, will I get to dance with you?" Mark asked.

She couldn't help herself. Being enclosed in his arms and moving to the music would be ecstasy. "I think... I'd like that," she said.

Mark gave her a last slow smile in the parking lot, and she watched as he slipped through the crowd. *He probably won't be at the dance.* Still, she etched his broad shoulders into her memory, just in case.

Kate sat up in bed wide awake that night. Powerful sensations raced through her mind. Was this part of the invitation she'd been given on the street in Portland? Mark seemed perfect, which made her wonder what would happen when they saw each other again. *Why would he be interested in me? My hair is a dishwater blonde. My teeth aren't even straight.*

If this was the start of something magical, could she trust the process? Her parents had loved each other once, too. She heard them arguing in the kitchen like they always did. Her dad couldn't seem to do anything right to please her mother, and she complained about everything he did. No wonder he drank so much.

Sometimes when their quarrels reached down the hall to her bedroom, she would run out of the house and into a nearby orchard for a good cry. But tonight, something else agitated her. Talking to Mark under the umbrella still made her pulse pound fast.

...

The next night, Kate met her friends at the teen dance and the loud DJ music pulsated core deep. Ron acted like she was his date and they danced to the music in wild exuberance, but between the sets of music, Kate kept glancing at the door. An hour went by and then a young man appeared in the hall's entryway. His muscular legs were encased in faded blue jeans; his broad shoulders sported a navy-blue sweater. He stood and surveyed the crowd until the song had ended.

Was that Mark? Yes. Kate caught her breath, wondering what he would do.

Mark spotted her and walked straight to them in the middle of the dance floor. The surrounding sounds seemed to fade as he came up and tapped Ron on the shoulder.

"Would you mind if I claim Kate for this next dance?" he asked.

Ron looked at her, perplexed when she nodded her consent. "I guess not." He shrugged and walked off the dance floor.

The DJ played a slow record next called "The House of the Rising Sun." On the first chords, Mark wrapped her up in his arms and, in perfect symmetry, swept her away into the rhythm of the song.

Kate liked the confident placement of his hands, although he held her tighter than he should. She could follow his strong lead until his arm around her back drew her in an inch closer, and then another inch again. Mark's breath caressed her forehead.

They floated above the floor as the crowd receded into a blur of movement. An electrified awareness between them became stronger every minute. Kate didn't want the music to stop or the exquisite sensations. But when it did, they ended in a final flourish and grew still.

Kate's eyes were locked on Mark's. His full sensual mouth formed a lopsided smile in slow motion, causing the sexual attraction to hit her so hard she couldn't move.

He lowered his head and whispered in her ear, "What's your phone number?"

"But how will you remember it?" She was quick to give it to him anyway, and he repeated it once before Ron returned to claim her for the next dance.

Mark nodded his thanks. Then he turned and walked out through the crowd of dancers to the door without looking back.

Ron acted as if nothing had happened. She guessed for him; nothing had happened. But Kate's mind was not on dancing anymore, and the rest of the evening dragged on. Would Mark call her? Would he even remember the number she gave him?

Once Kate got home, her mind churned with anticipation. She remembered sinking into his dark brown eyes and touching the tight skin on his muscled arms.

...

The next morning, the phone rang early. Kate ran to pick it up on the second ring before her mother did. It was Mark.

"See, I remembered your number," he said. "How would you like to go for a drive with me this afternoon? Say about two o'clock?"

"You have your own car?" Kate could hardly believe Mark wanted to see her so soon.

"Yeah, and I earned the money to buy it too," Mark said with pride.

"That's pretty cool. I'd have to ask my parents and you'd have to meet them first."

"I'll put on my best manners," he said, teasing her.

Kate hung up the phone and hurried to shower and wash her hair. *I can't believe it. What if I'm not allowed to go out with him? It would be so embarrassing.*

Mark showed the right amount of maturity and manners to impress her parents when he arrived. He told them he worked at a gas station and assured them he was a conscientious driver, and with that, her parents consented to her first proper date.

Mark helped her into the car and went around to the driver's seat. When he closed his car door, it was like they were under the umbrella again, only feet apart, and she didn't know what to expect.

"That went okay with your mom and dad, didn't it?" he asked, and she agreed. He leaned over closer to her. "What shall we do now?"

"I don't know." Kate risked a nervous glance at his profile, holding her hands in her lap. "What do you want to do?"

"I can't do… what I'd like to do." He studied her with a cocky grin. "Let's just drive around. We'll act like we're tourists and explore the valley going up toward Mt Hood."

"That sounds fun. Let's pretend we're traveling in a foreign country."

Mark drove up the east side on roads she'd never been on before. They stopped at viewpoints overlooking the rolling hills of orchards and farmland. At each intersection, he'd ask which way to go, and she'd choose. As he drove, they talked about all kinds of things. They both planned to go to college; she wanted to go into social work, and he wanted to be a doctor, so grades were important to both of them.

"I wish we went to the same school so we could see each other more," he said.

"That would be better." Kate agreed, elated with his projection of a future relationship. She wondered what Mark was like at his school. Was he popular? Did he have a wild reputation? She knew so little about him.

Mark pulled over to view a beautiful farmhouse with a wide veranda. "It looks so serene with that red barn in the background. Shall we buy the place and move in?" he joked. "We could become hard-working farmers on the land."

"There is an old-fashioned peacefulness to it." Kate laughed at his roleplaying. Their real world wasn't peaceful at all.

"Do you think there'll be a third world war?" Kate worried about the young men fighting the Communists overseas in Vietnam.

"I guess anything can happen now." He rubbed his forehead. "When Kennedy got elected as president, things seemed peaceful then."

It was true. Kate remembered back in 1963 when somebody shot President Kennedy during a parade in Dallas. The entire country had reeled in shock. "The patriotic speech he made sure excited my parents when they heard it on our television set. My dad kept repeating the President's words over and over again."

"You mean the slogan they put on the billboards? 'Ask not what your country can do for you but ask what you can do for your country.'"

"Yeah, that one. My father ranted about how he'd already done a lot, but I didn't understand what he meant."

"Did he fight overseas when he was young?"

"I guess he did."

Mark's voice grew quiet. "Well, that's what he meant."

Kate had never thought of her father as a young man in uniform before. She hadn't thought about war or politics until now.

Mark brought her home in the late afternoon, and she agreed to see a movie with him the next weekend. At the door, he held her hand to his mouth and kissed her fingers. Kate couldn't wait to tell Leah and Joey about him.

Such peculiar things had been happening to her. First, the radiant young woman she saw on the city street, then that strange invitation extended into her heart. Now, this handsome hunk of a guy appeared.

Her whole life was taking off at a galloping speed, and Kate had no idea where it was going.

Chapter 2

THE PASSION OF INNOCENCE

"I can't believe Mark's even interested in me. He showed up for just one dance on Saturday night. It was a slow one too." Kate shared the details of her weekend with Leah and Joey before class on Monday morning. They always caught up with each other like that.

"Then yesterday, he asked me out for a drive, and my parents allowed it." Kate tried hard to act like it was no big deal.

"Wow, that's so cool. You going to see him again?" Joey showered her with avid attention.

"He asked me out for a movie next weekend." Kate couldn't help but let her excitement show. "And Mark is drop-dead gorgeous, isn't he?"

"He's got the looks, all right," Joey said. "Hey, I have a friend who goes to his high school. Do you want me to see what I can find out?"

"Sure, see if she knows anything about him."

"He's at least a year older than us," Leah spoke up. "I bet he could be drafted and shipped off to Vietnam to fight in a year."

Kate was sick at that thought. "No, he has one more year to go. But that's true. Some of the guys we know will be forced to enlist in the military." The draft had been in effect for a few years already. Her family always watched the six-o'clock news and heard the broadcaster give the official headcount of the number of men killed each day. They saw the airstrikes happening in North Vietnam and the gory scenes in the burned-out villages afterward.

That evening after supper, her father was relaxing in his armchair in front of the television. "Kids," he said, "come and watch this black civil rights leader. They're interviewing Martin Luther King Jr."

"Isn't he the black man who gave the 'I Have a Dream' speech on civil rights?" her mother asked.

"Yeah, that's him. He's quoting from the Declaration of Independence."

Kate listened to the words. She was starting to understand a little about world affairs from her classes in school. She learned that racial hatred still ran deep in the southern states, even though the Civil Rights Act had passed a few years ago.

"Black men and white men, both are guaranteed the unalienable rights of life, liberty, and the pursuit of happiness," Martin Luther King declared.

During the next commercial, Kate asked a question. "Do black people still have to sit in the backseat of a bus in the south?"

"Yes, and they can't go to the same restaurant as the white people or drink out of the same water fountain." Her mother's face showed her concern.

"The water fountains?" Kate asked. "How do they tell which ones they can use?"

"The government puts up signs to tell them," their father said.

"What do the signs say?" her little brother, Barry, asked.

"What does it matter what they say?" Her father voiced his belligerence.

Her mother explained it. "They have the words printed, 'For Whites Only.'"

"But that's terrible. It's against the Civil Rights laws." Kate had to speak out.

"Hush now and listen." Her mother was the peacemaker in the family.

The television screen showed Martin Luther reciting his famous speech. "I have a dream," he said and paused for dramatic emphasis, "that one day this nation will rise up and live out the true meaning of its creed... that all men are created equal."

Kate's father scrunched back in his seat. "Oh cripes, what a bunch of hogwash. I grew up in Mississippi, and the black people there are worse than our white trash. Most of them don't have a pot to piss in."

Kate didn't say anything. Her father's opinion surprised her. Martin Luther King sounded like a good preacher, like the Sunday morning sermons her mother took them to hear. She hoped her parents wouldn't argue again that night. The Selective Service didn't care about skin color. They shipped both black and white boys off to Vietnam, whether they wanted to go.

Kate watched the rest of the broadcast with her family, but her focus for the rest of the evening was off. What if Mark was drafted? Or worse, what if he wants to enlist in the armed forces to go off and fight in the war?

...

Mark sat close to Kate in the movie theater on Friday. He slid his arm around her on the back of the seat. When they sat in his car afterward, she couldn't remember much about the movie.

"I'm an outdoor kind of guy. I learned all kinds of things in Boy Scouts. How about you, Kate?" He sat sideways in the seat, looking at her.

"My father used to take us hiking in the woods where I lived as a kid. He had an aluminum boat with a motor, too. We'd camp up at Lost Lake and go fishing."

"That's cool. Hey, do you know how to ski?" He reached over to take her hand. Snow-capped Mt Hood was the tallest mountain in Oregon. Its majestic splendor could be seen year-round all over the valley, south of Hood River.

"I love to ski." Mark's thumb moved back and forth on her wrist, and the warmth of it made tingling sensations shoot up her arm.

"Good. We'll have to go skiing up on Mount Hood together."

"I took a few lessons, so I'm okay on the blue runs," she said. "I'd love to learn how to ski down the moguls, though."

"I'll be your personal ski instructor. We'll have fun together, Kate." He seemed so sure of their relationship.

"What do you think about the war in Vietnam?" she asked, wanting to know how he felt about the subject.

"I don't know. I don't follow politics much."

"But why are the armed forces over there? I bet the common peasants want Americans to mind their own business."

Mark frowned before he answered. "Our military fights to protect us from the spread of Communism."

Kate wondered how the invasion of one poor Asian country was so crucial for their country's protection. It didn't make sense. "You're not going to enlist, are you?"

"I want to, but I won't be allowed."

"Why would you want to do that?" She cocked her head, a grimace on her face.

Mark fidgeted in the driver's seat. "Well, it's my patriotic duty."

"You'd have to kill people. You might even get killed over there yourself. It would be awful." She stared at him with concern.

"Don't worry about it. I doubt they'll draft me," Mark said and squeezed her hand.

But she worried because she didn't want him to be one of those statistics reported on television.

When they were at her front door, Mark tipped her chin up and lowered his mouth to graze hers. The kiss continued ever so softly, and he finished by nibbling her bottom lip. He held her tight, which was fortunate because otherwise, she may have fainted.

...

Kate saw Mark every Saturday after that first date. He took her for walks along the Columbia River in the fall. When they went to the drive-in to watch outdoor movies, he'd tuck a warm blanket tight around them.

The ski slopes at Mount Hood Meadows opened early that winter and Mark taught Kate how to ski down the moguls. It took an effort to navigate the hard, scalloped mounds of snow on the more challenging runs, but she pushed herself to the limit, exhilarated with every success. And each time they rode the chairlift to the top, Mark gave her kisses. Hot and moist. Chapped lips against frozen chins.

Early in the New Year, Mark surprised her with a special dinner date at a swanky restaurant in Portland. Kate was nervous about dressing up for that event. Would she even know how to act?

The maître de seated them on the upper mezzanine so they could look at the other diners below them. Candles glowed on each table, giving a romantic feeling to the expansive room.

Mark sat across from her and held her gaze. "How beautiful you are. But you don't know that yet, do you?" he whispered across the table.

"I… guess not." Kate beamed at his compliment. She wore nylons and heels, and a navy-blue scooped neck dress with long sleeves was the fanciest thing in her closet. Mark's good looks were devastating. His shoulders fit snug under a dark sports jacket, and the crisp white shirt set off his brown skin tone perfectly.

"You light me up inside like the sun is shining. I'm going to call you 'Sunshine.'"

Kate smiled at that. "You look very handsome to me," she said.

The waiter approached their table in a black suit and carried a crisp white towel draped over his arm. He presented a liquor menu, but Mark nonchalantly declined since they were still underage.

Kate studied the food menu, but she couldn't decide what to order. "Some of these descriptions are in French, right?"

"Yes, my mother likes gourmet cooking and recommended the place, so I thought we'd come here." Mark helped her choose an entrée and ordered the meals for them.

Kate was trying to appear sophisticated, but she soon realized she was way out of her league. Too many forks and spoons lay beside her plate. She wondered why a tiny spoon rested above all the others. *What kind of dining etiquette was required for fancy restaurants like this?*

Mark perceived her dilemma and whispered, "Just start the first course with the outside utensil and work inward." He smiled but seemed to enjoy teasing her. "If you're still not sure what to do, wait until others start to eat from their plates and follow their lead."

Kate was embarrassed. Yet Mark was so—what was the word? Debonair. He was considerate and yet devilishly sexy at the same time. She decided she would willingly accept his instructions if he wanted to educate her.

It had been a perfect night, and this time when he kissed her at the door, his kiss was deeper, so potent with tenderness it made her dizzy. She steadied herself in his arms for a minute until he brushed his lips against her forehead and walked off to his car.

Kate had a smile on that wouldn't stop as she got ready for bed. Her mother had insisted on saying prayers with her before going to sleep. She had long ago given that up and didn't even know if she believed in the God they taught in their church.

But that night, she wrapped her arms around herself and gave thanks to whatever higher power there was for bringing Mark into her life.

...

Time flew by, and then it was spring. Mark chose an exciting hiking trail for them to explore one Saturday, and Kate brought a picnic lunch. The steep trail led up to a wild green meadow where a flock of crows cawed out warnings of their approach. Mark found a spot of dry ground. He pulled out a thin blanket from his knapsack and smoothed it out on the grass.

"I Think we're Alone Now," Mark said, referring to a new release by the Shondells. It was a cutesy melody, but Kate's heart was thumping, just like in the song.

"We'd better be careful how we play." She smiled and taunted in a soft voice.

The sun's warmth and the gentle breeze satisfied Kate more than the picnic food they munched on. After eating, Mark stretched out in luxury, and she cuddled up at his side. He broke off the tassel end of a shoot of grass and trailed it over the skin on her cheek, causing her to shiver.

When Kate looked up at him, she wanted to beg for a kiss. He always made her hungry for him that way.

"Can't take it, can you?" Mark chuckled, continuing the torture.

"No. It tickles." She had to make him stop. She rolled on top of him and tried to pin him to the ground. Mark just laughed more, and they ended up kissing like crazy.

Kate thought this must be about the strange invitation she was given; she'd been invited to be loved. Because she had never been so happy, all wrapped up in his arms on their blanket island in the meadow. Things were getting hot between them, but then the sky clouded over and drops of rain hit their skin. They had to pack up fast and hike back down the trail before the actual storm began.

...

School hours bored Kate compared to the time she spent with Mark. She got to talk about him between classes with Joey and Leah, though. They asked, of course, for the juicy details of her recent dates.

"Aren't you worried about being alone with him on your hikes in the woods?" Leah asked.

"I trust Mark with my whole heart." Kate meant it too.

"But can you trust yourself? That's the question." Joey laughed.

"You're so bad. Don't be silly," Kate threw out her words. Yet, it was kind of true. Her passion scared her. She wanted Mark's respect, but she didn't want to lose the special connection growing between them. Were his feelings for her the same?

"What did your friend at Mark's high school say about him?" Kate asked Joey.

"She told me he doesn't have a wild reputation for sleeping around, but he hangs out with some of the guys that do." Joey shrugged her shoulders.

"He seems pretty cool to me. Just take care of yourself," Leah added. She had such a kind nature.

Weeks later, on a beautiful day, Kate and Mark drove east along the grassland overlooking the Columbia River Gorge. He parked the car on the side of the gravel road where there was a panoramic view. They got out and strolled along the edge of the cliff until they found the perfect spot to picnic.

The sun was a scorcher that day, and Mark pulled off his t-shirt. Kate rolled up her shorts even shorter. They chatted about their lives and dared to share dreams for the future.

Mark chuckled. "Hold still. Let me look at your face in the sunlight."

"Oh no, do I have a zit or something?" she asked. They were so relaxed with each other.

"Not you, ever. But you have tiny peach fuzz on your cheeks that I haven't noticed before." Kate squirmed away from his inspection, but he held her down on the blanket. He laughed hard, and the lines around the corner of his eyes deepened.

"You remind me of a thoroughbred colt. And you have the cutest littlest ears I've ever seen." Kate quit trying to get away. His mouth moved to the beads of sweat on her neck. He nipped at one ear.

Mark's kisses landed on Kate's breast as he nuzzled her T-shirt lower. Without warning, his face jumped to her waist and his kisses lingered there. He moved down and grazed the soft inner skin on her thighs, and then worked his magic all the way to her ankles.

Kate lay there, quivering, undone by a swirl of emotions.

Mark raised his head and noticed her agitation. "Don't be afraid," he said, trying to reassure her.

Oh, how she wanted his body on top of her. She ached for him. Surely, he must feel it, too.

But then he stood abruptly and pulled her up to stand beside him. For a while, they looked out over the spectacular view of the gorge and just breathed.

Kate's heart slowed down enough for her to think again.

My God, if falling in love is like this, it's sure is powerful.

Chapter 3

DOWN THE ROAD OF NO RETURN

Leah sat next to Kate in algebra class and waved her hand. "Yo, Kate, what's wrong?"

She mouthed the words in exaggeration as their math instructor scribbled equations on the board. The gray-haired teacher showed no patience for distractions from the life-saving mathematical formulas he tried to impart to them.

"I'm fine," Kate whispered. She had already told Leah about her last date with Mark, just not the intensity of her emotions.

"Love, sweet love." Leah touched her heart, whispering it behind the teacher's back.

Kate grinned. Perhaps Mark sat at a similar desk at his school, as bored as she was. She glanced at her classmates. Stanley fidgeted with a pen that didn't work, and baby-faced Michael had his eyes glued to the board like a mad scientist. The boys in her class seemed juvenile to her.

Kate pictured Mark. She imagined his finger lifting her chin for a kiss. Did he yearn for that, too? He knew how to arouse her, that was for sure. Was it because he had experiences with other girls?

Her mind spun in crazy circles. She wanted him to touch her in off-limit places, yet she feared it at the same time. Does he care for me, for real? Or is he seducing me just to have sex? Kate spent the next hour trying to find clues to his intentions, but by the end of class, she still had no answer.

...

It wasn't only Kate's inner world in turmoil that April. The news on every television channel was troubling. Someone assassinated Martin Luther King Jr in Tennessee. But now, the footage of his speeches came with a negative political slant because he opposed the draft and dared to speak out against his country. He said the government had created the Vietnam conflict itself by spewing out propaganda against Communism. He claimed the US was responsible for most of the violence in the world.

Kate figured that was why he got assassinated. Yet wasn't freedom of speech one of the great constitutional rights for every citizen in a democracy.

The newscaster quoted one of Martin Luther King's statements, and it seared into Kate's mind, molding her personal political stance. "There comes a time when one must take a position that is neither safe, nor political, nor popular, but he must take it because his conscience tells him it is right."

Huge demonstrations of university students protested the draft. They chanted, "Hell no. We won't go," and Kate knew why the young men didn't want to go. They'd be forced to kill people. She lived in an age of rebellion, and this political dissent filtered down into her everyday life.

At her high school one day, the boys in the senior gym class refused to do extra laps around the football field, yelling the same thing, "Hell, no. We won't go." They had to stay after class for an extra twenty minutes, but most of the guys thought it was worth it.

...

When Kate was with Mark, she didn't concern herself with the state of the world. He called her every other day, and each call made her light-headed and breathless.

"Hey Sunshine, I found a neat sandy beach I want to show you. Let's go for a swim on Saturday."

"It sounds fun, but isn't the weather still too cold?"

"I'll keep you warm."

"Mark!" Her objection was light-hearted.

"Let's do a picnic then. I bet we can find a warm spot out of the wind and sunbathe at least."

"Okay, let's try it." She'd follow him anywhere he wanted.

Kate and Mark hiked along the shore of the Columbia River until they found the perfect private beach. An old, weathered log became one wall, and the surrounding bushes created the other walls for a virtual room of their own. They spread the blanket down in the sandy hollow to protect them from the river's cool breeze.

Kate opened the picnic hamper and took out roast beef sandwiches, the brownie squares she had made the day before, and two large granny smith apples. She wondered why food always tasted so delicious out in nature.

The sun's rays were strong, and after they devoured their picnic, she and Mark stripped off their jeans and thick sweatshirts to let the sun warm their pale winter skin. They talked for a while, and Kate closed her eyes to daydream in the serenity of their surroundings. She zoomed up into the sky in her mind and pretended to be a bird looking down on them.

Two bodies stretched out, side by side. One wore a pink two-piece. This bright color and the young man's green swim trunks contrasted against the grayness of the blanket and sand. They looked good together from up there. The spring's toasty warmth soothed her, and she listened to the gentle rumble of the river in the background. Sandpipers squawked close by and pierced the silence off and on.

Mark rubbed tanning lotion on her back, and she sighed at the touch of his hands. Each caress heightened her senses, melting her body into the ground. Heat built up deep inside her and made her arch her back in response. She rolled over to face him and touched his chest. Was his heart beating as fast as hers?

Mark's words came out in a whisper. "I think I'm in love with you, Kate." He said and waited for her reaction.

"I'm glad, Mark." She should tell him she loved him too, but she wondered if he had said these same words to anybody else.

Mark took her lips in his. His hand slid under her bra and discovered a taut, round nipple. Kate experienced an unfamiliar physical ache that startled her, and she wanted… she didn't know what she wanted.

"No, Mark," she struggled to stand up and broke the spell. "Come on, let's go explore the shoreline."

Mark stood up with awkwardness and threw back his shoulders to take a breath. She took his hand, and they wandered along the riverbank. He tried to climb a limbless tree, and she chased the sandpipers while they laughed at each other's childish antics.

...

Kate tried hard to focus on her evening homework, but the television in the living room distracted her. It wasn't only that. School would be over in less than a month, and she would have all summer to go out with Mark. Her father seemed to read her mind when she glided past him to the kitchen in a cloud of bliss.

"You're seeing a lot of that young man of yours, Katie." Her father stated the obvious.

"I know, Dad. I like him a lot." Kate's parents struggled with their own problems and took little notice of her. But they seemed to approve of Mark, perhaps because their daytime hikes out in nature seemed so wholesome. Kate was heading to her room when her father shouted from the living room.

"Somebody shot another Kennedy."

"What do you mean?" Kate asked, seeing her dad shake his head in dismay. She remembered the family's shock when someone assassinated President Kennedy.

"They shot senator Robert Kennedy, just like his brother."

"But who did it? Why did it happen again, Dad?" It was eerie, another political murder in the news.

Her father couldn't explain it and shook his head. "I don't understand it either, Katie." The news broadcast offered no concrete answer to why two brothers high in the political scene got mysteriously snuffed out. Who was behind these assassinations?

Within a day or two, the media coverage ended. It seemed everybody was used to politicians getting assassinated. Kate counted them up. First, someone shot President Kennedy right beside his wife in the parade. Next, the black militant leader, Malcolm X, got shot on stage while he was speaking. Then Martin Luther, the peaceful black leader everyone respected, got murdered. Now JFK's brother, Bobby Kennedy, was killed. That added up to four assassinations in five years. The facts jolted Kate. *This isn't right. My country is supposed to be a democracy.*

But was it? Kate lay on her bed and stared at the ceiling. The government forced innocent boys to be drafted which forced them to kill or be killed in a war that made no sense. She closed her eyes to push away the world's problems. She had better things to think about. As her mind turned back to Mark, she snuggled into her cloud of bliss once again, expelling a contented sigh.

...

Kate's first job was working part-time at the corner café to earn money for college. Of course, she was going; her sisters both went, and her parents took pride in that. The waitressing job taught her to move fast and stay pleasant even when she didn't feel like it. She hated faking a cheerful social persona to earn extra tip money. It felt so false. But she and Mark both had jobs, and that was part of maturity.

"Want to go to the drive-in movies on Saturday night?" Mark asked on their Wednesday night phone call.

"Of course." Kate stretched out on the blue shag carpet in her bedroom and pulled the kinks out of the phone cord in her hand.

"Okay, I'll pick you up after I get off work."

"What's showing?"

"I don't know. Does it matter?"

"I guess not." Kate laughed and already, she anticipated the thrill of making out when they snuggled in his car. They'd had a few dates at the drive-in theater where even the windows got steamed up. They didn't care if it rained. Each date gave her a bigger rush than the last one. He touched her in places his hands shouldn't be, but it was so pleasurable she didn't want him to quit. Kate knew it wasn't proper and resolved to let him go only so far.

A few weeks later, Mark called her on the phone. "My parents want to meet the girl I'm dating so often."

Kate's voice came out soft. "Oh. But what if they don't like me?"

"Sunshine, what's not to like about you?" Mark teased. "Maybe you should cut that little wart off your chin before the visit, though?"

"That's not funny, Mark. I'm nervous."

He took her to his house to meet his parents on Saturday morning. His well-dressed mother bustled around in their fancy kitchen, making something special from the looks of the unfamiliar ingredients on the counter.

His father stood up from reading the paper at the table, and when he smiled, it was the way Mark smiled. Kate became more at ease after noticing that. She liked their upper-class casualness and the warmth they showed her.

Mark seemed satisfied after they left the house. "They liked you. I could tell."

"It seemed like they accepted our status as a couple, anyway," Kate said, leaning in for his kiss.

...

The summer months whizzed by, and Kate's world revolved around Mark; their friendship, the respect he showed, and his gentle touch made her swoon with love for him.

She often listened to the radio in her bedroom. When Peggy Lee came out with a new song called "Fever," Kate got up and danced around the room because that's what she and Mark had. The time they spent together was always fever-pitched, and that was her dilemma. *What am I going to do if he wants to go all the way? If I say no, will he find another girlfriend?*

One warm summer evening after going to the drive-in, Kate and Mark spread out a blanket in a soft meadow, way off on the side of a gravel road, to watch for shooting stars in the dark sky. The moon's light shone bright enough to see an intense eagerness on his face, yet there was hesitancy too.

"We're going to celebrate tonight," Mark said. He brought out two small crystal glasses and opened a bottle of cherry brandy. He poured only a small amount into each glass and put the bottle away. They clinked their glasses together.

"To us. to the future," Mark spoke the words as a benediction. Alone in the moonlight in the middle of the night, the darkness surrounded them like velvet. Sipping on the strong sweet ambrosia caused their talk to turn to silly things.

"Your hair looks like spun gold in this moonlight, like Rapunzel in the fairy tale."

His description thrilled Kate. She had always thought her hair was a mousy color. "I created it that way on my spinning wheel… just for you," she said.

"Do you hear the crickets?" He peered into the night's stillness.

"Yes, they sound pretty."

"They're serenading us."

"No, they're not… they don't realize we're even here."

"Those crickets know. They're hiding under the rocks all around us. The closest one is peeking out at you right now," he teased.

Kate and Mark finished their drinks. She relaxed with Mark's arms around her in almost a mystical connection. His hands swept the entire length of her body, and when he kissed her ear, his breath felt warm and moist. Kate cuddled up against his chest and smelled his Old Spice aftershave. She breathed it in and kissed his chin. She had so much love for him.

Mark lifted her blouse and cupped her breasts under the fabric of her bra. Every part of her body seemed to yield to him. He eased her flat on the ground and unzipped her jeans, sliding his fingers down to touch the fine skin below her belly.

Oh no. That drives me crazy. But she wanted it, almost needed it.

They had engaged in that electrical current before, and it was deliciously intoxicating. But Kate's moral standards had always held to these preset boundaries.

Tonight, Mark pushed his hand farther down and finger-played her where it was warmer. Kate quivered. She couldn't control her body from thrashing upward. She yearned to give herself to him like an unwrapped present. And she could. No, she would! There was no more hesitancy in her mind. That night, the only thing that would satisfy her long-awaited hunger was the real thing.

"I need to see you," he whispered. "Let me take your blouse off."

Kate nodded because she couldn't put words together in a coherent sentence right then. She helped him lift the material over her head, and then he unclasped her bra with dexterity. Now exposed halfway down, Mark's whistling sigh was a beautiful compliment and dissolved all her inhibitions.

"You're so lovely, Kate." He lowered his face and put his mouth on one breast and then the other, causing odd, exquisite sensations. She shuddered as he lingered there for a while. Then his kisses trailed down to her waist where her jeans gaped open. Kate's breath caught in her throat.

Mark stopped. He raised his head. With his eyes full of love, he asked the silent question.

"Yes," Kate said breathlessly, and it was such a bold word for her to say, not knowing what came next.

He stood up, removed his shirt, and threw it aside. Then he tugged off her jeans and dropped his own.

Kate saw his erection against the faint moonlight before joining her on the blanket again. He wriggled her panties down, so she was completely naked. She could feel the full, warm length of him, his chest on top of hers, and that part of him hard between her legs. Kate panicked. Sanity returned for a second, and she struggled to push him away.

"Wait. Mark, wait. It's not safe. What if…"

She jerked up and squirmed. Mark stopped her with a passionate kiss and dug a condom out of the pocket of his nearby jeans. She watched wide-eyed as he put it on.

Then he leaned over her. "This might hurt a little, Kate, but it'll be good."

Spellbound, she nodded. Their love was so strong, and she wanted him with all her heart. Yet when he tried to slip it in, she thought it couldn't possibly fit. *I'm not big enough for him!*

But Mark paused on entry for a few seconds. He kissed her mouth, his breath sweeping across her cheek until her insides expanded enough to hold him. He pushed in further.

It hurt. A lot. She whimpered, and Mark stopped moving inside her. The pain eased, and then it felt wet and smooth. She opened to him as Mark carefully slid in deeper. Moving slowly, shuddering and moaning, he seemed to fight for control.

Mark thrust deep in and out, and her sensations grew unbearably sweet, but they kept climbing. He moved faster, creating white-hot passion and desperate need. And faster still, until out of control, she called out his name. There, on the pinnacle of desire, they became one entity in strange, wonderful sensations Kate had never experienced before.

The tension drained from their limbs as she and Mark took in big draughts of air. Kate imagined them tumbling off a mountain and down the other side, wrapped up together, falling ledge after ledge until they bottomed out, exhausted. Reality came back into focus, and the stars twinkled above them once again. Kate heard the noise the meadow crickets made, or had they been chirping all along?

Mark rolled off and took care of the condom. "It was okay, then? I didn't hurt you too much?" Loving concern exuded from his voice.

Kate leaned up against her elbows, still panting, but she couldn't stop the serene smile from spreading across her face. "There was some pain, yes. But it felt so good too, all at the same time."

"It was perfect," he said simply.

"I never dreamed it would be like this." The sexual ecstasy stirred her belief in all things good and pure. It made her heart explode with love, and she would always want it. She had touched a slice of heaven and would never be the same. But then that thought shocked her. Because she had carnal knowledge and was not a virgin anymore. She had given that gift to him, betraying her Christian upbringing. They weren't married or even engaged, so sex was wrong according to what the church taught. But how come it seemed so right?

Kate put away her thoughts for later, and they hugged each other, standing up naked, unabashed in the cool air.

"You're gorgeous," he said, caressing her like she was the loveliest thing on the planet. "I love you, Kate."

"I love you too, Mark." At last, she said the words, and she meant them, too, in this evening of perfection. "Hey, look, you can see our shadows in the light from the moon." Kate stepped away and did a little dance.

And still naked, they chased each other's moon shadows around the meadow, just like little kids, laughing in the glory of it all.

Chapter 4

THE MAGIC OF LOVE

At sixteen, Kate was in a blissful state of love. Her life was complete. She and Mark would be going back to school that September; he for his senior year, and she with two more years to go, but they had a future together.

Gordon Lightfoot sang "The First Time Ever I Saw Your Face" on the radio while she was doing homework one evening. She cried at the beauty of it. The first time she saw Mark's face was under the umbrella at the football game, but now she imagined romantic proposals, engagement rings, and the wedding dress she would wear one day.

Kate woke up at five-thirty the next morning with the scent of dewy green grass drifting in through her bedroom window. She hurried to dress in cutoffs, a T-shirt, and her Doc Martin boots. It was a glorious morning for a stroll down her country road. The sun hadn't yet peeked above the horizon, and only a few cars passed her.

She walked halfway to town, keyed up with amazing energy, and decided to walk to Mark's house. But when she arrived, nobody was up yet. She stood outside the old two-story character home with its stone foundation. What should she do?

She couldn't ring the doorbell this early in the morning and wake up his parents, so she picked up tiny pebbles from the ground and gently tossed them at Mark's upstairs window. She stopped and waited.

Mark appeared in his plaid pajamas with his hair tousled from sleep and slid up the window. "Can't wait to see me today, huh?" he said with a grin.

"Come out and go for a walk with me!" Kate stretched her arms wide to embrace the fresh morning air.

"Sh." Mark held his finger to his lips and pointed to the neighbor's house. He danced a few steps to show off and motioned that he'd be down in a minute. She and Mark always did spontaneous things. When they walked around town, he would pick flowers for her or challenge her to a race to the corner. And each time he pulled her into his arms for an unexpected kiss, her heart melted.

Months flew by and life was busy with school, homework, part-time job, and Mark on the weekends. The only thing Kate didn't like was working at her greasy spoon restaurant job.

"You don't have to stay there, Kate. You can apply to other businesses in town." Mark encouraged her; he believed in her.

Kate got brave, typed up a proper resume, and applied for a job at the local drugstore. The interview went well, but it was a surprise when they contacted her a week later. Kate's new boss, Joanna, was a gracious older woman. At the beauty counter, she explained the use of cosmetic creams as if they were aphrodisiac love potions.

"You must put on moisturizer every night, even if you think you don't need it at your age. That way. it'll be a long time before you notice wrinkle lines around those pretty blue eyes of yours."

"But these products are expensive, and I'm saving money for college."

"Oh, honey, good skincare doesn't require expensive products. Here's a secret. Noxzema and baby oil work almost as well." Right then, Kate knew she would like her boss.

Mr. Bertram was an older pharmacist and friendly in the quiet atmosphere of the shop. When business became slow, he asked her questions as if she alone represented the younger generation. "So, this handsome boy you like, will he enlist in the military when he graduates?"

"I don't think so," Kate said.

"Young people ought to fight in the Vietnam War, serve their country with pride."

Kate didn't know how to disagree. "Is it fair for half a million troops to invade one small Asian country?" she asked instead.

A frown crossed Mr. Bertram's face. "Those patriotic boys are protecting us from Communism."

Kate thought of how the Vietnamese people might view the US invasion. "Last night on the news, they said the Viet Cong killed over five hundred soldiers last week."

The pharmacist nodded. "And that's a genuine tragedy, all right. But I guess your young man won't have much of a choice if he's drafted."

An icy shiver ran up Kate's back. Mark would face the draft soon. She had to talk to him about this.

"Unless, well, you heard about Muhammad Ali?" Mr. Bertram asked.

"The famous black boxer who wins all his matches?"

"Yes, he refused his induction notice, and the army sentenced him to five years in jail. It ruined his career."

Her discussion with the pharmacist worried Kate. Mark called her as usual on Wednesday night.

"Hi, Sunshine, what's new with you?"

"Not much. My father's been talking about how they're still bombing North Vietnam. How long can it last, I wonder?"

"If Richard Nixon gets elected president, we're in it for the long haul. My parents say he's a political hawk."

Kate picked her words, hoping to get his perspective. "It's so sad and scary at the same time. I hope you don't get drafted."

"I can't do anything about it," he said, and was quick to change the subject.

...

Mark traded his old car in for an antique 1949 Nash Ambassador that late summer and showed it off to her. The rear of the vehicle looked like a dark green frog to Kate, although she'd never tell him that.

"See, there isn't a scratch on it, and the dashboard has real leather," Mark said. "And guess what? The seat in the back actually folds down into a bed. I bought this car for us!"

"Well, that's suggestive." Kate rolled her eyes with a shy grin.

"A guy needs to think ahead and prepare for cold weather, doesn't he?"

Kate had to admit, at the drive-in movies, the back seat of this car would be comfortable to stretch out in. But for privacy and parking somewhere after a date, it would be dangerously seductive.

Mark's family owned a few acres of vacant property off one of the country roads in the valley. They drove up there one night, and he opened the old wooden gate with a copy of his father's key. After going through, he stepped back out of the car to lock the gate again before driving to the top of the hill. There, in the privacy of their backseat-bedroom-on-wheels, their lovemaking became magical.

Kate no longer talked about her sexual escapades with her girlfriends. They weren't going steady with anyone and didn't know what it was really like. Mark didn't seem to have any close friends to share details with, either. They lived in their own private world. *We have something rare and wonderful. This kind of love will last forever, won't it?*

...

In Kate's political science class that fall, she tried to make sense of the country's turmoil. Lyndon Johnson didn't run for his second term for the presidency, and Richard Nixon got elected. Kate's worry about Mark's draft status grew obsessive. In the past, wealthy families arranged their son's exemptions by sending them to college, so only the underprivileged boys were sent off to the battlefield. It wasn't fair, but Kate wondered how much wealth Mark's family had.

In December, the public put intense pressure on the government to change the draft laws, and a fair lottery system went into effect, activated only by random selection. So, if a guy was born before 1950, his draft number could be drawn, and he'd be drafted. Mark was eighteen. He was eligible.

Kate called him on the phone. "I read in the newspaper you have to register for the draft within three months of turning eighteen."

"Yeah, I already registered."

"Oh," Kate took a breath. "Have you heard from the Selective Service?"

"Nah, I don't think I'll be drafted."

"But they might draw your draft number anytime. Aren't you worried about it?" Kate was panicking. It would devastate her if they pulled his name.

"I don't want to talk about it," he said.

"But Mark…"

"Hey, let's go skiing this Saturday. You want to drive up to the mountain with me?"

"Of course, we have so much fun," she said.

...

Mount Hood was Oregon's famous year-round snow-capped mountain with two ski resorts on it. The trees were loaded with sparkling snow, and the mile-high run above Timberline Lodge matched the height of her enthusiasm. Each time she swished to a stop on the slope, she shrieked with exuberance.

Mark suggested special plans for this ski trip. Kate told her mother she would spend the night with Leah after skiing. But instead, she and Mark went winter camping.

He locked their skis in his car at dusk and slung on their backpacks to hike over the slopes, away from the lights of the ski lodge. Still, the yellow glow filtered through the trees with a mystical ambiance as her vision adjusted to the dark, frozen landscape.

She helped Mark pitch the nylon tent he'd brought, and since there was only frosty snow to sink the tent pegs in, they tied the four corners of the tent to stunted alpine trees.

Inside their little fabric home, Mark unrolled two foam mats and a sizeable down-filled sleeping bag. Off came their ski boots, parkas, and pants, right down to their long-johns. Kate's teeth chattered until they climbed into each other's arms. Then they slept in toasty warmth, while Mount Hood's massive white peak stood over them.

...

Those winter months of courtship bonded them even more. In the spring, Kate still worked part-time at the pharmacy, and Mark did his hours at the gas station. Both sets of parents seemed to accept the seriousness of their relationship.

"Mom, Mark invited me to go to his prom! What should I wear?" Kate asked.

"That's nice, dear. Anna's or Sherry's old dance dresses might fit you. They're in the laundry room closet."

Kate looked, but between the yellow Cinderella chiffon and the pale blue organza with frayed straps, she wouldn't be caught dead in either of them. She joined her mother in the kitchen.

"I was thinking I could spend some of my college savings to buy a new formal for the dance. I want to look my best. This is Mark's last prom, and I'll be meeting all of his friends."

"Hmm, that is special. Why don't you and I drive to Portland on Saturday and have a shopping day together?"

"Just you and me? That sounds cool." Kate had never spent a whole day alone with her mother before.

At the Lloyd Center, Kate tried on dress after dress at different stores. They were all either cheap-looking or too expensive. After hours of searching, she tried on a deep purple gown and fell in love with its elegance. It had an empire waist and a long, straight skirt that fit her to perfection. Best of all, the fabric was soft velvet, like tummy fur on a kitten.

Her mother frowned at her in the full-length mirror. "Oh, dear," she said. "That style is too mature for you, Katie."

"But it looks sophisticated. It's perfect. And look, it's twenty-five percent off." She twirled to check out the back of the gown in the mirror.

"Well, I guess if you wear long white gloves to conceal your bare arms, the dress certainly would be stunning. It's your money, dear."

Kate thought the gloves would be overkill, but she would go along with her mom's suggestion just to get the dress.

On the night of the long-awaited dance, Mark brought her an orchid corsage, and his eyes lit up when he saw her. He stepped in close to pin it on her dress. She did the same with the yellow rosebud she had purchased for his lapel. Mark looked mature and handsome.

The prom decorations in the gym had an old-fashioned romantic theme. Kate felt like a celebrity when Mark's friends came over and he introduced them. "Wow! You guys look good together," one of them said.

Kate and Mark danced all the slow dances as though glued together. They showed off for everybody on the fast ones. A hired photographer took professional pictures of them that Kate would cherish. The evening of Mark's prom ended in his car behind the closed gate, with Kate's high heels on the dashboard and her dress draped over the steering wheel. The touch of his hands through her nylons was exquisite until they too, came off. Their lovemaking was always powerful and this time, in the glow of the aftermath, they discussed living their lives together, forever in love.

...

In the outside world, the number one topic was still the Vietnam War and Mark refused to discuss it. Kate needed to know how they could plan their future when the draft hung over his head? "Did the Selective Services contact you yet?" she asked a few days later.

"Yes, I got assigned a draft number," he sighed, but the look he gave her was peculiar.

"You did? You didn't tell me. That's terrible. The draft board could call you at any time." Kate was rattled.

"No, it's not terrible." He stared off into space. "Kate, I can't be drafted. I can't even enlist."

"But why not? Why wouldn't they want you?"

"Because I have a physical condition that makes me exempt. I can't hear from my right ear." He looked embarrassed.

Kate hadn't noticed the hearing loss, but when she thought about it; he sometimes cocked his head to one side when he listened to her. She found the habit endearing. "I didn't know. I'm sorry," she said. "But I'm thankful it will keep you out of Vietnam."

Had he known all along? "Why didn't you tell me before?" she asked.

"I don't know. Guess I didn't want you to think I was handicapped."

"Oh, Mark, you're perfect in every way. I've just been so worried." Kate let out a huge sigh; he would not be going off to war. She would not be left behind, wondering if he would ever return.

"You don't think I'm less of…."

"Absolutely not." Kate hurled herself at him, smothering his neck with kisses. The war in Vietnam couldn't touch them now.

Yet Kate's joy was short-lived. September was coming, and all too soon Mark would go off to college, leaving her alone back in their hometown. Kate had to resign herself to the separation with occasional weekend visits.

But then a far more serious problem arose.

Chapter 5

THE WAKEUP CALL

Kate's period was late. Real late. She couldn't believe it was happening. *We've been careful, and Mark uses condoms. This can't be happening.*

Kate appealed to God, to Jesus, and whatever angelic cosmic power that might listen, but each day, her panic grew. She went for long hikes up in the hills past the orchards until she was panting with sweat, hoping to bring on her period. She rode her old bike down the bumpiest trails she could find. Every day, she prayed to see a bit of blood on her underwear, but nothing happened. *What will Mark say? How will I tell him?*

Mark seemed to sense her distance the next time she visited him. They sat in his living room on the couch, sipping Cokes for a while since his parents weren't home. Kate was quiet. She couldn't fake the natural camaraderie they usually had together.

"Hey, where's my sunshine girl?" he asked, pulling her up off the couch.

She remained quiet. She didn't know how to bring up the subject.

"What's happening in that pretty little head of yours?"

"I don't know how to say it." She stood close to him and yet felt so alone.

"What's wrong? Did I do something?"

"No. Yes, but…" And then, as if only she alone carried the shame, Kate spoke the words every unwed woman of her generation dreaded to say. "I think I'm pregnant."

His eyes bore into hers. Then he whispered. "Are you sure? How late are you?"

"It's been three weeks." Kate dropped her gaze. "And I chart my periods every month. I didn't want to tell you."

Mark just stood there. Then he held her, rocking back and forth in silence for a minute. "How could you be pregnant?" he whispered. "I used a condom. I always put one on."

"But a couple of nights, it was messy." Kate whimpered, choking back her tears.

Still holding her, he paused to think. "Don't cry; we'll figure this out."

"Mark, if I'm pregnant, I wouldn't want an abortion."

"It would be easy, though. There are doctors who can help with this problem."

"No, I've thought about it. I can't do that." Kate wondered where her resolve had come from.

"You don't know for sure if you're pregnant yet, do you? Maybe you've stressed yourself out by worrying, and that's why your period is late."

"I've never been late before."

He rubbed her back for a minute. Then he kissed her forehead, and his comforting arms enclosed her.

"If you're pregnant, I won't let you handle this alone." Mark drew apart to face her, revealing his lop-sided smile. "I feel weird about all this."

"What do you mean?" She faced him head-on. Fear of his rejection hit her hard.

"I'm sort of proud of myself. Isn't that funny?"

Kate smiled through her tears. "No, it's beautiful," she cried. "Our love created something together."

"I'll stand by you, Kate; I love you. If that's what you want."

Kate's heart melted. How could she saddle this on him? "But how would we even take care of a baby, Mark? We're too young to be parents."

"Let's wait for another week or two and see what happens. You probably just missed a period, and there's nothing to worry about."

...

Kate panicked when three weeks late turned into four. Young and unmarried, she wouldn't be allowed to go to high school. She'd have to drop out when her pregnancy showed, and how disgraced her parents would be. Kate didn't pray very often, but now she sent up a fervent one, asking Jesus to allow her own blood to flow.

For the first time, Kate considered the sex they had enjoyed might be wrong, a sin with inevitable consequences. She believed they loved each other, and lovemaking with Mark was fantastic. So why the dreadful panic? Shouldn't they be celebrating what their love had conceived? But Mark never asked her to marry him. He could walk away at any time.

She had to make a doctor's appointment to find out if she was pregnant or not. And if she was, there was no one else Kate could turn to but God. He was supposed to help those in trouble, right? Maybe she better believe in him.

Dear God, please do this for me. Don't let this happen. Make my period start tomorrow!

...

The long weekend was coming up. Her family planned to drive to Seattle to visit her oldest sister, Sherry, and her husband. It was a family trip planned months before, and Kate had to go. Her other sister, Anna, home from the university, and her younger brother, Barry, would all be squished up in the back seat of the family car.

Kate had to put her worries on hold. Did she dare talk to Anna about her situation? How was she going to tell any of them she was pregnant? Anna and Sherry didn't have babies yet; Kate would be the first of her sisters to have one.

The trip to Seattle took six hours, but at last they were there and greeted Sherry with hugs. She and Anna were going to sleep in the attic, and Kate thought it would be fun. A set of steep stairs ran up to a long narrow room with dormer windows on each end, overlooking the yard.

That night Anna talked about her college life. Kate told her about their father's drinking and how it was still causing havoc at home. She wanted to talk about being pregnant, but her sister fell asleep before she had the chance.

Kate lay awake, massaging her flat belly, and considered her predicament. If she was carrying their child, perhaps Mark could get a job somewhere after graduating from high school, but would he want to do that? Would she be able to finish her schooling at home?

It would be tough to have a baby, but not impossible. And if she had to do it alone, she would. There was no other choice. A surge of adrenaline went through her. *What would it be like to hold a child of my own? Would it look like Mark? Would it look like me?*

No, wait. Kate corrected herself. *It isn't an 'it'. Our baby would be a little boy or girl!*

Despite Kate's growing anxiety, her family had plans for the next morning. They were going to tour the spectacular new Space Needle built for the World's Fair. Anna dressed early, eager to go downstairs. Kate moved slower. Her head was full of private thoughts. She pushed her concerns to the back of her mind, determined to enjoy the family outing. After dressing, she spent a few moments looking out the window, dreaming of possibilities.

"Katie, we're going to go now. Are you ready?" Anna hollered up the attic stairs.

"Okay, I'm coming." Kate found her purse, grabbed her shoes, and started down the narrow stairwell. On the second step, her stocking feet slipped. Her right shoulder bounced against the wall. Her bum hit the next step, hard. Then she tumbled and crashed against the other side, going way too fast to brace herself anywhere. At the bottom of the stairs, she lay in a heap.

Oh... Ouch. Dazed, Kate stretched her limbs and found no broken bones, but between her legs, blood gushed out.

My period now? Kate squealed in alarm.

The bathroom door stood open on her right. She crawled through, locked the door, and barely made it to the toilet in time. Great big clots of blood plopped into the water. Then she realized she had been pregnant, but she wasn't going to be.

Kate's shock turned to joy at not being pregnant. Then her emotions flipped and morphed into grief—for not being pregnant. The facts sank in. She had been carrying the early stages of a tiny person, part of Mark and part of herself. Now she was losing that precious little embryo. She had prayed for this to happen and now she was having a miscarriage.

Sadness engulfed her in waves. She turned and looked into the bowl of water, staring at the clots of blood as if she might see a tiny human tadpole caught up in the red tissue. The awe and the tragedy mixed as intense pain cramped her stomach again. She cried her anguish without a sound. How long would this go on? What if the bleeding didn't slow down?

Anna came back into the house and shouted through the door. "Mom's wondering where you are, Katie. Everybody's in the car waiting for you."

"Ah… I'll be out in a few minutes," Kate yelled back.

Excruciating cramps continued to twist her insides, but the clots she passed were getting smaller. She couldn't stay on that commode forever. Her mom came and rapped on the door, and Kate sat up straight.

"Are you okay in there? What's wrong with you? You've been in there for a long time."

"I'm not feeling so good." She flushed the red water away again.

"Is it something you ate? Have you been throwing up?"

"No."

"Do you have stomach cramps or diarrhea?"

"Kind of." She gritted her teeth as a fresh wave of pain gripped her inside. "I should be done soon."

Her mother sighed in exasperation as she walked away.

Kate cried alone in silent despair. Shielding the leakage with gobs of toilet paper, she searched the drawers and the cabinet under the sink. Yes, there was a box of large sanitary napkins. She discovered safety pins in the top drawer and secured four pads together. She washed out her panties, the spots on her jeans, and dried them with a towel. *Okay, this is just going to be a horrible period. I'll get through it.*

Kate flushed the toilet once more and cleaned off the floor. She figured there wasn't any evidence at the bottom steps where she had landed, or someone would have noticed already. She washed her hands, stuffed more napkins into her pockets, and listened for noise outside the door.

Only then did she realized no one needed to know about the miscarriage. She didn't have to say anything to her family. She didn't need to share this with Joey and Leah, or anybody. It would be a solitary, private incident in her life. *And isn't this precisely what I asked for from God? My prayers; are they that powerful?*

She had lost a baby, created out of beautiful, intimate moments shared with Mark. But instead of being relieved, sorrow permeated her to the core. She lost a child that no one but her would ever mourn. She had flushed it down the toilet. *Oh God, I didn't realize. What have I done?*

That weekend in Seattle seemed like it lasted forever.

. . .

"Hello, Sunshine." Mark leaned over and nuzzled her neck with a kiss when she saw him next. "How was the trip with your family?"

Kate settled herself in the car seat before she answered him. How much should she tell him?

"Well, I'm not pregnant anymore." She spoke in a monotone and stared straight ahead. "But I was. I'm having my period now."

"Oh. That's why you're looking so serious." He looked away and ran his fingers through his hair. "Whew. I guess that's it then. We don't have to worry anymore. That's a good thing, isn't it?

"I had a miscarriage, and it was awful," she almost shouted. She couldn't, wouldn't, pass it off as if it was nothing for Mark's sake.

"How did it happen?"

Kate explained how she fell down the attic stairs and the cramps and bleeding that followed. That was enough for him to know. She didn't share her deeper feelings, the relief and afterward the despair, not to mention the remorse for praying to get rid of their baby. She had asked God for it to happen. How could she make Mark understand the guilt-trip she was on?

"It must have been awful. I'm relieved though, aren't you?" He took her hand to pull her closer across the seat.

"I guess so. But I'll always wonder what it would have been like to hold our baby in my arms."

Mark's forehead furrowed as he absorbed her words. "We might be ready for that someday," he enunciated slowly, "but it's not a good time. Just be my girl for now." He kissed the tip of her nose.

Kate decided right then and there that she wouldn't be anybody's girl. She'd be responsible for all her actions. Mark's calm acceptance of her miscarriage horrified her because it had been his baby too.

With that, Kate stepped into full womanhood. After a simple slip on a set of narrow stairs, her life veered off in a completely different direction.

Chapter 6

KILLING TIME ON THE TIMELINE

Kate and Mark continued to spread out their blanket for picnics. They visited their romantic parking spot through the gate in the late evenings. Yet, the intimacy that bound them together wasn't easy anymore. Kate didn't trust condoms, despite how careful they both were.

Besides, it got more complicated. Kate's menstrual periods came on every two weeks, so they had to plan their dates to have sex. That halted the spontaneity.

"You look so tired lately," her mother said.

Kate let out a deep sigh. Nothing seemed important enough to put forth any effort. "For some reason, my periods come twice a month. Would that be making me tired?" she asked.

"For heaven's sake, child, yes. Let's get you a doctor's appointment and find out what's wrong."

Four days later, Kate had her first pelvic check-up in a private exam room, which seemed weird because, until then, Mark had been the only one to see her naked. She didn't have to tell the doctor what happened to her. Somehow, after the examination, he knew she had been pregnant.

"It seems you've had a rough go of it in the last month or two, haven't you? Was it a miscarriage or an abortion?"

Kate was relieved her mother wasn't in the room. "It was a miscarriage," she said but didn't add any details to that admission.

"You're having bi-weekly periods because your body is still trying to adjust. It's no wonder you're always tired. I won't ask any more personal questions, but just one. Do you plan to continue having sexual relations?"

"Yes, but I don't want my parents to know about it."

"How old are you?" he asked.

"Seventeen."

"Ah." He noted something down in her file, then opened the door and asked a nurse to bring her mother in.

Kate caught her breath. *Is this doctor going to tell her what I've gone through? Will he honor my request for confidentiality?* She sat and chewed on her thumb while the doctor wrote out a prescription. When her mother came through the door, he addressed them both.

"Everything seems fine, but I'm prescribing birth control pills for your daughter. This will work best to regulate her bi-weekly menstrual cycle into a regular monthly pattern again."

"I never knew those kinds of pills could cure irregular periods. But if you say so, I guess that would be okay." Her mother was always skeptical but she respected a professional.

Kate hardly contained her relief at the doctor's discretion. She had wanted a better method of birth control, and here it was. *Well, I'll never have to worry about getting pregnant again.*

She should have been glad to have this sexual freedom. But she thought about the miscarriage and erased the image of the small house with a white picket fence from her mind. *I prayed for a miscarriage to happen, and it did. But perhaps I asked for the wrong thing. Mark and I might have been young parents, but it could have worked. It would have been so wonderful.*

...

Kate wasn't the only one with a heart full of aching regret. In the spring of 1968, young men were being discharged after serving in Vietnam. They stumbled back home, but not as heroes. Half a million Americans believed the war was ridiculous insanity. Plagued by the trauma the young soldiers endured, they returned as empty shells of what they once had been. They didn't share their experiences because nobody wanted to hear about it.

Kate didn't talk about her miscarriage for the same reasons. There was a cynical song being played often, called "What are We Fighting For?" by a band called Country Joe and the Fish. The lyrics summed up how Kate felt about the war and the apathy in her own life. She didn't give a damn about anything either.

Kate had a few months left with Mark before he left for college. Could the two of them still make plans for their future, despite her miscarriage?

That summer, Mark found employment with a logging contractor and worked across the Columbia River in Washington.

"I have to take the job. The pay is a lot more than what I can earn pumping gas." He explained how he'd be living in a small logging camp.

"But I thought we'd have this last summer together." Kate's voice quivered.

"I know. But that's not the worst of it. I have to sell the Nash to buy a half-ton work truck."

"But you love that car." Kate knew he was being mature in making the decision, but the sale of the Nash would surely end the magic of their lovemaking.

Mark came home every other weekend, but the two-hour drive separating them made the commute difficult. It wasn't enough, and they planned a rendezvous at a midpoint near the Portland Airport for the next Saturday night.

He drove south, and she borrowed her parent's car and drove west to meet him on a small access road near the airport so they could watch the jet planes take off. Mark set up two large camp chairs in the back of his pickup, and in the dark, they had a makeshift living room surrounded by live entertainment on the airstrip.

"My logging job is…" he shouted.

She didn't hear the rest of it. "What did you say?" The jet rolled down the runway and left the tarmac in a horrendous roar.

"It's building muscles I never had," he said. "I guess from holding the chainsaw all day."

"It sounds grueling. Are you going to last the summer?"

"I've got to. How about you? Have you mixed up any love potions in that pharmacy of yours yet?"

"I'd get rich if I could do that. All the women customers would buy it." Kate gave him a dreamy look. "Do I need to use it on you?"

Mark grinned. "Nope, not on me. We could fly away in one of these jets with the money you'd make and go live in the South Pacific."

Kate smiled at his humor. Ribbons of light decorated the night as the jets took off and landed. Their lives were poised to take off too, and the sky was no longer the limit. Didn't Neil Armstrong just walk on the moon? They had both watched the footage on television a few weeks ago. Later, Mark spread his sleeping bag down on the bed of the truck so they wouldn't be seen by the passing cars. The sex was still hot, but their furtive actions made Kate feel more like a call girl picked up on the side of the road instead of a cherished girlfriend.

Kate drove home after a tearful goodbye and remembered their lazy picnics and intimate hikes in the woods. *Nothing stays the same, does it? Life was so simple when I was young, before the miscarriage.*

That summer, the school board posted office jobs and hired Leah and Kate to type up curriculum materials for the district teachers. It differed totally from the jobs she had before and would look nice on her resume. Joey was the first to buy a car with her wages from a job at the bakery. Her father, a used car salesman, helped her purchase a light blue Cutlass convertible, and Joey always invited Kate and Leah to ride around with her.

"Come on, baby! Let's see what you got." Joey's thick, dark hair streamed straight back from the driver's seat.

She pushed the speedometer up to eighty miles an hour on the freeway. It was their first road trip together, and they were off to Portland for a shopping spree.

As Kate and Leah leaned back in the racy sports car, they must have looked glamorous because quite a few men in the oncoming vehicles stared at them and smiled. Joey waved exuberantly, and Kate and Leah couldn't stop laughing. But suddenly, the car wobbled out of control. Joey held the steering wheel tight, jerking it back and forth while she pumped the brakes. She finally got control and brought the car to the edge of the road.

"Hot damn! That was close." Kate exclaimed.

"What the hell happened?" Leah's face was all eyes.

"Does anybody know how to change a flat tire?" Joey asked. Leah and Kate groaned at the same time. But they praised Joey's excellent driving skills, considering the circumstances.

Kate laughed. "I think 'race car driver' should be your career choice, Joey."

A fleeting smile crossed Joey's face. "That's an idea. But now we have to figure out how to jack up the car and change the flat tire."

"No, wait, we don't need to change it. We'll lift the hood and stand here looking pretty," Kate said.

A good-looking man in a gray sedan pulled over to a stop. He had their spare tire on in less than ten minutes and acted like it was a pleasure to help. They charmed him with appreciative comments and set off again in their powerful femininity. But this time, Joey drove a lot slower.

...

Leah asked Kate and Joey for a slept over at her house one night. The evening was full of light-hearted fun until the conversation became serious. Leah talked about seeing Billy Graham for the first time at a recent Christian youth rally that she and Joey had attended. Kate hadn't gone but wanted to know what they thought about it.

"The worship service was so cool," Leah gushed as they lounged around in her bedroom. "What Billy Graham said, it touched my heart."

"Yeah, maybe God really does exist," Joey said.

"Do you mean you're going to make Jesus Christ your Lord and Savior?" Leah asked Joey, trying on the new terminology.

"I don't know, but it kind of makes sense." Joey hugged herself as she spoke. "Jesus loved all kinds of people. He sounds like a cool hippie to me."

Kate noticed their glowing rapture as they relived the event. Wait a minute, she thought to herself. *They don't know much about Christianity. I was brought up in it and it didn't do me any good.*

Kate had once enjoyed hearing about God in church, but it didn't come close to the intimate love she was experiencing with Mark. Her girlfriends were still virgins and didn't understand the pleasures of sex. In Kate's opinion, grown-up love made religious passion seem silly.

"You guys won't become goody-goody girls and go to church every Sunday, will you?" Kate whined.

"We might." They both exclaimed in unison.

"Oh, brother." Kate rolled her eyes and fell quiet until Leah changed the conversation to another topic.

Later, Kate wondered why she had responded the way she did. She believed in God when she had asked to have a miscarriage, but she didn't want to believe in him anymore. But then an uncomfortable thought formed in her mind. Was she blaming him for what happened? That was a question she couldn't answer.

...

Kate and Joey planned to share an apartment after graduation near Oregon State University, where Mark would be attending. Neither of their parents could help pay expenses for higher education, so they took on a temporary second job that summer. The fruit packing plant hired them both for the swing shift, which started at six o'clock at night and continued until two in the morning. There was barely enough time to grab a bite to eat between when their office job ended, and their night job began. But that worked for Kate because she wanted to stay busy and not think about Mark all the time.

Ten women at their assigned table sat on stools while they worked. Apples tumbled along the wide tabletop like red balloons bobbing down a river. They had to move the top-grade fruit onto a higher belt and the damaged fruit to a lower one as fast as possible.

"Can you believe it? I'm eager to go back to school already. This working for a living is exhausting," Kate said as their shift ended one night.

"We need a break from our summer break," Joey answered, looking half asleep. They walked out of the warehouse like zombies.

Kate thought wistfully of Mark, but his logging job wouldn't end until the beginning of September. "I wish I had somewhere to go on a vacation."

"You could visit your older sisters," Joey said.

"Yes, but Sherry is living in Alaska now, and my other one just moved to Canada with her husband."

"Is he the draft dodger?" Joey asked.

"Yeah, after he received his draft notice, they left the country. My sister supported his decision to go."

"It's better to go north than have to fight in a war you don't believe in," Joey said with passion, and Kate agreed with her.

...

In early August, Kate received a letter from Beth, a close childhood friend who had moved a few years ago to Colorado. They wrote letters back and forth as pen-pals, and Kate hatched out a crazy idea. Mark was always working. Perhaps it's her turn to travel out into the big world and could talk to Beth about Mark and her miscarriage.

"Mom, you remember Beth, don't you?" Kate asked, holding her latest letter in her hand as her mother was preparing supper that evening.

"Of course, I remember your friend."

"Well, I want to fly to Colorado to see her before school starts." Kate had done her research for the trip.

"Katie, you've never traveled on your own before. That would cost a lot of money." Her mother didn't like the idea at all.

"I can fly on a student standby ticket for half the cost and then take a bus to her town. I'll use some of my savings."

Kate's father seemed to understand her determination. "Our daughter has grown up, dear. We should let her go." With her dad's support, her mother gave in, and Kate had permission to travel solo on her first jet plane.

At the airport, she thought about when she and Mark had watched the jets take off in the middle of the night, but now she was on one and roaring down the runway herself. The wheels lifted off the ground, and they were free from the confines of gravity. A smile spread out on Kate's face because she, too, was escaping the weight of what had been holding her down.

The landscape below receded until she no longer saw any cars or roads, only a vast display of green and brown rectangular patterns. And from that perspective, her personal problems seemed small and insignificant. Soon they entered a layer of misty white clouds that formed a soft billowy mattress around them. Kate wanted to jump out of the plane and bounce around like a kid on a trampoline. She pressed her face against the glass, and as the plane rose above the whiteness, it broke through into an orb of pure blue. The higher altitude gave her thrilling clarity because above all the dark clouds in the sky; the sun was always shining. She'd remember that perspective when the burdens she carried became too heavy.

A string of soft words flashed and echoed around in her head.

~~MY~~LOVE~~SHINES~~
~~THROUGH~~ANY~~DARKNESS~~

The peculiar message saturated her with peace. The words were crystal clear, just like when she saw the girl on the street and was given that subliminal invitation. It had to be Spirit talking to her, God's Spirit, and she savored the joy that filled her heart.

Kate was poised with confidence when the plane touched down in Denver. She made all her taxi and bus connections without a hitch. She acted like one of those sophisticated models featured in a Seventeen Magazine and found traveling alone was not that hard.

Beth and her parents were waiting at the bus station as planned, and they gave her a warm welcome.

"Wow, you look so much older," Beth exclaimed, giving her a hug.

"You do too. Isn't this crazy?" Kate said. Beth's father put her suitcase in the car's trunk, and the girls climbed into the back seat.

"It'll be so cool to hang out again. I'll show you around after supper." Beth giggled at the plans she had made.

They walked around the town that evening and talked for hours about fashion and guys they had dated. Kate described her concerns with Mark going off to college, but because she hadn't seen Beth for so long, she didn't share about her miscarriage or her shame over wanting it to happen.

"You can come to my first day of school tomorrow as my guest. The principal gave me permission." Beth mumbled later that night before they drifted off to sleep.

The next morning, Beth was at the sink applying a fancy mascara, which made her eyelashes a half an inch longer.

"You look like Marilyn Monroe with your blonde curly hair," Kate said as she peered in the mirror at her own bare face.

She put on more makeup than usual, but her style wasn't the same. Did she even have a style? Later. when the guys at Beth's school flirted with her, Kate grew more confident.

"Hey, you must be one of those west coast hippie girls," one said to her, and Kate flaunted herself just a little with them.

Beth's parents took them high into the mountains for a day trip that Saturday. They rode on cushions in the back of a pickup, with the aroma of dry pines all around them in the late summer air, just like they did in Oregon. But Kate's four-day visit with Beth was soon over. On the plane flying home, she realized their friendship was gone too. They never would recapture the closeness they once had as children. So why had she made the trip?

What is it I'm searching for?

Chapter 7

A COLD DAY ON THE MOUNTAIN

The world had changed over the summer, and so did Kate. Woodstock happened, a rock festival in New York's Catskill Mountains drawing the most massive crowd of young hip people that ever came together. Big-name bands played non-stop music for almost half a million people. They smoked doobies, drank beer and wine with abandon, and flaunted their disgust for the establishment. Her parent's generation couldn't understand it, but Kate thought she could.

Mark finished working and was coming home. She dressed in a tight T-shirt and her favorite jeans for their last date before he left for college. Without words, she ran to him, and he picked her up and twirled her around in a big hug. He was lean and strong from his summer logging job, and his hair was longer. But his arms felt the same, and she knew their lovemaking on the hill behind the gate that night would be special.

"I've sure missed you, Sunshine," he said afterward as she cuddled beside him. "But darn it, I'm only home for a few days and have to pack and do stuff with my family."

"You're excited to leave, aren't you?" she stated the obvious, her tone full of petulance. Surely, he could make more time to be with her.

"You'll be keen too when it's your turn to leave this town. But I promise we'll get together as often as we can on the weekends."

Kate struggled to act mature and hold back her tears as they talked about their summer experiences. Their lovemaking was incredibly tender. She inhaled the scent of his body and tried to capture the texture of each lingering kiss. Then Mark brought her home, gave her a last squeeze, and left. Kate went to her room and cried her heartfelt tears alone. Could their relationship survive yet another long-distance?

...

As fall leaves drifted to the ground, Kate's senior year classes started in bleakness. How was she to endure the months ahead without the excitement of seeing Mark all the time? His whispered endearments on the phone once a week only increased her loneliness.

"Mom, do you remember where those knitting needles are? Did we put them in the sewing cabinet?" Kate learned how to knit in a grade school 4H class and had made a sweater for herself.

"Try the bottom drawer, dear."

Kate found them next to an old pattern book and decided to make a sweater for Mark to wear on campus. She bought expensive yarn in a rich moss green color and followed the directions meticulously. It took weeks to finish, and at the left bottom edge, she knit in two small pink hearts spaced above the ribbing. When Mark came home on his first visit in October, Kate gave him the present.

"What a groovy sweater. Where did you get it?"

"I made it for you." Her voice came like soft velvet.

"You're kidding. No way."

"I did. Every single stitch went on and off my needles." She watched his odd smile spread across his face.

"That must have taken a long time." Mark rubbed the softness against his cheek.

"Look what I knitted on the bottom."

"But how did you get those tiny hearts right into the stitches?"

"I tied in another color of yarn. Here, try it on."

He pulled the sweater over his head. "It fits great. I'll wear it all the time."

The sweater sat well over Mark's broad shoulders with the color accentuating his lingering tan. He would wear a garment she designed, and those two hearts stamped her specific claim on him.

...

In early November, Mark called her one night and invited her to spend a long weekend with him in Corvallis. The idea was tempting since Monday was a Teacher's Prep Day at school.

"I'd like to come. Do you think I should?"

"Definitely. I need to see you." He tagged a husky note to his words.

"My parents would be flabbergasted. I can't tell them I'd be staying with you."

"Tell them you'll be staying with Susie, a friend of mine. But I'll sneak you into my room, and we can sleep together the whole two nights."

"I won't get in trouble with the Housing Office, will I?"

"No, it's cool. Come on, Sunshine. I'm dreaming of those tender lips of yours and you know how I like to nibble on them."

"I bet you're dreaming of more than that," she said.

His laughter made the phone line crackle. "My friends don't believe me when I tell them I have a girlfriend back home. Let me show you off a little."

That convinced her. Kate's mind raced to figure out how she'd get there. "Okay, I'll try to come. My sister Anna has to go back to college in Eugene near there, she might give me a ride. I'll ask Joey if she'll drive down to pick me up after the long weekend."

"Great. Tell Joey I'll pay for the gas. You should come."

"I really would like to see you." Kate ran her fingers through her hair, nervous about meeting his friends on a university campus for the first time. Would she even know how to act? But if there was competition from his female friends, she needed to be seen with him.

"And listen, Kate. I'm not staying in a regular dorm room, so you don't have to worry about appearances. My place has lots of privacy."

"Where do you live then?"

"Just wait. I'll show you."

In Kate's mind, she only saw Mark's eyes crinkle up at the corners through the telephone line. How she wanted to be in his arms again, all night long! To wake up in the morning and still be in his bed would be pure bliss.

That next weekend, Anna dropped her off at the Oregon State University campus near the Student Center to meet Mark. She saw him first, walking in with a group of friends.

"Mark," she called out.

He glanced around, and his eyes locked on hers as he paced toward her. "You made it. I'm so glad you're here." He wrapped her up in a long, tight hug, and then he introduced her to his friends. Kate found it hard to respond to their chatter about classes or the campus news when they hung out for a while. Mark was popular with his good looks and personality, and as words bantered back and forth between his friends, Kate sensed the two other girls were not so keen on meeting his younger, naïve sweetheart. She felt like Mark's kid sister, two years younger and without a clue.

"Hey, let's find some privacy." Mark took her hand, and they strolled outside across the campus, taking a path around a large building. He pointed out the landscape work he did on his job as a part-time ground's keeper.

"We're here," he said, taking out keys and opening a maintenance service door on the backside of the building.

"Where are we going?" she asked, raising her eyebrows.

"This is my place." He grinned. It was coal-black inside until he flicked the light switch. The one large bulb only illuminated a small part of the interior. The dirt basement stretched out as far as Kate could see, with an assortment of garden equipment stored in one corner and a small bathroom in the other. Mark led her down a trail of boards further into the darkness.

"Cripes, where are you taking me?" she asked, straining to see ahead.

"It's a surprise, a secret underground cave," he said with boy-like pride.

Kate saw the bed first, then a beat-up old dresser and some of his clothes hanging from nails on the ceiling rafters. But there were no walls to that island in the dark. The floor was constructed with rough boards laid side by side. Mark turned on the one lamp that sat beside his bed.

"This is where you sleep? But why in this place?"

"Because I can live here for free."

"Oh. How did you discover it? Aren't you trespassing?"

"No, the ground supervisor offered it to me. But I have to be discreet about using the space. I shower at the gym and study in the library, so I'm really not here much."

"But–your bedroom has no walls." The blackness seemed to stretch out forever.

"I bet you'll light the room up with me tonight, though. You're my sunshine girl, remember?" Mark reached for her then, and despite the odd location, Kate was finally alone with him with all the privacy they needed. Their intimacy built up, intense and sweet, and ended up with sparklers burning clear to the end. But afterward, Kate had tears in her eyes.

"Why are you crying?" Mark asked, raising his head to look down at her.

Kate didn't understand the reason for the wetness on her cheeks. She was all mixed up. "I don't know; I've just missed you so much."

Mark held her tight, with her head resting on his chest until they both fell asleep. That entire weekend revolved around his campus life. Kate tried to show interest in his activities, but she had nothing in common with his classmates. What was worse, Mark hadn't even asked how she was doing at home. He was different, and Kate thought the nighttime magic wasn't quite the same either. They weren't embracing each other under the stars; they were hiding their love in a dark hole of a basement.

On Monday, Mark resumed his class schedule, and Joey arrived to whisk Kate away, back to their dull, black-and-white high school existence.

...

Winter arrived early that year. The next time Mark came home, they planned a day of skiing up at Mount Hood Meadows. Kate was eager to ski with him on the white slopes like they used to do.

"I shouldn't be going skiing because I have so much studying to do," Mark complained when he picked her up.

"Oh, please, I want to spend the day with you." She understood his university classes were challenging, but it was her turn to spend time with him.

"Okay, but I can't ski all day. And I need to talk something over with you," he said.

"That's fine. Let's go for half the day then." The sun made sparkles on the cold, snow-covered trees as they sped up the mountain road to the ski resort. Mark filled her in on what he was learning in classes and shared news about his friends. Kate sat and let him talk. Gordon Lightfoot's song, "If You Could Read My Mind," played from the cassette player on the dashboard. She and Mark were out of sync with each other. The tender looks of love she used to cherish were missing. Still, it was a perfect day for skiing, and at least they were together.

Mark stopped his truck in the parking lot as Kate slipped into her ski jacket, eager to get on the slopes.

"Kate, hold on." He reached across the front seat to detain her. "Remember, I said we should talk about something?"

"Yes, but you've been talking." She pouted and turned to face him, waiting.

"Well… Oh, how can I explain this? We've gotten pretty serious in the last few years, right?"

"We have." Kate smiled. Then her breath caught in her throat. "What are you trying to say?"

"I've been thinking about how young we are. These years are supposed to be the best time of our life."

"They have been wonderful for me, but not so much now because you're so far away." The space in the vehicle seemed to close in, and everything became silent. What he was leading up to.

Mark sighed. His words came out like bent, blunted arrows. "I think we should break it off for a while and, you know, date other people."

The shock of his words hit hard. Kate froze like a cold stone in a snowstorm. Her eyes blurred because his declaration was unthinkable. Their years of intimate dating flew across her mind. *I've given him my innocence, and he still doesn't value what we have.*

"Kate?" He reached over to touch her.

But she pulled away and sat still. Her world tilted on its axis. *How can his love stop like this?*

"Kate, say something. Hey, I still want to see you," he said.

She looked down at her shaking hands. Her thoughts swirled in a fury. *What am I, some dirty little rag he used? Now he wants to try sex out with somebody else? I can't compete with sophisticated college girls.* Then her words tumbled out fast. "I won't be just one of the girls you make love to. If you don't want me anymore, it's over."

She stormed out of the cab and struggled to grab her skis from the back of his truck.

"Wait. Let's not end it like this," Mark shouted through the open door. "I said I'd ski with you today. You don't even have a way to get home."

"I'll find one then." She threw the words back at him. "Obviously, you don't care about what happens to me."

For a second, she held her skis and drank in Mark's image one last time until tears blurred her vision. How could God be letting this happen to her? But it was. She slammed the side door, hoisted her gear to her shoulder, and stomped off into the freezing cold. When she got to the lodge, she spotted him already driving off down the road.

Kate skied the slopes alone that day, icy rivulets of tears freezing on her cheeks. Late that afternoon, she cuddled in a quiet corner of the ski lodge and cried some more. Her chest ached with an actual physical pain within her.

A young couple sitting in the common room noticed her obvious despair and the woman came over. "We couldn't help but notice your tears. Are you okay?"

"My boyfriend just split up with me." Kate knew the words sounded childish, but she couldn't elaborate to a complete stranger how Mark had just severed their years-long perfect relationship.

"Do you have a ride? My husband and I are leaving to head back to town now. We could take you home."

By that time, she realized Mark was not returning. In her distress, she hadn't yet figured out how she was getting back to town. "I guess I need a ride." Kate got herself together and left with them to go down the mountain. The couple was very kind and drove out of their way to drop her off. Kate thanked them, but when she entered the living room, she broke down again into fresh tears.

"Katie, what happened? What's wrong?" Her father jumped to his feet to give her a hug.

"Mark broke up with me," she sobbed, pouring out the events of her miserable day and explaining how she had gotten a ride home with strangers.

"He left you up there alone? I'll have something to say to your young man when I meet up with him next."

"He's not my young man anymore." She choked the words out. "I'm never going to see him again."

"Now, dear," her mother said, trying to console her. "These things happen. You two can work it out."

Kate shook her head and blindly stashed her ski equipment in the closet. She trudged to her bedroom as her father spoke in hushed tones to her mom.

"Good grief. I've never seen our Katie this upset."

"It's a young lover's quarrel, but he's a nice boy. Whatever happened up there on the mountain, they'll both get over it."

But somehow, Kate knew Mark would make love to someone else soon… or maybe he already had. And that was something she would never, ever get over.

Chapter 8

A FOGGY NIGHT ON A CLIFF

"Hey Kate," a senior student called to her in the school hallway a few weeks later. "I heard you broke up with your college boyfriend."

Pete played a forward position on the basketball team. He seemed to approve of her plaid miniskirt by the smug smile on his face. But wore his unkempt hair a little too long, in Kate's opinion.

"If it's true, do you want to get together sometime?" he asked, raising one eyebrow.

"I don't know. Maybe." Kate was shy and hurried past him. And just like that, she became available—not the overlooked, studious girl anymore. She figured the boys were checking her out because of the sexual experience they imagined she had after dating Mark for so long.

Kate asked Joey about it. "Guys I've never spoken to are saying 'hi' to me today. One even pointed me out to his friend in the hallway. Did a rumor go around that Mark and I broke up?"

"Oops. I told Kevin. I guess he must have spread the word." Kevin was Joey's latest flame.

Kate grimaced and rolled her eyes.

Joey put on a clown face without an apology. "Look, you didn't drown," she said.

"I wish you hadn't told anybody." Kate knew she wasn't ready to date anybody yet, although she'd stay on the pill.

"You might as well throw yourself into the dating pool again." Joey nodded to encourage her.

Kate wasn't whole anymore after Mark left her on the mountain that cold winter day. She had given him every piece of her heart and all her body. She ran naked with him in the moonlight. They wished on falling stars, and she had carried his baby for a short time. How could that magical rightness ever happen again? She must be flawed if Mark's ties could be severed so easily. And if he couldn't return the love she gave him, would any other man love her back the way she needed?

Kate had taken pride in being a nice girl. She attended church sometimes and didn't lie, steal, or cheat. She knew you weren't supposed to have sex until you married. But they loved each other, didn't they? They'd talked about spending their lives together. Was the sexual intimacy so wrong because they hadn't waited until the legal ceremony? She wondered what the religious word for sex before marriage was and then remembered it was called fornicating. What an ugly word. In slang, that meant she was, what, a tramp?

If she had waited and kept her virginity, would Mark have married her to have sex or just found someone else? If she hadn't fallen down the stairs and miscarried, they'd have a child by now. *He would have married me then. But what if he played around after we were married? Is matrimony even a guarantee of faithfulness in this world?*

Kate's thoughts were poisoning her mind. She had lost something far more than her virginity; she lost her ability to trust men–and to trust God. *Life is a stupid game to play. Why should I care about having high morals? It doesn't seem to matter anyhow.*

...

Time, colored in grayness, swept her along. Kate still had no word from Mark after a month passed, and the pain of rejection cut deep. She applied herself to classwork with busyness and joined the debating club to build a social life. Her daily routine that February was depressing, but the weekends were brutal. She had pity parties in the privacy of her bedroom, playing the what-if game. *What if I had made different decisions? But what if all guys are like that?*

Then one evening, out of the blue, Mark called her on the telephone. "I'm coming home this weekend. I'd like to take you out to dinner, you know, as friends?"

Kate trembled. She tempered her voice. "I guess we could do that." They didn't talk long, but Kate danced a jig when she got off the phone and shared her exciting news with her parents.

"Guess what? Mark asked me out for next Saturday. Do you think I should go?"

"How wonderful for you, dear," her mom said. "He must want to patch things up."

Her father wore a strange expression. "Do you really want to see him again after the way he treated you?"

"I have to, Dad," she said.

...

That Saturday night, Kate curled her hair and dressed in her most mature outfit. She waited by the front door, thankful her dad wasn't around. When Mark arrived, she wanted to fall into his arms, but she held back, remembering they were getting together only as friends.

"It's good to see you, Sunshine."

"You too," Kate said. She tried to be nonchalant and talked about how busy she was after joining the ski team and making new friends.

The dinner date resembled the others they'd been on, except the conversation stopped and started like a taxi trying to get through a busy city. Yet the sexual tension still sparked between them across the top of the table.

"I didn't think my college courses would be so challenging. I'm in the library every night studying hard, but I miss you, Kate."

"I feel the same," she admitted. Mark's eyes didn't sparkle like they used to do. They reminisced about earlier times they had spent together, but their conversation fell flat. Kate didn't know how to be just friends. When Mark drove her home, she couldn't think of anything more to say. He hadn't said he wanted her back and they could have cut the tension in his pickup with a knife.

Abruptly, he exited off the freeway to a rest stop and parked the vehicle. "Let's go for a stroll before I take you home. Remember those starlit evenings we spent together?"

"I'll never forget those nights." But there were no stars out on this cold, cloudy night, just a small breeze whistling through the bare branches of the trees. They followed a path through the dimness to the picnic area in the clearing. Kate sat on top of a table, hoping they might discuss things better in the natural setting.

"Where are we in our relationship, then?" Kate asked. "I need to understand because...."

Mark was quick with a kiss to stop her from speaking. His breath, visible in the winter air, formed a ghostlike essence that caressed her face. Mark's hands slid under her sweater to the softness of cold skin. He pushed up her bra and kissed her breasts, and the magic of their passion replicated itself once more.

Kate couldn't make herself to stop responding, and her hot craving built up to a crescendo. Her body belonged to him. She wanted it too, right there, on top of the picnic table. She leaned back and granted him the right to enter, with only the promise of enduring love hanging in the chill night air.

Mark quickly sheathed himself and took her hard and fast.

"Mark, wait," she cried out. But Mark didn't hold back for her to reach any kind of climax of her own. It left Kate wanting and incomplete.

"Whoa, that came on quick," Mark smiled, straightening up afterward.

Kate sat still. She had to be clear about their relationship. "So, we're going to be exclusive, right? That means you won't date anybody else?"

"It doesn't have to mean that exactly, does it?" He handed her some tissue from his pocket.

"But isn't this precious to you? Isn't our love 'real' enough?" She struggled to get off the table.

"Sure, but we don't have to get all serious about it," he said.

Kate adjusted her clothes and glared at him. She rushed back to the parking lot without saying more. Instead, she screamed the words inside her head. *You want me to keep loving you, and you want to sleep around with other girls? It's not going to happen like that. If you're chalking up experiences, I'll have them too. I'll have them with a vengeance.*

...

The silent ride home and Mark's peck of a kiss for a goodbye didn't help her calm down. Jealousy had come weeks ago, but now the desire to get even swept over her like a tsunami. She wasn't Mark's special sunshine girl like he once had told her. She'd been used, meticulously groomed, to be his first virgin lover. He had cast her aside like a faded flower and went off to pick some fresh ones. What was the adult phrase? A secondhand rose is what she was. Well, she might never be a virgin again, but she wouldn't be an old maid either. Kate had discovered the pleasure of sex. She had opened Pandora's Box and would always crave the sweet intimacy she once shared with Mark.

Kate's anger took over her grief. She vowed to stuff her feelings and paste on a smile. She'd learn to flirt with the guys and strut down the hall. There would be sex with others because she was sure Mark was having it, too. And what did it matter? Everybody was doing it. One thing she knew; she'd never love anybody like that again. It just hurt too much.

...

Kate went back to school that Monday and a new version of herself emerged, cultivated out of necessity and self-pride. When a dark-haired guy named Tim asked her out for the next Saturday, she accepted. He seemed nice, wasn't bad to look at, and they made plans to go to a movie with another couple.

After the show, the chitter-chatter between the four of them seemed pointless to Kate. She felt separate from them. Tim dropped off the other two classmates, and then he was quiet, not at all sure of himself.

"I don't want to go home yet," Kate whispered, even though it was close to midnight. She watched the dark scenery flash by outside the window. The winter snow had melted, but it wasn't yet spring, and that matched her cold distance from him and everybody.

"Sure, let's pull off somewhere. Is there someplace you'd like to go?" Tim said eagerly.

Kate glanced at his profile with a frown. *Go park and make out, he means? Well, why not? But on my terms.*

"There's a side road up ahead with a view overlooking the gorge. I used to hike to the place sometimes because you can see the Columbia River below." The cliff was one of Kate's special thinking spots.

"Sounds good to me." He acted keen on the idea, but that didn't break her melancholy mood.

The spot was beautiful, even at midnight. Black scrub trees edged the clearing, and opaque moonlight paled the sky. The scent of wet pine needles perfumed the air. They followed the path to the edge of the cliff where swirling mist lay like a carpet at their feet. Four hundred feet below, faint sounds from the freeway traffic rose up to meet them, muffled by the fog.

Kate stepped closer and held out her hand to touch the exquisite, otherworldly scene before her. Oh, to walk out on that white carpet and dissolve into the mist was tempting. To merge into a higher realm and be alive with charging energy. She tried to imagine what it would be like to fall down through the cloud, hit the earth, and shatter into a million billion pieces. Why should she go through years of struggling through all the trials in life? There might be joy in parts of the journey, but she knew there would be much pain ahead to endure as well.

"It's beautiful," Kate whispered, projecting her inner thoughts into the gray expanse of fog. But there was no purpose to her life, anyway. Why not end it now?

The cold dampness caressed her, and she stepped closer…. She was ready to walk out into the scene, when crystallized words echoed from the dark void.

~~MY~~CHILD~~
~~THAT ~~I~~ MIGHT~~
~~SPARE~~YOU~~THESE~~TRIALS~~

Kate almost stumbled, startled by the voice in her head. Then Tim grabbed her arm. "Hey, you're scaring me. Let's go back to the car." He put his arm around her shoulders and led her away, impatient with her lack of desire for him.

Kate allowed herself to be dragged away from the grassy edge of the cliff. She knew she could have jumped easily, but the loving concern in the voice had stopped her.

...

Kate didn't sleep well that night but decided she wouldn't consider suicide or listen to stupid voices in her head, either. If life was a game, she would play it with gusto, not as a victim, once chosen and then tossed away. She'd hold on to life and shake it, take what she wanted from it. To hell with values and having to be kind and feminine to men. To hell with sweetness and purity! She'd make up her own rules as she went along.

Kate played a record of Peggy Lee's song, "Let's keep Dancing," and she learned all the words that night. The third verse perfectly expressed her cynicism because if that's all love was, then it had little worth to her.

Chapter 9

PLAYING THE GAME

Kate threw herself into party-mode with those song lyrics as her mantra. The guys in her class also wanted to cut loose and bring out the booze because the draft board was calling young men with birthdays in 1951. They knew anyone of them could be next. War was the insanity they all faced, which suited Kate's mood perfectly.

"Look what I brought for us." Joey pulled off the road and waved a pack of Camel cigarettes in front of Kate and Leah's faces. They had skipped out of classes that afternoon and were driving around in Joey's baby blue convertible.

"You want us to light these up?" Kate asked, taking one out of the pack.

"Well, duh," Joey said with exaggerated sarcasm. "If we hold our hands out like this, we'll look like elegant, sophisticated ladies. Guys will think we're twenty instead of seventeen."

"Don't cigarettes taste disgusting, though?" Leah wasn't sure about smoking them, but she held one in her hand. "They'll make our breath smell terrible."

"Nah. These little babies give you a buzz, and then they calm you down." Joey lit one up and showed them how to inhale a cigarette.

Kate's first intake made her dizzy. With the second one, she started coughing. She was careful to inhale only a little on the next drag, but they sure looked cool while they held their cigarettes and tapped the ashes off out the window.

...

Kate hung out with a girl named Jessica from her poetry class that spring. She was a little wild. She invited Kate to drive up to a gravel pit for a different kind of high.

"It's a gas," she joked. Her boyfriend, Paul, and two others were in the car. "Freon gas. It makes you laugh and frees you up from all kinds of crap."

"It's the stuff they use in refrigerators to cool the temperature down," Paul explained, stopping in the privacy of the graveled area.

They all got out, and one guy held a small narrow hose connected to the tank of Freon gas while they took turns breathing it in. Each person slipped helplessly into fits of hysterical laughter as the others cheered them on. It was uncontrollable laughter in a can. Kate's circle of friends expanded. The small crowd often met together in an orchard, deep in a maze of apple trees. Other nights, everybody drank in an empty field near the river and hung out around the vehicles with their car radios cranked up. The guys were under the legal drinking age, so they asked older relatives, or sometimes complete strangers, to buy cases of beer for them.

Kate kept her rebellious activities a secret from her parents. Her overbearing mom and her alcoholic father were drowning in marital problems, and they had enough conflict to handle. Besides, it was easy to play the role of the dutiful child for them.

"What are you doing with your friends this evening?" her mother asked one Friday night, drying her hands on a dishtowel after supper. She seemed relieved that Kate finally had a wider social life.

Kate gave an honest answer. "We'll probably find some booze and sit out in the orchard. We have to party now before all our guy-friends get shipped off to Nam."

"Katie don't be silly. You're such a smart girl. You aren't really going to do that." Her mother chuckled.

Kate didn't say anything else. She just gave her mom a cheeky smile, waved goodbye and out the door, she went. Her mother always believed the best in her. Kate found that rather humorous, but it was an endearing trait.

...

One evening, Kate, Leah, and Joey didn't have dates, and they decided it would be a girl's night out. The trouble was nobody they knew would buy them any alcohol.

"I bet you'd be able to purchase some at the corner store, Leah. You could pretend you're a young mother in that flowered blouse you're wearing." Leah wore clothes that sometimes were way too prim and proper, in Kate's opinion.

"I have an idea," Joey said. "What if you buy diapers and hot dogs and then put a case of beer on the counter? The check-out clerk will assume you're over nineteen and just bringing the booze home for your husband."

"I don't think that would work." Leah giggled, shaking her head.

"It would. You could get away with it. Here, wear this scarf around your neck," Kate said.

"And she needs to wear my glasses. They'll look nerdy on her."

Leah pulled her hair back into a bun to humor them and adjusted the scarf and glasses. Kate and Joey agreed she looked at least ten years older.

"But I can't see with these glasses on."

"Wear them on your nose then, and you'll look like a studious teacher. You'll be great."

Kate and Joey waited in the vehicle, cheering Leah on as she entered the store. Minutes ticked by, and they saw her standing at the cash register next. They watched through the window for the cashier's reaction. Sure enough, Leah paid the money, picked up her bags, and hurried out of the store, smiling. She had scored!

The three of them hung out often after that. They shared knowledge about men, making love, and even politics in great gabfests late into the night. There was a first-time experience for everything.

"Hey, Joey, pour me another one of those, will you?" Kate loved the feeling she got from drinking cherry sloe gin. They were at an older girl's slumber party with the parents gone for the weekend.

"Chug-a-lug, girlfriend," Joey said, refilling her own glass too.

"It's not cool-aid, you know," Leah said with caution.

"Tastes like it," Kate slurred out her words.

Kate missed half the party that night after getting horribly sick. Leah, with her sweet compassion, stayed by her side and held her head over the toilet. The party wasn't so fun after that.

The summer flew by. Kate still worked part-time at the pharmacy and spent her free time hanging out with friends. She often played tennis with Leah, or she and Joey dove off the big dock into the Columbia River. School started up way too soon in the fall.

...

Sam, a good-looking guy in her math class, invited Kate to the Homecoming dance. She didn't know him very well but hoped it might be the start if something good. She wore a pink formal that Anna had worn, not quite her color, but it was fancy. The one she had bought for Mark's prom still hung in the closet. Two hours before her date was going to pick her up, she stepped on half a toothpick embedded in the shag carpet of their living room. It rammed in deep with no way to get it out. Her father took her to the emergency where the doctor cut around it and used long-handled tweezers to yank it free.

She couldn't walk on the foot, but her mother said it was too late to cancel her date and made her go to the dance, anyway. It was mortifying. There, she sat on the sidelines while her date danced with everybody but her.

That winter, Kate drove up to the ski hill with her girlfriends instead of Mark. She pushed old memories aside, determined to enjoy skiing again. The three girls attracted a lot of attention with their exuberance as they skied down the runs together. Leah spotted James, a guy she had met before from Portland. He and his friend traversed across the slope and swished to a stop in front of them, with skis spraying powder all over them.

"I thought it was you, Leah. Hey, my friends and I are having a party tonight. You girls should come over when you're done skiing for the day." James was tall and wore a swanky ski jacket and mirrored sunglasses. His parents owned a vacation cabin on the mountain.

"Lots of people will be there. and James has the newest records." His friend butted into the conversation, bouncing on his skis.

"Thanks for the invite," Leah answered after getting affirmative nods from Kate and Joey. "It sounds divine."

James gave her the directions to his chalet and added, "Oh, and if you want to ski again tomorrow, you can crash there tonight. We have lots of bunk beds and couches."

"Maybe. We'll see you later, though," Leah answered for the three of them. They talked it over as they waited to get on the ski lift.

"So, we're going, right?" Joey asked, sliding her skis forward in the line.

"Yeah, let's go. James' family is rich. I bet their chalet is gorgeous." Leah was game to go.

"We can't drink much if we're driving down the mountain tonight." Kate pointed out.

"Come on. Let's be daring. We could crash at their lodge and ski all day tomorrow." Joey beamed with excitement. "We can stick together at the party."

"We'll have to tell our parents something," Leah said.

"Look. You guys can call home and say you're staying with me tonight," Joey said. "I'll tell my parents I'm staying at Kate's." They agreed with the plan.

The party was in full swing when they arrived, with a large kegger dispensing cold beer. The young skiing crowd mingled in the spacious living room and fancy kitchen, talking about the black diamond runs they took that day. Kate and her girlfriends geared up to meet the sophisticated crowd from Portland.

Fortified with a tall, cold beer, Kate lost her shyness. She looked around for guys that looked like Mark, but there wasn't anybody to compare with him. Yet when people started jiving to the loud rock music, Kate found herself on the crowded floor for the rest of the night.

Hours later, after many drinks and wild dancing, James shut off the music to assign rooms and bunk beds for his guests. Kate crawled into a bottom bunk with her head spinning and was drifting off when the guy in the top bunk engaged her in late conversation.

"Hey, down there. We'd sleep better if we cuddle up together." He hung his smiling face over the side, flirting outrageously.

"I'm already sleeping," Kate mumbled.

"But I can't sleep. You got to help me out here," he insisted.

"Why do I have to help you out?" She couldn't do anything but laugh at him.

"Because you're a cute chick and that's what's keeping me awake."

Kate was quiet, not wanting to encourage him. She wondered if they had danced together earlier, but she didn't recognize him or his voice. With a soft, exaggerated snore, she slipped off into nothingness.

Sometime in the night, he climbed into bed beside her. That woke her up quick, and she pushed him away.

"It's okay. I'm wearing pajamas. We'll only cuddle."

Kate's mind was still hazy, drunk. She had no energy to make a fuss and fell back to sleep. But her eyes flew wide open when she felt him fondling her breast.

He shifted his body then and pinned her outside arm against his leg. Holding down the other one, he struggled to still her thrashing.

"Get out of my bed. I don't want sex." Kate hissed at him. "I don't even know you."

He only grunted and pulled her pants down with one hand. "Well, now you'll get to know me," he said, lowering his heavy body weight on top of her.

Kate fought furiously, but he spread her legs, forced himself into her, and was moving fast. When it was over, Kate lay there, whimpering, unable to move.

"Oh, come on. You wanted it too, or you would have hollered for help." He said as he staggered back and climbed up to the top bunk again.

Kate knew that wasn't true, but why hadn't she screamed at him to stop? Her body was numb, as though it wasn't hers, like a dirty rag doll thrown on a rumpled bed. She couldn't stop sobbing. She never dreamed the second man she'd sleep with would treat her with such disrespect. Was she stupid or just not cool? She did drink too much. But perhaps everybody paired up, and she didn't realize it was that sort of party. This was rape, wasn't it? Above her on the top bunk, he snored lightly. At the bottom, she sniffled and cried herself back to sleep.

The next morning, out in the kitchen, the guy acted as if nothing happened between them. She doubted he even told his friends. Kate didn't tell Leah and Joey either, not because she cared about her reputation. They knew she had experienced it with Mark. She didn't talk about it because it had been so demeaning for her. Casual sex was becoming the norm, and she guessed she had to come to terms with it. It didn't seem to mean anything special to anybody, not like when she and Mark had made such sweet, innocent love.

Kate filed the ugly memory away in the back of her mind; she'd be smarter and more cautious next time. Then she remembered he hadn't used a condom. *Yuck. Thank God. I'm still on the pill.*

...

Kate went out with Ed Johnson that Spring and smoked her first joint of marijuana in the front seat of his pickup truck.

"Inhale, and then hold it as long as you can." He gave a how-to demonstration, then handed the doobie over to Kate.

She took a puff, held it in, and then let it out to breathe again. After they each took another toke, Kate discovered that inhaling the chemicals in Ed's homegrown weed had caused her reality to shift. *It definitely wasn't like smoking a cigarette.*

Kate turned to face Ed in contemplation. "I see why they call this stuff 'mind-blowing.'"

"Yup, it's pretty rad." He said, letting his smoky breath hiss out of his mouth.

"It's like my body is drunk, but not my head."

Ed laughed. "Watch this," he said, holding his hand out in a flourish to draw figure eights with the swirling loops of smoke rising from the joint. Then he brought it back for them to each take another toke before he put it out. He leaned in closer and slid his thumb across her lower lip.

"Your eyelashes are way too long for a guy," Kate gazed at his face up close. She didn't worry about how that sounded. She had no worries.

"Can I kiss you?" he asked after their perception of things had gotten rather strange.

Kate nodded; her emotions intensified. A desire for intimacy again was a surprise. He wanted her, and she just let things flow. Each breath, touch, and kiss were intentional and sensual. She discovered making love while stoned was uninhibited, wild passion in slow-motion. Oh, how she had missed it.

After that experience, Kate decided the whole hippie movement into drugs and sexual freedom might really be a social evolution. Perhaps they'd fall in love. She thought it might happen because the sex was so intense. But Ed didn't want any permanency, and after they had sex a few times, their dates soon fizzled out. He had moved on.

One warm Sunday afternoon, Joey picked up Kate in her snazzy convertible so they could hang out together. They stopped at a wide spot on a small gravel road, and Joey pulled a joint out of her purse.

"Ta Daa! Let's smoke this little joint." She lit it up, and they each took tokes. Then they fell into a philosophical discussion about peanut butter and the value of jumping into icy rivers.

"We're not making much sense." Kate chuckled. "Let's turn on the radio." She twisted the knob full blast to tempt Joey, who had taken years of jazz class dancing.

Joey's moves were contagious. Soon they spilled out of the car and danced around the vehicle to a heavy jungle beat. Even the leaves on the trees seemed in sync with the music. Their graceful arms flowed in the air, and their feet pounded the ground. They were Amazon women, reveling in their power.

...

Kate's school bus dropped her off near her driveway. She pulled letters and the newspaper out of the mailbox as usual. After she walked home, she left them on the coffee table for her father. Then she read her mom's instructions on the kitchen counter for making supper. This was her mother's way of teaching her how to cook, and most of the simple recipes she followed turned into tasty meals.

Kate found a snack and then plopped down on the couch. A large photo on the front page of the newspaper showed a male student sprawled out dead on the ground. Another belligerent young man was standing up, and in the middle, a female student crouched between them. Her hands stretched out in rage; her eyes glared with anger at the madness of men. Kate had to read the article.

Kent, Ohio. May 4, 1970 "Four students at Kent State University, two of them women, were shot to death this afternoon by a volley of National Guard gunfire. At least eight other students were wounded."

"Holy cow," Kate mumbled as she read about the latest anti-war demonstration with a thousand students involved. A quote from President Nixon said, "This should remind us all once again that when dissent turns to violence, it invites tragedy."

What the hell, she thought. Was the President threatening young people not to demonstrate? It seemed the government had sent in the same number of guardsmen to put a stop to stop the protestors. Kate wondered which side became violent first.

The guardsmen threw tear gas at the crowd, but the protesters flung the canisters back. Then the guardsmen marched forward and threatened them with bayonets on loaded M-1 rifles. The students threw rocks back at them and called them pigs. That was a nickname unfamiliar to Kate. Kate slapped the arm of the couch in shock. *It's a war zone right here in my country, and they're all Americans.*

The government claimed a student sniper fired first from a nearby rooftop, but the reporter who had been there hadn't heard anyone shooting. The newspaper article made Kate want to go out and demonstrate herself. Wasn't the finest power in a democracy the privilege of free speech? The government's actions were outrageous.

Kate considered the men involved in the Vietnam war: those who enlisted and were eager to fight, those who held their draft numbers praying not to be called, and those trying to be Conscientious Objectors to avoid killing anybody. What about the power-seeking men perpetuating the whole war machine? Or the generals with all the medals plotting war games inside their safe little bunkers?

Kate figured out why they needed to draft soldiers. The US military put the draft into place because there weren't enough young men crazy enough to sign up. Those boys were just cannon fodder for the harvest.

And what about the rich weapon manufacturers behind the scenes? The military-industrial complex manufactured the guns, tanks, and fighter jets to reap hundreds of billions of dollars in profits. Taxpayer's money bought them all because the government approved the war to make the mega-corporations rich. The logic of that meant there always had to be a war going on some place on the planet so weapons could be sold. Testosterone's love for money and power.

Kate thought if women were making big political decisions for the country, they would never go to war to prove their superior strength on any level. Women, with their maternal instinct, would value all human life.

The female gender should rule the world. But what can I do about that?

Chapter 10

ON STAGE IN THE LIGHTS

"It's spring already. Look how warm it is. We don't want to stay inside with weather like this." Joey complained to their group of friends during the lunch break in the cafeteria.

"Well, we can't all skip out," Kate said.

"We could if we figure out how to shut the school down." Ed was always up for a challenge.

"Then get the guys together and figure out a plan." Joey and Kate encouraged them and started chanting. "We want freedom. We want freedom."

Ed and Paul started scheming, and by lunchtime, the word was out. Everybody synchronized their watches. Ed assigned them to their stations: each shower in the locker rooms and every toilet, sink, and water faucet in the entire building. Kate was sent to a drinking fountain, and at precisely twelve-forty-five, she and all the others opened the taps.

Some invisible events happened behind the walls because no water came out anywhere. The pressure burst the pipes at some connection deep down in the infrastructure because none of the faucets worked.

"We did something," Joey exclaimed in the hall.

"We got the power." The guys whispered, giving each other a thumbs-up as they hurried back to class.

An hour later, their well-orchestrated scheme closed the school. The principal released four hundred high school kids from school early because toilets could not be flushed. Much to the students' delight, the plumbing repairs would take a couple of days to complete.

The outraged school principal couldn't pin the blame on the ringleader because there wasn't only one person who orchestrated it. She and her friends were all guilty. They had tested the 'power of the people,' and that was what the anti-war demonstrators were currently doing. Yet Kate had some deep thoughts on it later. She knew their actions were fundamentally wrong. Their group had damaged public property, and their parents would pay for it in taxes.

Why had she been swept away by the enthusiasm of a crowd? It made her realize how young soldiers in a mob could do atrocious things without considering what was right or what was wrong.

Herd mentality, that's what it was, she thought. *Like sheep.*

...

Joey caught up with Kate at school on Monday. "Hey, you want to skip class and sneak out to the orchard for a smoke?" She had a wayward little smile on as they pulled books out of their lockers.

"I can't, darn it. I have that appointment with the school counselor right now," Kate explained.

"See you later, then." Joey sang her farewell and sailed off. "Hey, it's no big deal about the counseling session; it's a summary of those tests we did, and it only lasts half an hour," she said.

Mrs. Larson was hip for an older woman, and she dressed in classic clothes with big, handcrafted silver jewelry. The counselor had been around long enough to remember Kate's two older sisters, Anna, and Sherry. Kate dreaded the meeting because she would be expected to live up to their sterling reputations for honor-roll grades.

The senior students were each given scheduled time slots to discuss the results of the Stanford-Benet Intelligence Scale test they'd filled out. That was a mouthful. The school had sent a letter home claiming it calculated a student's IQ and learning style. The second form they had filled out was the Myers-Brigs Test. It was supposed to help people understand how to process facts to make better decisions in life.

Kate sighed in resignation. *Shoot, I've already made major life decisions. And my school counselor is going to tell me how best to live my life? Yeah, right.*

Mrs. Larson called Kate into her office and greeted her with enthusiasm. "Thanks for coming in, Kate. I'm going through the students alphabetically, and you're one of the last I've had the pleasure of chatting with."

"Gee, I bet you're tired of saying the same things to all of us," Kate said, leaning against the back of the chair.

"In your case, I've been looking forward to our meeting because your assessment data ran outside the ordinary." Mrs. Larson flipped through the colored charts as Kate drew closer with curiosity.

"The Stanford-Binet test finds your IQ above normal for your age group." She quoted Kate's score but explained how social and emotional IQ differed. Then she described fluid reasoning and quantitative reasoning, the two methods people use to make decisions.

"Okay, but I'm not sure how important any of this is." Kate pushed her hair back and hoped to look like Mrs. Larson when she became that old.

"Let's examine your results on the Myers-Briggs test, then." She laid another graph sheet on the table and continued.

"Most young people gather facts to make up their perception of reality. Here we see your answers to the questions show quite the opposite. You seem to start with truths you've already predetermined, and then you search for evidence and experiences to back them up."

Kate saw her darker green line skewed off from the norm.

"What do you think accounts for the way you make your decisions?"

"I'm not sure." Kate shrugged her shoulders.

"This profile puts you in the INFJ personality category, out of the twelve types." Mrs. Larson took her glasses down from her head and put them on to read again. "INFJ types are rare, intuitive, and introverted individuals, making up less than one percent of the population. They have a high degree of idealism and morality that influences their judgment."

She paused and glanced over at Kate. "Does this sound like you?"

Whoa. She's reading some serious stuff here. Kate thought, but she stayed quiet, and the counselor picked up the page and continued reading.

"Students in this category tend to be serious workers who contribute to society. They are private and reserved, but they can be easily hurt. Sometimes their peers think they're too intense because of these traits."

"Actually, that definition might fit me," Kate said, sitting up straight.

The counselor nodded. "Let's look at the next chart. Most students become uncomfortable when they find themselves in a stressful situation, but it looks like you're able to thrive on challenges. I think this trait is quite special, don't you?"

"I don't know if I'd call it thriving," Kate answered, "but I've faced a few challenges already."

Mrs. Larson offered her a genuine smile and ended the appointment with a career counseling chat. "What are your plans after graduation?"

Kate's oldest sister graduated with a master's degree, and her other sister was finishing her bachelor's degree. Her parents expected Kate to excel in the same way, although they couldn't help with the finances. "If I can save up enough money, I plan to go to college and take sociology or psychology," Kate said.

"Either of those choices would be an excellent fit for you." Mrs. Larson handed Kate a few scholarship applications to fill out and then checked her watch. "I'd love to follow up with you in ten years' time or so to see what you do with your life." She gave Kate a nod of respect and stood up to end the interview.

Kate left the counselor's office in deep thought. *Am I so different from others? What am I going to do in life if Mark isn't going to be a part of it?*

...

The Elks Lodge sponsored a Junior Miss contest in the city each year, a sort of beauty pageant. Kate heard the cash rewards for first, second, and third prizes were substantial, and that interested her. She thought about entering, but not about winning first place because the winner had to compete in the state contest and make appearances at civic events. That didn't appeal to her. Still, Kate couldn't shake the idea. She was bored and decided to enter for the experience in case there was a chance of winning third place. After all, it wasn't a beauty competition; it was a talent contest. There was no parading around in swimsuits. The contestants would only be judged for their appearance in evening gowns.

But talent? She didn't have any exceptional talent that she knew. How would she compete with the girls who had already signed up? The ballet dancer, the pianist, the one that sang like a canary bird; they had wealthy parents who had paid for ongoing lessons for their darling girls. What could she do for talent? Kate knew she had a passionate nature, but that didn't count as a talent, did it? *Maybe she could read poetry or something.*

Sure enough, they listed a dramatic reading as a talent category under the contest rules. Kate signed herself up. She chose a poem she liked for the contest and had fifteen days to practice it.

The evening of the Junior Miss Pageant arrived. Each contestant had to appear in a formal gown and introduce the next girl in line to start it off. The judges would score each of the ten young women on poise and stage presence during these presentations. They drew straws to see which order they would go out on stage, and Kate ended up with the longest straw. It pleased her to be first and not have to wait in jitters for all the other contestants.

Kate sewed the peach-colored floor-length gown she wore. It had invisible pockets on the side of the skirt, and Kate put her shaky hands into them. She loved the simple lines of the dress, fitting snug in the bodice and flaring out gracefully in the skirt like a bell.

The Master of Ceremonies would open the gala event. He was a top-ranking man in the Elks Lodge, and his humorous comments made her laugh while they waited together off stage. He treated her like an adult, which boosted her confidence in facing the sizeable crowd seated in the auditorium.

The lights flickered. The pageant began. The MC moved onto the stage, welcomed the audience, and introduced the first contestant. Kate held her head high and walked into the bright lights to open the competition. Her brief speech introducing the next contestant went well. She smiled and nodded to the audience as she spoke. Then she curtsied like a princess and headed to the risers on stage to wait for the rest of the girls to give their formal introductions.

It was mayhem back in the dressing room after that. Kate had drawn a shorter straw for the pageant's talent part and was almost the last contestant. She encouraged each of the girls as they prepared to show off their talent before the judges and audience.

Kate had taken Modern Poetry for an English class, and the poem she chose was titled 'The Hoods.' It was written by a Russian poet she admired. Her choice was political and daring because the Russian communists were the enemy of the Cold War going on. The poem described a generation of youth on the verge of changing the world. Kate thought the words also represented young Americans because the hippie movement wasn't only about love and long hair, but about freedom from war and racial oppression. They were demonstrating against the military-industrial complex, making profits from the sale of weapons. They opposed US imperialism, the raping of natural resources from third-world countries. Kate was determined to play a small part in that rising tide of dissatisfaction.

Then it was her turn to go out front and share her talent on stage. She wore a shirt-waisted, green-and-white checked dress. She strolled to the front stage on her patent leather Kelly green heels and then paused for a dramatic effect. Gazing out over the crowd, she made eye contact with as many faces as possible in the dim auditorium. She spoke clearly, her words amplified by the microphone clipped to her dress.

"I'd like to read a poem called 'The Hoods,' meaning, of course, my younger generation." Kate added that for humor, and the audience chuckled.

"It's written by Yevgeny Yevtushenko, a popular Russian poet, yet this poem is international. To western observers, Yevtushenko is a symbol of the growing intellectual freedom in that country and in ours. He wrote the poem to bridge the generation gap, and he ended it in almost a prayer." Kate began to read Yevtushenko's poem with loud, heartfelt emotion and poignant pauses.

"So, this is the Great Twentieth–Century of the
Sputnik...
What a scary and scared century.
A fine century, and a century of quicklime and
pits.
A century of fine ideas and a century that eats
those ideas again.
A century to be hated by those who are young in
it.

Yes, they hate it all right; they hate their
governments.
They hate their politics; they don't like the
Church too much.
They don't have much use for philosophers,
They don't much like the world, to tell the truth.
They don't much like its banks and cashiers,
They don't like themselves, for not liking
anything much.

The Great Twentieth is just their bad old
stepfather.
They hate him all right.

And their hatred is strong, moving fast, beating
along the dark banks
Of the Hudson, the Tiber, the Seine, and the
Thames.
They're tough, they're hip, they're cool and
they're very strange.
This is the first century they've ever been here…

I know there is truth, somewhere there is–in this
century too.
There is truth in the things you can work with,

And when I come fighting here, I know I'm
fighting for friends…
Even when I'm fighting against them.

But you, what happened to you?
Is it some truth like this you are waiting for,
scowling in pain?
You go on shuffling across two continents,
On the road in Europe, on the American road.

The Great Twentieth–the Sputnik Century.
You're not dead yet.
Why don't you shake them up and out of that
endless, sinister groove?
Don't hand them any "security" crap, Century.
Give them something to grab hold of…
Something like a belief in the right things, the
good things you have.

They're not your enemies, Century.
These kids, your kids, can't be enemies.
You've got to do something for them. Do you
hear me? You've got to give,
You've got to give them a new road. I'm talking
to you, Century!"

Kate finished the last line in a loud plea and stood still in silence, frozen in the spotlight. The audience was quiet. Then the clapping began, and it grew in volume. In excitement, she said a formal thanks to both sides of the auditorium; and turned to promenade back down the short runway. Kate had already won something amazing. Because even though she might not be good enough to win the contest, she had shared her strong beliefs with the audience, and she could tell they liked her.

At the end of the pageant, all the contestants lined up once again on stage in their evening gowns. Kate was glad it was over and waited for the runner-up winners to be announced. The judges pronounced the third-place winner, and it wasn't Kate. They announced second place, but again, it wasn't Kate. She was disappointed but pasted a firm smile on her face. She had dared to speak her truth, and the pride in her performance was all she needed.

The first-place winner was announced, and the Master of Ceremonies called out her name! Kate couldn't believe it—total shock set in. She panicked, and her hands covered her face. *The ballerina was supposed to win this thing. How can I be the winner by just reading a poem?*

The MC beckoned her down on the runway to receive a dozen red roses. Last year's Junior Miss lowered a sparkling tiara to the top of her head. She waved Kate off to walk down the runway once again to the applauding crowd.

With a broad smile, the MC called Kate's parents to come up on stage and stand beside her, too. The honor given to their youngest daughter stunned her mom and dad. And like her, they didn't quite know how to act.

That night after all the excitement, Kate tried to comprehend what had taken place in those hours on stage. What had made her confident enough to enter the pageant in the first place besides trying to win the scholarship money? It wasn't arrogance in her looks or abilities. It was the hunger for truth, for the rightness of things, and her love for others that was important. She had shared these traits with the people in the auditorium in boldness, and there was power in sharing them.

All the tension and stress disappeared when Kate sank into bed. In that satiated state, some invisible pulse shimmered, and she heard words again.

~~LOVE~~TRUTH~~INTEGRITY~~
~~BRING~~JOY~~

Those were some of God's character traits, and the words satisfied her in the most profound way. She had won the contest because the audience, maybe even all of humanity, hungered for these same qualities of love, truth, and integrity. *Could she live with those and build a belief system on that simple philosophy?*

Chapter 11

OUT INTO THE BIG WORLD

Kate studied diligently for the final exams in her last high school year. Her parents still argued about her dad's drinking, and she was done with it all. Soon, she'd be out of the fishbowl and into the bigger world around her.

Joey met up with her as usual before their Monday morning class. A substantial dark bruise mottled her leg just below the miniskirt she wore. Joey's chin was scraped raw in places, and one forearm had a severe case of road rash.

"What happened to you?" Kate asked.

"Richard came back from Vietnam. He took me to the show on Saturday night." Despite her bruises, Joey purred like a cat with a bowl of cream.

"Cool. The older guy you were serious about a couple of years ago, but why all the bruising? It looks like he beat you up."

"Weirdest thing, we were just walking down the road together when a car backfired." Joey touched the bruise on her leg. "You know how the sound comes out of a muffler? Well, he panicked and threw me down on the sidewalk." Her hands gestured the dramatic scene.

"But why? That's crazy."

"He just returned from Nam, remember? If he hears any loud noise, he violently, automatically reacts. Boy, is he a mess."

"That's awful. Is Richard going to be okay?"

"Physically, I guess. But it was so strange, him pushing me down like that. He was trying to protect me, like I was right there in the jungle with him."

"He must have lived through hell. Did he tell you what it's like over there?"

Joey pursed her lips and shook her head. "Not much. He admitted they passed out drugs like candy before being sent out on patrol each morning. He said they needed the amphetamines to face surprise attacks by the Viet Cong hiding in the jungle foliage."

Kate looked at Joey with concern. "It's so sad. He enlisted, right?"

"Yeah, but he's not getting any respect for serving his country." Joey hung her head.

"You used to be crazy about him."

"I know, but now I don't even want to date him. It's scary not knowing how he'll react to loud noises that might happen."

Kate thought Richard and Joey would have made a delightful couple together, but the war was screwing everything up. Later that same day, she heard Ed and his friend Charlie talk between classes in the hallway.

"What are you doing after you graduate?" Ed queried Charlie as he opened the locker nearby. "Are you going to enlist?"

"Shit no. I'm not stupid. My parents are sending me to college." Charlie played defense on the football team, and his tall, bulky form guaranteed respect for his sheer size.

"What if you still get drafted?"

Charlie leaned his frame against the wall. "I thought if a guy enrolled in college, he could avoid the draft."

"Nope, not anymore, because it's a whole new lottery system. Once we turn eighteen, the draft board can pull our name out of a hat, and there's not a thing we can do about it. We get that letter, and we're off to boot camp in just a matter of weeks."

Charlie closed in on Ed and lowered his voice. "But I don't think I could kill anybody. Could you if you had to do it?"

"If I had to, I would. But if you want to be a conscientious objector, you must prove you're religious to get that classification. Besides, they still make you serve in the war, just not in combat."

Steve, a clean-cut guy from her Social Studies class, joined the conversation. "Well, I'm man enough. If they call my number, I'll serve my country." He stood up straight which made his pointy chin jut out even more.

Kate thought of the young men she knew creeping through the jungles with stealth. She tried to imagine her classmates trained as soldiers, brainwashed for the sole purpose of shooting smaller Asian men to survive. After graduating, they would enlist or wait in anxious silence with their draft numbers memorized. It was the air they all breathed.

Kate's brother-in-law had left for Canada when he received his induction notice in the mail. It didn't mean he was anti-American, just anti-war. He and Anna lived up in the west coast province of British Columbia, or BC, as the Canadians called it. He found a teaching job, and they liked their new country.

...

One sunny afternoon, Kate sauntered down the street in her favorite patched blue jeans, her macrame purse swinging from her shoulder. Out of the blue, Mark sprang out of a shop door right in front of her. His eyes crinkled when he saw Kate, and his lopsided smile beamed with pleasure.

It had been over a year since they broke up, and yet Mark chatted as if everything between them was normal. Kate responded with clipped words and pulled out her mother's car keys to make a quick get-away. Her Marlboro cigarettes fell out of her bag and onto the sidewalk.

Mark's face turned stony as he picked up the pack of smokes for her. "What are you doing with these things?" he said with disgust. "I don't want you smoking these cancer sticks."

Kate stiffened in anger. Then she glared at him. "Who are you to tell me what to do?"

The words surprised her and came out hard between set jaws. "You gave up that right a long time ago. I'll do what I damn well please." She grabbed the pack from his hand and stormed around him.

Behind the wheel of her parent's car, Kate took deep breaths to stop her shaking anger. Wiping the tears off her face, she started the vehicle. Then she drove home as though nothing happened, and nothing had happened, really. Like thousands of other high school girls, she still grieved over the loss of something precious. It wasn't just the virginity thing; it was the innocent beauty of that first love. Instinctively, she knew that was the strongest kind of love a girl would ever have.

...

Kate put the chance encounter with Mark aside because her life was changing fast. Portland State University had accepted her application for the fall semester, and she and Joey had saved enough money to get a place together. She attended her high school graduation ceremony, but it wasn't a big deal to her. A week later, when Kate and Joey drove to Portland to rent their first apartment and find summer jobs, that was a milestone.

"Come on, let's rent this one." Joey bounced from room to room as they inspected the place. "We'd each have a bedroom, and we can walk to our university classes in less than ten minutes."

"It is close to everything, all right. But the rent is higher than what we planned." Kate knew they'd have to budget to the bone to make their savings last.

"Look, it's on ground level. We can climb out of the window and pretend we have a patio." Joey pushed up the battered window frame to show how they could access the concrete yard outside.

Kate had to admit that although the apartment was run-down, it was perfect for their first home, and the city's pulse beat out a tantalizing welcome. "Okay, let's rent it."

Kate found summer employment in the cutting room at the Pendleton clothes factory, and Joey worked at a bakery again. They made homemade soups and stews to save their money for college tuition.

One afternoon, Kate tried to find the street where she'd seen the powerful aura around the strange young woman, when that peculiar invitation had popped into her head. That calling had started a spiritual hunger making her want to know what purpose she had in life if there was one. Kate walked around for a while and discovered the right street, but the Salvation Army center wasn't there anymore.

In the big-city atmosphere of Portland, it was easy to slide into the hippie movement. Demonstrations against the war were still happening all over the country. Rock festivals were everywhere too, so Kate and Joey called Leah, and they tried out a local festival for themselves. Loud music blared from live bands and echoed out into the grassy field where six hundred young people sat, stood, or lay wrapped up in each other's arms. Skunky fumes from finger-sized joints were available to anyone for the cost of a smile.

Joey was the extrovert, chatting and beaming at everyone she met. Leah drew people in with dreamy, sweet affection oozing from her heart. But Kate, the quiet introvert, wandered around on her own, an observer out of sync with her peers. She didn't understand why she felt disconnected that day. Perhaps it was because that particular love-celebration seemed so fake. She'd known the real thing with Mark.

...

Kate landed a part-time secretary job in the University's Psych Department when classes started in the fall. She was majoring in psychology, and she soaked up fascinating knowledge from each course she took. The inner-city campus was small, spreading over a few blocks with giant graceful trees, living umbrellas over the walkways. Kate stopped to listen to a flute player on a park bench one morning. His notes drifted up into the beams of sunshine and filtered into the leaves. She had learned about Maslow's peak experiences in her Psych 101 class, and the haunting flute music put her into a state of transcendent joy. Kate knew she was right where she was supposed to be, at a pivotal point in her life.

She and Joey made an assortment of new friends and settled into campus life, mixing their class time with weekend parties. Their tiny living room filled up with guests, and often, someone would roll up a joint and pass it around, which made the evenings mellow. Joey's latest guy, Ryan, brought over a friend with him on Saturday evening. Kate sat in the corner with Jim and chatted until most of the others had left for the night.

135

"Do you want to try something better than grass? Joey asked her into the kitchen. Ryan's got some psychedelic drugs. He's invited us to trip out with them."

"What? I don't know, Joey. How well do you know these guys?"

"They seem nice. You're being cozy with Jim, aren't you? Come on, it's the weekend, and the night's still young."

"Jim isn't my type, but what the heck. Why not?" Kate said. "We smoked marijuana, and nobody went crazy like the school brochures said would happen. Maybe this will be good, too."

The four of them huddled together, and Ryan offered a small pill to each of them. It looked like aspirin, but whatever it was, it didn't take long to kick in.

But this was not like smoking weed. Toking on joints had laid her back so she could hardly move sometimes. The pill she just popped in her mouth revved her up with energy.

"Hey, let's jump in my car and see the city lights," Ryan suggested.

"You can drive on this stuff?" Jim laughed, fitting his arm snug around Kate's waist.

"Sure, I'll be your taxi man tonight. What far-out worlds can we discover with this drug coursing through our veins?"

Kate got in the back seat with Jim and felt like she had entered a jet-set vehicle. Neon city signs lit up in rhythm and synced to the music on the radio as they floated over the streets. Vehicles sprouted free-flowing psychedelic tails behind their bumpers. And when they crossed over the Willamette River, it took forever to fly through the maze of cloverleaves in the air.

Ryan put in a cassette tape, and they all sang along with "Lucy in the Sky with Diamonds." The Beatles played the song in the car full blast just for them. She didn't know how Ryan stayed on his side of the road, but he was maneuvering the car like a magician.

"Hey, we're tripping anyway. Let's go to the airport and pretend we're leaving on a jet plane." Jim's enthusiasm was contagious.

"Perfect man. Let's go there." The others chanted. Even the car obeyed and headed in that direction.

Ryan slid into the short-term parking lot, and they danced toward the terminal to the roar of planes just landing. Inside, the corridors of shops were almost empty that late at night, but they strolled along, acting nonchalant, as though waiting for their flight to be called. Everything seemed funny because inside their heads, they were already on a trip. There was a forgotten balloon hanging on a row of seats that seemed lost and lonely, so Kate rescued it and tied the balloon to her wrist by its string. She talked to it as it bobbed along beside her like a pet. Ryan and Jim were laughing at her, but she didn't care.

"Kate, try to act normal," Jim whispered. "Then nobody will notice we're so strung out."

Kate appreciated the practical advice but every time she looked at Joey, they broke down giggling.

"Maybe you girls should go to the restroom and get it together." She heard Ryan tell Joey.

Joey led her off to the woman's bathroom where they tried to get serious, but since no one else was around, they doubled up with laughter until they almost cried.

Kate peered into the mirror above the sink. Her eyes looked stark, but her skin was alive. The pulsating blood in the veins under her flesh captivated her. She watched it move along the narrow blue pathways back to her heart.

"Hey Joey, look at my skin. Can you see the blood flow?" Kate held out her wrist.

Joey looked and then examined the blue veins in her arm, tracing the surging movement. "Far out! That's so trippy."

"Our hearts are pumping the blood; this throbbing must be what creates our pulse."

"That's got to be it. How awesome is that?"

"Look, it beats in every vein. I think I can hear it." Kate stood stock still, holding her wrist to her ear. A faint sound of drums in the background of her bodily functions sounded loud and clear. That altered perception of their physical anatomy was mesmerizing until they remembered to join the guys back in the airport corridor.

By two in the morning, the fascinating hallucinogen wore off. Kate didn't remember how they all got home, but her pet red balloon went with her.

...

Joey wandered out to their messy kitchen to help Kate clean up after the party. "Wasn't that a trip at the airport?"

"Oh, my God! It was like we had x-ray vision or something." Kate peered at her flesh, amazed at the difference. "I can barely notice the veins in my arm now. What sort of drug did we take, anyway?"

"It had to be a psychedelic, that's for sure." Joey held a plate up like a mirror and pretended to gaze into it.

"But what we saw was real, wasn't it?"

"I don't know. It sure makes you question reality, doesn't it?" Joey pointed out.

Kate wiped down the counter and pondered the risk they had taken. *But we could have had a car accident. Ryan's reality could have killed us all...."*

Chapter 12

A TASTE OF HISTORY

The subjects in her university classes that winter stimulated Kate. Her sociology professor taught them how to use critical analysis to make sense of the rapid political changes in society, but there was much Kate didn't understand. Walking to class one day, she passed a gas station where vehicles were in a line-up almost a block long. The government's official story stated North America was running out of fossil fuel. But the university students she talked to believed it was just one more government lie.

Kate still couldn't figure out why the US troops were over in Vietnam. Did oil seep up out of the ground in the green jungles of Asia? She hadn't heard about it. The only reason that seemed logical was the huge profits the big corporations were making from the sale of military hardware. Kate took her critical analysis a step further.

They wouldn't stop with Vietnam. If American corporations stage-managed war to make mega-profits worldwide, they'd have wars going on continually. And if that was true, what a horrible betrayal to the working-class families who sent their boys off to fight. What's real when everything might be national propaganda?

Kate had met people who still didn't believe the Nazis exterminated millions of Jews during the Second World War. She proved that history to herself outside of a classroom. She went out on a lunch date that spring term with a man who had been there.

Well, Kate didn't exactly date him. Professor Wagner was an older instructor who taught Abnormal Psychology. They often chatted after class because she worked part-time in the Psych Department and got to know him there. She typed up curriculum materials for his classes. It surprised Kate when he asked her out for lunch, but he was an attractive, interesting man, and she accepted his invitation.

Despite their different ages and backgrounds, the conversation flew fast over the table in the restaurant.

"Ah, my young friend, you are naïve in geography and European history."

Kate nodded. "I guess so, but I'm learning. I grew up in a small town, so that's my excuse."

The man across from her smiled with kind eyes. "Don't worry. Your views are refreshing." He shared some of his background and when she discovered he was a Jew who grew up in Austria, she took the opportunity to ask questions.

"So, you must have been right in the middle of things when Hitler was in power?"

"Yes, but I wasn't more than a child then," Professor Wagner said, rolling up his shirtsleeves. "They sent my whole family to one of the death camps."

"But that's horrible." Kate regretted asking him about it.

"It was inhumane." He pointed to the blue-inked numbers tattooed on the inside of his forearm. Like a cattle brand, the small triangle and six digits half an inch high, marched down his left forearm. The light brown hair on his pale skin could not disguise the permanent markings.

"You must have some awful memories," Kate responded in sympathy.

"Yes, I and many others," he said. "The Nazis murdered six million Jews in the gas chambers of those concentration camps."

Kate sat and stared at him. She didn't know what to say.

"They sent us to Auschwitz, the biggest camp. I was young enough to still be alive when the Allies finally reached us.

"Yet you survived somehow. What about your family?"

Professor Wagner shook his head. "No, they're all gone." He grew quiet, as if he had shared too much. His gaze focused outside the lattice window beside their table.

"What brutality and deprivation you've endured."

"The smoke, you know? It was a constant reminder. We could see it...." He cut his sentence off short.

Kate caught her breath as she visualized tall chimneys in a gray landscape, billowing out the smoke of burned flesh. What was that smell like? She looked at his tattoo again. The horror of living through that atrocity engulfed her with a flood of emotion.

"Oh, dear, I apologize," her professor said in such a gentle voice. "I did not mean to give you a history lesson over our pleasant lunch together." Then he redirected the conversation back to more mundane things.

Kate hurried to the library on campus after the lunch date and did some research. His tattooed markings and the facts he gave her were all true. Her older friend must have been one of the young, incarcerated skeletons who walked out of Auschwitz when the Allies liberated the Jews. Professor Wagner had miraculously survived.

...

Kate and Joey moved into a bigger house in the spring where they each rented a bedroom for a lot less money. Joey worked full time so she could do some traveling, but Kate continued her college classes, soaking up knowledge any way she could.

Cheryl was a student in her sociology class. She was a tall, fun-loving girl with strawberry blonde hair but no freckles. One Sunday morning, they decided to go to a Peace Rally. They walked across the Burnside Bridge and continued to follow a side street along the Willamette River.

"That must be it, just ahead," Cheryl said, picking up her pace.

"Wow, hundreds of people are here already." Kate had expected some college kids milling around, but many older professionals had shown up, too. The park was on the banks of the river overlooking the city skyline, and as they waited for the rally to begin, the sun's warmth felt good on Kate's shoulders.

Then a man with blue jeans and a bright white T-shirt walked to the top of the steps to address the people with a microphone.

"Everyone, hello." He paused and took his time to let the crowd settle down. "We've assembled to protest the military presence in Southeast Asia. Why are we here again, you might ask when the government led us to believe the war is winding down? Well, today I'm here to tell you this aggression continues to grow. Not only are we still fighting in Vietnam, but we've just found out our military forces have also been bombing the nearby countries of Cambodia and Laos."

Disgruntled groans of shock rippled through the crowd. Kate couldn't believe it either.

"Yes, it is true. The military is taking these aggressive actions—without the knowledge of Congress or the American public. President Nixon's administration tried to stop the facts from leaking out, but recently published Pentagon Papers confirm this deception."

Those people standing around Kate first mumbled and then shouted out their outrage.

"But today, we celebrate the Supreme Court's decision to uphold our First Amendment. Justice Black's closing statement in the case confirms what we know to be true. 'Only a free and unrestrained press can effectively expose deception in government.'"

"So, we say, 'Bravo for the New York Times,' who is brave enough to challenge the US government in the Supreme Court."

Kate knew she stood at a pivotal point in history. She studied her surroundings. The Willamette River swept along beside the group as though it carried the political toxins to the ocean to cleanse the land.

The speaker's voice picked up in volume. "Thomas Jefferson gave us 'unalienable rights to life, liberty and the pursuit of happiness.' Therefore, we have the right to refuse arbitrary rules like the draft requiring us to take actions against our conscience. May we each find the courage to do what our hearts tell us to do."

The crowd cheered in agreement, and a young woman moved to the steps and lifted her palms upward. She sang an old spiritual folksong that Joan Baez made famous, and her voice rose like church bells tolling over the river. Kate joined with the others in a sacred outflowing of emotion, singing "We Shall Overcome." Those strong affirmations sunk heart-deep, and Kate swore to stand up for what she believed; war was wrong.

After that morning, Kate fell into a melancholy mood. She picked up Joey's guitar and plucked the notes from the lyrics of the song, except the words echoed back to her with deep personal meaning:

~~SOME~~DAY~~
~~YOU~~WILL~~OVERCOME~~

There were lots of free concerts in the city parks that summer and she and Joey enjoyed the hot weather in their free time. They only drove back home to Hood River to see their families twice.

Kate got a job as a gardener in the cemeteries for the city of Portland. She had to laugh at this odd employment, but working for the Municipal Parks Department paid well, and she knew how to pull weeds and rake flower beds from helping her dad in their garden. She wore cut-offs and T-shirts and listened to music on her ghetto blaster as she worked in the beautiful landscape dotted with gravestones. One day, a couple of gravediggers were doing their job nearby. She walked over to visit and sat on a tombstone to talk and eat her lunch. "Where's the body?" she joked. "When is the funeral?"

They looked at each other and then back at her. "This is the pauper's area. The body is that box of ashes by your feet, and I guess you're at the only funeral this poor sucker's going to get."

Sure enough, on the ground beside her was a small wooden box, and it shamed her to be so flippant. No mourners were ever going to honor this person, now reduced to so little. After that, Kate took her job more seriously and respected the dead by playing only beautiful melancholy music for the remains of those bodies in the ground. She read the epitaphs on their tombstones and wondered what would be written on her own. Their lives were history. She had hers still to live.

Chapter 13

TRIPPING THROUGH A MEADOW

Kate bought her first used car that fall to get back and forth to classes. It was an older baby blue Volkswagen Beetle, the same color as Joey's convertible. Kate drove her car with pride because the shape symbolized a rebellion against the long, sleek cars of The Establishment.

She was lucky to get the courses she was wanted at the start of her second year at university. In her Astronomy class, the study of outer galaxies fascinated Kate, as well as the tall, good-looking guy she was getting to know. Doug wore his hair in a ponytail like a blond Viking and was also in her psychology class. They'd gone out on a few dates, and a calm strength about him was appealing. He gave her soft kisses that tugged at her heart.

One day, they wandered out of the classroom discussing the lecture on black holes in deep space. Kate found the concept thought-provoking, but when Doug changed the conversation to a whole new subject, she became even more intrigued.

"I got a hold of some windowpane acid yesterday," Doug said when the halls were quiet.

"What's windowpane acid?" Kate asked.

"It's a mind-altering drug called LSD, a chemical they're studying for use in psychiatry." Doug leaned against the wall to let other students pass by in the corridor.

Kate lowered her voice and looked around. "I've heard something about that research."

"Well, I know a guy who works in the lab, and this stuff has a reputation for opening spiritual connections."

Really?" Kate's miscarriage had changed her beliefs, and she hadn't gone to church in a long time. But those subliminal messages she had heard in her head might be a type of spiritual connection. She pulled her attention back to Doug. "So, they're going to use it to treat psychiatric patients? That's interesting."

"This Saturday my friends and I plan to drive up to Mount Hood to a gorgeous meadow we found. We're going to drop some acid there." Doug raised one eyebrow and grinned. "Do you want to do some personal scientific research and try some with me?"

Kate's first experience with hard drugs had been bizarre, but it also gave her breathtaking new insights. Besides, Doug was a handsome hunk of a man. She'd love to share this experience with him.

"I won't need much if I take it. The only other time I tried hard drugs turned into a crazy trip just walking around the airport. I don't know what kind it was."

"Windowpane acid is the absolute purest. The lab techs drip the liquid onto cellophane paper and cut it into eighth-of-an-inch squares that melt in your mouth. That's why it has the name, but we can cut it in half and share it, okay?"

"Will I'll fit in with your friends, though?" Kate remembered when she met Mark's college pals and felt left out.

"Sure, you will. I've known them since we were kids."

Kate bounced a little in excitement. "Okay, I'll try it with you." The consciousness-expanding drug intrigued her. What would her next trip be like?

...

It was warm for the end of September. After driving halfway up the mountain, Doug pulled off on a side road and cautiously unfolded a gum wrapper. He showed her the protected translucent square inside. The piece was so tiny, hardly bigger than a pinhead. Doug took a razor blade from a plastic case and split it in half, and they laughed at how insignificant it appeared. He put one rectangle on the tip of his finger and licked it off. Then he placed the other on her tongue and sealed it with a kiss and a grin.

They continued up the gravel road for half an hour until they met his friends parked at a turnoff. An emerald-green meadow stretched out before them with snow-capped Mt Hood standing on the far end in all its majesty. By then, the acid had kicked in.

"Hey, you made it, man." Doug's friends greeted them as they milled around his car.

"Sure did. We had a good drive up here."

"You drop yours yet?" one of them asked.

"Oh, yeah!" Doug smiled emphatically. "Kate, this is Mario, Alana, Jorge, and Ruth."

Kate said hello but knew she wouldn't remember all their names.

Jorge took a Frisbee out of his knapsack and sailed it through the air. Back and forth it went as they made their way out into the meadow. Soon their frisbee play turned into a gentle body-checking game of tag. Then, when things became a little spinney, the group stretched full out on the soft grassy ground. They moved so their heads came together forming the center of a star, and they held each other's hands. Feeling so much tingling energy, they tried to channel it across the synapses, from one mind to another. Everyone's feet pointed in all the directions of the compass, and their individuality fused into a living Borg, bound, and saturated in an all-consuming love.

Flat out on the surface of the field, the group gazed up into the heavens. Someone pointed out the oddity of the clouds, a mackerel sky quilted into puffy squares. The blanket of white spread across the whole curvature of the earth and paralleled the wide mound of ground they lay on. Mt Hood towered overhead, filling up half of the horizon, an ancient god of purity, their own "Stairway to Heaven."

In time, their collective snowflake broke apart. Kate and Doug drifted off by themselves to explore that strange new world, like the actors on Star Trek in the new television series. The grass in the field grew in dark vibrant color, with tassel-tops of gold reaching upward. Tall fir trees at the edge of the meadow circled their emerald island.

Kate held up a handful of dark, rich soil. With magnified eyesight, she zoomed down and tunneled into the fullness of each living component that made up the whole. Tiny bits of multi-colored organic matter, specks of sand, active organisms, and shiny minerals all throbbed in her hand.

"Look at this! No wonder plants can grow from dirt." Kate showed the handful to Doug.

"Wow," he said. "The dirt is alive."

Kate plucked a single blade of grass, and her vision zoomed in on the fiber. There she discovered a green machine, a factory manufacturing chlorophyll. Each pinpoint of neon color burst into being on the outer edge. They pulsated with life in a steady beat, marching inward to enter tiny capillaries. She watched the bright dots thrust into the stem of the grass and merge into the flowing liquid like microscopic cars on a freeway. It was the water mixed with minerals brought up from the soil.

Kate confronted a profound truth. Vegetation grew because soil and sunlight existed in a loving symbiotic relationship. It was a sacred connection! Then she remembered to examine her skin. Just like before, the intricate surface of living flesh captivated her. She ran over to show Doug and the others.

"Hey, you guys. Look at your skin up close," she said.

Doug and his friends studied the veins in their arms and saw the same thing.

"That is so radical, man!" Jorge said. "Far out!"

Alana was dancing. "I can see my blood pumping in my arms."

"Like we're outside our bodies looking at them," Ruth added.

Doug jumped to his own conclusion. "Skin must be the outer layer of our energized molecules."

"Look at a blade of grass. You can see the same thing happening in leaves." Kate plucked a green stem and held it up.

After that, they all peered at pieces of grass and weeds and saw the neon molecules on the move. Mario expanded the concept perfectly. "I got it. It's the pattern of creation. The little capillary veins in our skin are like the twigs on the branches of a tree!"

Kate thought of another epiphany, but it was too personal to share. Joy must be the physical sensation of interacting with other energy sources, just like the sunlight does to the leaf. That's what pleasure is! She thought of the wind on her face, the feel of dirt on her bare feet, and the simple pleasure of holding someone's hand. Then another truth telepathically flashed across her brain.

~~I~~LIVE~~IN~~ALL~~THINGS~~

She burst out laughing. "Ok, I can see you, God. You're all around me!" Kate stood still, electrified, as tiny flares of brilliant color burst forth from every nerve ending under her skin.

Doug seemed to understand her reaction and stretched his arms wide, twirling in circles. Kate imitated him, absorbing exquisite feelings. She became teary-eyed from the beauty of nature surrounding her, made by a loving Creator for the sole purpose of providing pleasure for human beings.

Kate and Doug joined the group again, and Mario got their attention. "Isn't that a farmhouse way off at the end of the field?"

"Let's hike over and check it out," Doug suggested.

Jorge was already moving in that direction. "Yeah, let's meet the inhabitants who live in this paradise."

"We should thank them for letting us spend the afternoon here," Alana said, and the others thought it was a most excellent idea.

Ruth wasn't looking at the farmhouse, though. "Kate, where are your shoes?"

Kate realized she was barefoot. "I don't know. It doesn't matter to me." She loved the texture of the brown earth squishing between her toes.

Alana and Ruth hugged her with concern. "Maybe we can find some shoes for Kate to wear at the farmhouse."

So off they went down the long stretch of the meadow, arms linked to form a straight front line of unity. Mt Hood was huge, the sun was shining, and they had a mission to accomplish in that foreign land.

The farmer's home was built with squared timber, and it had a solid, weathered door. Wildflowers grew around the front porch. But before they could even knock, the door opened, and out came the ugliest man Kate had ever seen. His head was disproportionate to the shape of his gaunt frame. He wore glasses so thick his eyes appeared huge and took up the top half of his face. However, the man's strange appearance didn't faze Doug as he introduced each of them.

"We wanted to meet the person lucky enough to live in this beautiful spot," Doug explained. Then they all bubbled over in their eagerness to engage in conversation.

"You have such a splendid view of Mount Hood.

"Thank you for letting us visit your meadow."

"What a gorgeous day this is." They voiced their thoughts in simple harmony.

The man with the thick lenses quickly became their friend, and they all chatted in an old-fashioned neighborly visit.

"But this girl here," the ugly man stepped closer to Kate, and the enormous eyes behind his glasses peered down at her feet. "She has no shoes."

"She lost them in the meadow." Her friends erupted in laughter with their explanation.

"That won't do," he said. "Follow me to the hay barn. I keep a family trunk of old clothes there. We'll find some footwear for you, girly."

The six of them peered up into the rafters, the high spaciousness of the barn, and their nostrils filled with the aroma of fresh hay. Rays of sunshine found their way through the cracks in the rough walls, and dust motes danced in the beams. The strange farmer led the group to a dim corner where an antique wooden chest sat. They gathered around it, not sure what to expect.

He opened it, and out came the most outlandish, outdated clothes imaginable. Dresses with ruffles and gathered organza, pinstriped suits, and fancy men's boots were lifted out of the box. Under these, the ugly man picked up a pair of red leather strapped heels. And somehow, when Kate tried them on, they were exactly her size.

"Here, it is my gift to you," the odd man said when she resisted.

Kate thought how kind he was, even beautiful, in his grotesqueness. How like the universe to provide for her every need with humor and abundance. The odd-looking man worked for God somehow. Kate knew it without having to understand it.

She thanked him graciously and gave him a warm hug. Then, like Dorothy in the Wizard of Oz, she walked away in elegance.

Each of them thanked him profusely for his kindness and they all trekked back down the green field where the sky had lost its sharpness. The day was ending, and vivid colors paled into muted tones. When they reached their cars, Doug made plans with the others to rendezvous at Jorge's house until the acid completely wore off. He and Kate climbed into his car to start driving around the mountain again. Doug followed the road at a slower pace this time, and Kate was glad. She was having trouble merging back into the real world, and she thought he found it hard, too.

Only a few vehicles passed them by. The moon climbed over the black horizon as shafts of pale light splintered through the trees, spilling out onto the highway. They were on a moonlit fluorescent ribbon meandering through the forest while odd shapes and shadows did a bizarre dance in front of them. Kate's mind was drifting out of her head, penetrating through the glass window and into the empty spaces outside. She focused on keeping her thoughts held tight inside her skull.

"What if we can't find our way home?" The question slithered out of her mouth in a little mouse's voice.

Doug didn't answer, concentrating on the road ahead. They pushed on for what seemed like forever.

"What if we travel off into this emptiness and can't ever find the way back?" Kate was a little… no; she was a lot freaked out by then.

Doug cleared his throat to project his thoughts. "We just need to keep heading into time. Then we'll arrive in the place we're supposed to be."

Something about his words unsettled Kate. On the ribbon of life, where were they on the timeline? Returning to reality depended on whether they could find the correct porthole to merge back. Kate experienced such exquisite details in a paradise world, but now they were thrust into fearful exile on a menacing highway.

Please, God. Get me back to my own time. Kate repeated the sentence with fervency. The beautiful life force she had recently experienced was gone, and fear had her in its grip. *Please God, bring us back to safety.*

Eventually, the acid trip leveled off in subtle increments and they arrived at their friend's house. Everybody found beds and couches to crash for the night, but for Kate, the final sensations of the day still haunted her in nightmares.

...

It took Kate a couple of days to process her windowpane acid trip because the ramifications were huge. If she could see a living force of energy pulsating in her skin and in the sky, in the leaves, even in dirt, all from taking a teeny speck of a psychedelic chemical, then that knowledge changed everything. It meant that all living things were exquisitely interconnected for mutual benefit.

This beauty in the natural world was what people were supposed to be experiencing all the time. All things pulsated with life and that connected her to every living thing. Maybe even non-living things were somehow connected. *Darn it, I should have looked at a rock.*

Their group had bonded together in love despite their differences. There hadn't been an ounce of judgment by anyone, and the day was sheer perfection. Who was the ugly man then, with the glasses thick as Coke bottles? If she returned to visit the old house in the meadow again, would he still be there? He had showered her with kindness, and genuine caring sparkled through the thick lenses of his spectacles. He provided the very thing she needed and exuded love and acceptance to all of them. To exist in this state of universal energized love would be… She tried to come up with a word. *It would be heaven on earth.*

Kate had tasted a slice of heaven. She had met the personification of God himself. She couldn't have learned that truth from a psychology course. On the other hand, she remembered her terror when they were driving home. Things had unraveled, and her mind had drifted off into the menacing nothingness outside her body. That didn't come from a source of love, and it had a powerful influence. Perhaps negative entities existed, not at all supportive to humans such as herself.

The acid trip was only a chemically generated experience, but didn't it prove the existence of a Higher Intelligence in a parallel dimension? How could she blend that esoteric knowledge into her academic pursuits in psychology? Are the two systems of learning at odds with each other? Hard drugs might be dangerous counterfeits, but they showed her alternative realities did exist.

How she wanted to merge with the presence of God, for real! But wasn't that impossible to manifest in her real life?

Chapter 14

A CHANGE OF PACE

Kate returned home after classes one day in time for the postman to hand her the mail before he left. She opened the letter from Joey and Leah, who were hitchhiking down through Mexico. Kate had envied their free-spirited adventures all winter term while she plodded along trying to get a college education. But this letter differed from the others. Joey's scrawled handwriting told her something was drastically wrong.

"We're heading next to a picturesque little fishing village called San Blas north of Puerto Vallarta. A lot of hippies from the west coast stay down for the winter. Kate, do you think you can meet up with us there? I need your help. Leah overdosed on drugs at a beach party, and she's acting like she lost her mind."

Oh no. Not gentle-hearted Leah. Kate's hands gripped the letter and looked out the window in her room. The university term wasn't quite over, so how could she offer any help? Besides, she'd have to dip into her small savings to travel anywhere. Yet Joey had never asked anything from her before, and if Leah was that troubled, she wanted to be there for her friends.

Kate had written all her term papers, regurgitating what she had read from the assigned readings except for Political Science. That one class held her back, and she didn't want to lose the course credits after paying for it.

Kate tapped on Professor Andrews' office door the next day. "Excuse me, Sir. Could I talk to you?"

Professor Andrews had such charisma in class. It was still there as he hitched up his hip-looking denim overalls and motioned her to take a seat. "Come on in. What brings you by this early in the morning?" he asked.

"I have a dire emergency with a girlfriend who ran into trouble in Mexico. I need to leave and help her return to the States, and I won't have time to write the final research paper for your class, Professor."

"This term is almost over. Perhaps the rescue mission for your friend can wait for a week?" He didn't seem condescending, but she wasn't sure he was taking her seriously, either.

"I can't put off this commitment," Kate said. She told him about her friend's accidental drug overdose and how she was acting totally out of character like she'd gone mental.

"That is an obligation you might need to honor. However, it would be a shame not to receive University credit for the course if you drop out now." He rubbed his chin with his forefinger.

Kate tried to win him over. "I like your class. It taught me how our political system works and how corrupt it can be. I want to be an activist to change things, at least for the people I know."

"Under the circumstances," he gave her a steady look, "how about I give you an oral exam instead? I have half an hour before my next appointment."

"You mean, right now? You'd give me the exam here?" Kate gulped and chewed on her thumb in sudden nervousness when he nodded.

"Sure, tell me what you would have written on your term paper had you written one." Professor Andrews leaned back in his chair.

Kate took a deep breath and summarized the reading material he had assigned by explaining how the Civil Rights movement set the foundations to fuel the anti-war sentiment and demonstrations. She interpreted what she'd read in the news and expressed her shock at the students who were killed at Kent State. She told him how appalling it was to discover how Nixon secretly bombed Cambodia a few years ago without the consent of the House and the Senate.

"They called it 'Operation Breakfast,' but it's been exposed only recently. And it happened all while the government claimed to be deescalating the war." Kate ended there, wondering if she had done a good enough job on her verbal dissertation.

Professor Andrews ran a hand through his already messed-up long hair. "I see you've done the assigned lessons and have a good grasp of the troubled times we live in. I'll give you an above-average passing mark for the class."

"You would? That's fantastic. It's so cool to let me take the exam this way."

"That's done then. Now go off to Mexico and rescue your friend. You'll discover more about politics by visiting foreign cultures than I can teach you next term. We can't all be academics stuck in these lifeless rooms of learning and I'm a bit envious of you." Then he stood up to shake her hand.

Professor Andrew's unexpected approval made Kate's decision to drop out of college an easy one. Her landlord said she could store her belongings in his basement so Kate sent a letter to Joey and Leah's last address confirming she'd meet them in San Blas as soon as she could.

...

Kate shared her plans with Cheryl, her study partner in their sociology class in the university cafeteria the next day.

"You're not going to hitchhike down to Mexico alone, are you?" Cheryl quizzed her with concern.

"Well, just down through the states to the border. Lots of kids are on the road hitching rides like that. It'll save money for other expenses on the trip."

Cheryl's blue eyes stared at her. "When you get to the border, what will you do then?" she asked.

"I'll take a train south; I hear it's a cheap way to travel."

"Hey, you know what? Let me come with you!" Cheryl threw up her hands in excitement. "Let's both take the Spring term off and have some grand adventures."

"It would be good to have company." Kate's voice raised a pitch in eagerness. "I didn't really want to hitchhike alone."

"When are you leaving?"

"The day after tomorrow."

"Whew, that's fast," Cheryl said. "Then let's start packing." They gave each other high fives and hurried off to buy maps of Mexico and get traveler's checks. By the end of the day, Kate had put most of the things she would need in her backpack.

Cheryl asked her a question on the phone that night. "Do you mind if my friends Kris and Joanne come along?"

"They want to come too? I guess we could hitchhike in pairs for a couple of days and then meet in Tijuana at the railway station. We have to get our Visa cards there first before we cross the border."

"That sounds like a plan."

"What are your friends like?" Kate asked, thinking about four girls traveling together.

"Joanne is game for anything, and Kris is pretty cool, too."

The next morning, Kate and Cheryl piled into her brother's car, and he drove them to the freeway ramp. They started laughing when he shoved in a cassette tape of James Taylor singing his popular song, "Mexico" for them, and it was the perfect sendoff.

Joanne and Kris were waiting at the designated time and place. Joanne was the youngest with honey-blonde hair, but Kris seemed more mature with her short, brown pixie cut.

"Isn't this outrageous?" Joanne shrieked with excitement after the introductions.

"Talk about spontaneous travel plans," Kris said, laughing as she rested her pack on the ground.

"Okay, you guys. Let's get our maps out and mark our destination." Kate passed around a red pen, and they each placed a dot on San Blas, on the west coast, in the state of Nayarit.

"Wow, we're going a long way south, aren't we?" Joanne shouted over the roaring traffic, and the others agreed. Kate and Cheryl gave the other two girls a hug and walked a short distance away, but it required a bit of bravado to stick their thumbs out on the freeway for the first time.

A small car soon stopped for them, and they scrutinized the driver. Trusting their gut instincts, they nodded at each other before climbing into the vehicle.

"Bye! See you in three days at the Tijuana train station," Cheryl called out to Joanne and Kris, who stood waiting for the next car to stop.

Kate discovered hitchhiking was an exciting, easy way to travel. It was cheap, and you met all kinds of friendly people who shared unique perspectives on every topic imaginable. When dusk arrived, they walked off the freeway and stayed in a small, inexpensive hotel for their first night on the road. Then at the Mexican border, they showed their ID, applied for their tourist cards, and walked across into the town of Tijuana with no trouble at all.

"We have to find a Cambio first to exchange our dollars for pesos," Kate said. There was one on the street up ahead, and it didn't take long to stash away the strange colored bills in their money belts.

"Now, let's find a clean little room somewhere," Cheryl said. "But look, there's a liquor store. We could buy something to celebrate our first day in a foreign country." They ducked in and bought some cheap tequila, but it was exotic because it had a pickled worm at the bottom of the bottle. After they booked into an inexpensive hotel room, they poured an inch of the amber liquid into two water glasses and clicked them together. "To life and adventures," they toasted. Their drink was harsh to swallow, but it sure packed a kick.

Kris and Joanne were waiting for them in front of the railway station in the morning, just as they had planned. After the four of them chattered about their hitchhiking experiences, they climbed on board a dusty, antiquated train for a grueling thirty-nine-hour journey through the central states of Mexico. They took up two of the cracked leather bench seats that were facing each other, and their island of pale skin stood out against the dark local Mexicans in the train car. Kate greeted one woman with a smile and her high school Spanish broke the language barrier.

"Buenos días, señora. Como esta usted? Good day! How are you?" Kate asked.

"Bien, gracias, y tú?" the older woman returned the greeting and asked where they were going. Kate explained and was amazing how much one could communicate using gestures and a few simple words. When nighttime came, the Mexicans stretched flat out on their seats. The girls put their backpacks on the floor between their two benches to keep them safe, and it formed a lumpy bed for them to lie on. The evening became hilariously good fun with discreet sips of lemonade mixed with their tequila. They fell asleep with their feet tucked into the armpits of the others.

The train seemed to have only one slow clickity-clack speed the next day, and Kate worried about Leah and Joey during the long hours on the train. Was Leah's mental state getting better or worse? How was she going to help her friends after meeting up with them?

At every small village, the train slowed down to a screeching halt. Local vendors carried baskets of food on their heads, selling hot tacos, warm cinnamon pastries called churros, and exotic fruit to the passengers. All they had to do was reach through the open windows with their pesos to buy the food the village people offered. Kate's first choice for a meal became hot tamales wrapped in banana leaves.

Most of the Mexican people were friendly, except at one stop when she tried to step down the metal stairs between the train cars to stretch. She followed a swarthy older man in khaki pants and shirt, but turned to glare at her in disgust, and slammed the heavy cover to the stairs down almost on her feet. Kate stepped back just in time, wondering what events in his life had made him act that way. Were there anti-American sentiments down here, too? She spent hours watching the small communities and rural scenery rolling by the window. Farmers worked in their fields, and others on horseback traveled on horseback. Once she saw two teams of horses hitched to wagonloads of hay. They stood picturesque against the sunset on the horizon, waiting for the train to pass.

After two days of weary rail travel, Kate and her friends reached Tepic. Bone-weary, they stumbled off the train and asked for directions to the nearby bus station. Then they shouldered their heavy backpacks and shuffled down the street in a single file.

"This place is a madhouse," Joanne murmured. The bustling waiting room of the bus station had old-fashioned wooden benches filled with people.

Cute little kids played among the satchels piled high around their parents. Hardworking farmers punctuated their conversation with intense gestures, while influential businessmen clad in brown suits stood aloof. All the locals stared at them as they pushed through the crowd.

"Where's the bus schedule? I don't see any brochures around," Kris asked.

"Look at the man on the ladder." Joanne pointed and laughed. "He's writing the schedule on a huge chalkboard." The bus to the coast left in an hour, so they stood in line to purchase the tickets they needed.

A tired-looking old yellow school bus whisked them out of town on a two-lane country road that wound through lush green hills of vegetation. The driver had draped a string of miniature Christmas lights across the top of the front window and hung a plastic Jesus that danced on the dashboard. Kate was glad Jesus was up near the driver because when the bus tilted around the hairpin corners, Kate had to grip the edge of her seat and say a prayer or two. Huge semi-trucks wanted to pass while oncoming cars came at them. But that was no problem for their bus driver, who simply swerved off the road to make three lanes to allow one vehicle to drive down the middle of the narrow pavement. Graciousness seemed to be applied even to the rules of the road in that country.

The bus crept down through the hills to the coast and into San Blas in the late afternoon, where tall coconut trees and flowering bougainvillea grew abundantly. Shops and businesses stood shoulder to shoulder around a small plaza in the middle of town. Exhausted and ravenous with hunger, the four of them stumbled into the nearest restaurant.

"You girls, you just get in?" A couple of young gringos, foreigners like themselves, asked in friendliness.

"Yeah, what a ride down through the mountains that was!" Kate answered for all of them.

"Welcome to Paradise! This restaurant has the best tacos in town. Where are you from?"

They exchanged the usual travel chatter and ordered dishes from the menu. Kate wolfed her tacos down when they came and wondered if Joey and Leah had arrived already. She got her phrase book out and first asked the waiter for directions to the post office in her broken Spanish. "Hey, you guys, I need to check for a letter from my other girlfriends."

"We'll wait then. Meet you back here," Cheryl said. "We can't wait to walk around the town and see the beach."

"Shall we get rooms in the same hotel?" asked Joanne. "It'd be good to stick together." They all agreed with that plan. Kate hurried away to find the Post Office, but there was no letter addressed to her. Kate frowned with concern. *Where are Joey and Leah? After rushing to Mexico, why aren't they here to meet me?*

Chapter 15

A CLASH OF CULTURE

Kate and her friends checked into a hotel right on the beach that night, but it was small and dingy. Their two match-box-sized rooms smelled disgustingly stale, and at nine o'clock, the electricity shut off.

"Do you hear that?" Kate sat up in the dark on her lumpy bed.

"It sounds like a rat, or maybe a cockroach," Cheryl said.

"Oh, yuck. There must be a lot of them then."

"Quick, turn on a flashlight." The beam of light illuminated giant brown crusty creatures at least a couple of inches long. The cockroaches scurried over the scarred-up counter and tabletops looking for crumbs.

"Gross!" they both screamed, which made the giant bugs disappeared into cracks in the walls. Kate and Cheryl cleaned up the best they could, but they slept little that night. They learned the first lesson about budget traveling in Mexican. Put all your food away before lying down to sleep.

Kris and Joanne had roaches in their room too, so despite the beach location, all four girls decided other accommodations were necessary for the next night.

"Hey, I wonder if we'd be able to rent a tiny house together," Cheryl, the most experienced traveler, suggested as she packed her bag. "It might be cheaper than two hotel rooms in some other dive."

"Wouldn't that be cool?" Kate hoped to make this trip a real vacation for herself. "We could rent for a month even if we all don't stay that long and it would still cost less than hotel rooms by the night."

Kate used her broken Spanish to ask around at the local businesses as they explored the quaint little town. They found an owner who gave them a tour of his small brick house that had three bedrooms, an outdoor shower with a rusty spigot, a two-burner stove, and a beat-up old fridge. A small walled garden had a tall banana tree in the back of the house, with ripe bananas, and that sealed the deal.

Kate and the others moved in and slept in comfort. During the coming times, they emulated the lifestyle of the Mexican locals who knew how to slow down and enjoy life in a charming manner. In the center plaza, after the sun set, friends and extended families mingled together after the heat of the day. Old folks on the park benches smiled at the antics of their grandchildren and couples squeezed up close and made googly eyes at each other. Young men threw their arms over each other's shoulders and talked about their workday, while dark-haired girls held hands and flirted with the guys who strolled by.

The gringos imitated the manners of the locals in the market, too, where friendly bargaining for food and clothing at the stalls was such a contrast to the hustle and bustle of the world back home.

Each morning, Kate checked the post office, and after that, she and Cheryl walked to the beach and hung out with a variety of young hippies. Fashion wasn't important; bikinis, old, frayed cut-offs, and neon T-shirts were all one needed to wear.

Kate found a funky cantina on one of the dirt side roads, and it became their favorite place to gather in the warm evenings. They sat on the leather padded cane chairs with other young gringos and drank margaritas. Local guitar players strummed out beautiful Spanish music for entertainment.

"I'll show you the proper way to drink tequila straight. It's cheaper that way." A good-looking guy bought two shot glasses for them, eager to share his valuable knowledge. "First, you wet the pad of your thumb and sprinkle it with salt."

"What? That's crazy," but both she and Cheryl followed his instructions.

"Now, squeeze a slice of lime into your mouth. Then lick the salt off your thumb and suck back the shot of tequila." A small crowd nearby applauded as Cheryl and Kate entertained them with the process. Tequila was cheaper than beer, and the taste rush was one to be savored.

Walking home late at night held no dangers because of Mexico's heavy Catholic influence. The fabric of society was knit together with moral standards and held firmly in place. The only thing Kate had to look out for was the herd of pigs roaming about the streets. The farmers let them loose to scavenge and eat the organic waste people left out. The pigs acted as natural garbage collectors and solved the sanitation problem in that tropical climate.

The San Blas business owners realized hippie-gringos had little money, but even so, that tourism added to the community's wealth. Thus, the gracious local citizens shared their village, and the grateful foreigners showed them respect and took on the simplicity of their lifestyle.

Kate loved the village life and admired the hard-working Mexican people. On Sunday morning, she walked down the dusty streets in the poorer side of town, and immaculately dressed families came out of tidy thatched huts, all ready for church. The men wore crisp white shirts, and the women dressed in freshly ironed colorful blouses and skirts. And still no letter came from Joey, so all she could do was wait and worry, hoping they were doing okay. Then she met Miguel.

One evening, Kate and Cheryl swam naked with other young hippies in the ocean waves just to see the fluorescent plankton sparkle on their bodies in the moonlight. Miguel was one of the other gringos and he came out of the water like a black Aztec god, completely unabashed. After they all toweled off and got dressed, most of the group headed back to the cantina. Miguel, well-built and deep charcoal brown, took her hand and asked her to take a walk down the beach along to town.

Kate found him mysterious and educated, even if he spoke a strange broken English. His charisma and sultry glances drew her in. Miguel named all the constellations in the sky as they walked alongside the ebbing tide of the shoreline. Moonlight after midnight on a warm ocean beach played havoc with Kate's sensibilities. When he tilted her chin up for a kiss, the reflection from the moon danced across the black pupils of his eyes.

In the following days, they discovered places of local beauty most tourists never visited. Miguel took her inland on a flat riverboat tour to see monkeys swinging in the trees. Leathery, huge iguanas lay on the overhanging green branches. They watched fishermen bring in their morning catch on the beach and bought fresh shrimp right off the boats for their breakfast. The fishermen's wives cooked them over a small nearby barbecue and served them with seafood sauce in tantalizing aroma.

"In the sun, let us eat here." Miguel said, patting the warm sand beside him.

Kate sat down to shell her hot shrimp, dipped them into the sauce, and devoured each one. After the impromptu brunch, she told him her reasons for coming to Mexico was to help her girlfriends. She stretched out her white legs and bounced them up and down on the hard sand. His dark ones did the same and Kate commented, "They look like…"

"Piano keys!" he said and laughed at their mutual observation. Miguel hummed a melody to match their movements.

As the days went by, Kate thought of him as her Mexican boyfriend. He was intelligent, with integrity she admired, yet she noticed a distinct energy and paradox to his mannerisms.

"Where did you live before coming here?" she asked, curious about him.

"I do not come from Mexico," he said.

"What country do you come from, then? Where were you born?"

"I was not born, not in manner you know." Miguel had the most penetrating black eyes, so deep they were like black holes in outer space. He enunciated his next words with care. "I simply arrived."

"From where?" Kate peered at him.

He lifted his shoulders and hesitated at each word. "No explanation will make you believe."

"I'm not judgmental. Try me." Kate saw a compelling strangeness overtake him, and he said the next words in a monotone.

"I am not from this planet. Two years ago, I land on deserted beach in Tamaulipas on east shoreline of Mexico."

"Oh, from a spaceship, perhaps?" Kate rolled her eyes. He was usually so sincere; she couldn't fathom why he would concoct such a story to impress her. Didn't he realize she was already attracted to him?

"My people have current space station on your moon's dark side. Others like me, in capsules, arrive for earth study in... how would you say, in slice of time."

They sat close, side by side, and his dark brown hand held hers on his thigh. Kate couldn't help but compare the contrast in pigmentation. But really—not from this world?

"You landed in a flying saucer, and you claim to be an alien." Kate summarized his explanation.

"Not like saucers that fly, but in force-field, egg shape capsule. I splashed down in ocean for soft land."

Kate giggled at the picture he described. "So, the egg cracked open, and you climbed out?"

"See, I think you do not believe me." He formed a tolerant smile.

"No, I don't, but we can still be friends. It's fun to hang out, and…" she looked him up and down, "you're a handsome specimen from outer space if what you say is true," she teased.

Kate filed the conversation away and continued to enjoy his company. Miguel lived in a one-room thatched cabana on a dirt road at the edge of the community. Inside, a few quality possessions and artwork turned the small place into a semi-classy home. When they eventually made love in his large wide hammock, her white-skinned arms and legs all tangled up with his dark ones, the coupling was divine. His caresses felt like he worshipped every inch of her as his first earth goddess.

Kate relapsed into long-term thoughts of ever-after-love. Was this the man she was looking for? *I could learn to sleep in a hammock beside him like this every night. We'd have a simple house in the village, and he would start up a Mexican business. Our lovely brown skin children would play under the coconut trees in the yard.*

After that night, Kate didn't see him again for a couple of days. She wandered to his hut the next afternoon, looked around the yard, and knocked on his door, but no one answered. Kate turned the knob and discovered the door unlocked. "Miguel…" she whispered, but the cabana was utterly empty.

He didn't even say goodbye. What does that mean? She was stupid to even consider the validity of his story. An exploratory mission, a splashdown arrival from space, and he emerges from his force-field egg capsule; it was too far out to believe, wasn't it?

Yet the odd details almost made sense in the shy, straightforward way he had explained it. Kate shook her head in chagrin. *What a unique pickup line. I am so damn gullible. But then, where did he go?*

Kate asked the locals and other people they had met together, but nobody knew him well. She found no clues to where he had disappeared, and the mystery lay unsolved.

Maybe he…well, she would always remember the slice of time he had chosen to spend with her.

Chapter 16

A NEW WORLD

Kate was often the first to wake up in their household of hippie girls, and the next day was no exception. She put on her faded cut-offs and the T-shirt that she had fringed on the bottom. Then she braided her long hair to keep it off her face. The early mornings in San Blas were deliciously cool and balmy, so she took her hot Mexican coffee and sat under the banana tree in the backyard. She deserved a pity-party.

Why hadn't Miguel said goodbye? Why did men come and go out of her life so often? And if her old girlfriends didn't need her, what was she doing down in Mexico, anyway?

Cheryl came out to join her, still in her pajamas, and she sensed her pensive mood. "Hey, we're in paradise. You're supposed to look happy." Cheryl loved the Mexican culture and wanted to stay forever.

Kate sighed because it wasn't just Miguel's departure that upset her. "I'm worried. I figured by now, Joey must have got the letter I sent before we left the states. She could have written to me at least."

"Maybe your friend Leah recovered from her drug overdose, and they're just having fun, which is what we should be doing."

"You're right." Kate took the last slurp of her coffee and stood up. "Let's go early to the stalls and buy our fresh meat before the flies get too bad. I want to barter for more of those delicious mangos." A trip to the marketplace was always fun, and after they made their purchases, they detoured over to the post office.

"I got mail, at last!" Kate was handed a letter from Joey, and she stepped outside to open it. After scanning it, she shared the distressing news with Cheryl. "Leah has gotten a lot worse. They've run short of money and have been hitchhiking. Joey can't push her to travel any faster, so it'll be another week before they arrive."

"Oh dear, but that's good news for you. You'll have days to explore the area before you rendezvous with your old schoolmates and have to go home."

"That's true."

"Let's go to Guadalajara by bus to see the huge craft market there," Cheryl suggested.

"It sounds possible, and it'll give us a chance to see a little more of Mexico. Let's go tomorrow."

At the corner of the plaza the next morning, a crowd of locals stood waiting at the bus stop. Kate and Cheryl read the schedule and found out they'd have to wait until the afternoon for the first-class bus to Guadalajara, but the super-cheap, third-class bus was leaving right away.

"What do you think?" Kate asked.

"It would save us money. We might as well go now and not waste the day waiting," Cheryl said. They hurried to buy their tickets and were the only gringos in the line-up waiting to board. It turned out to be quite a process.

First, the driver stood on the top of the bus. The people would hold up their suitcases and duffel bags, and he'd tied them securely to a rusty metal rack on the roof. After climbing down, he opened the door to the bus, and the crowd started pushing in a frenzy to claim a seat. Kate and Cheryl managed to board, but all the by then all the seats were taken and they had to stand in the aisle. More locals got on, squishing them tighter than kernels on a corncob clear up to the door. The driver even had to climb through a side window to get to his seat in the front.

"Isn't this bizarre?" Cheryl peered back at her in alarm. She was five people ahead of Kate, and halfway up the aisle. "How long will it be this crowded, do you think?"

"It can't stay this way for too long," Kate answered, hoping she was right.

The bus eased onto the asphalt, and the old vehicle built up speed with rumbling determination. Top-heavy with freight, it leaned dangerously to either side around the corners, so it was hard to keep their balance in the aisle. Kate had an older man with two children in tow crouched down on the floor in front of her. A large round woman in a colorful dress pressed up against her backside. Kate held her position and waited for the next village to come into sight, but the bus passed right through the next town, leaving the people at the bus stop rejected.

Time passed as heat thickened the air. Little children sunk into sleep in their parent's arms, and flies buzzed at the windows. Underarm sweat from nearby passengers emitted a sour odor as they all stood erect, swaying upright for what seemed like hours.

"I don't know how long I can last," Kate shouted up to Cheryl, around the heads of the other local passengers. They didn't understand their English words, anyway.

"I know. Me too," Cheryl called back.

When the bus slowed down to a stop in front of a few houses on the road, everybody shifted, and a handful of people scrambled their way out. But new passengers crowded in, and the bus driver still had trouble closing the door. Kate couldn't believe it, but the locals acted like it was normal. Then the bus took off again through the open fields on a highway that seemed to stretch forever.

The woman standing behind Kate sunk into a blob on the floor in a cross-legged squat, and Kate had to adjust her aching muscles by picking up one foot to stretch the kink in her leg. The surrounding bodies were quick to shift, and when she tried to put her foot back onto the floor, she couldn't. Bundles, satchels, feet in sandals, and the woman's stout body spread out, covered every inch of the dirty aisle. *This is ludicrous. I can't keep standing here on one leg!*

Claustrophobia hit her and increased by waves. Ahead, Cheryl grimaced, looking panicky in the same way. So, when the bus pulled over at the next stop, they silently questioned each other and gave vigorous nods.

"Un momento, vamonos ahora mismo!" Kate shouted at the bus driver to wait for them to get out. She and Cheryl frantically climbed over the people in the aisle, stepping on bags and legs to escape from the bus. The locals were disgusted at their rude actions and called them gringas estúpidas.

Stupid or not, Kate and Cheryl somehow made it out the door. They stood on the side of the road as the noisy old bus pulled away. For a minute, they just breathed in the dry clean aroma of the air, staring at the vast countryside, empty except for two poverty-stricken farms in the distance. Then Kate burst out laughing, and Cheryl did the same. It was a classic scene off a movie screen, standing in a foreign land in the middle of nowhere. They kept laughing until there was no stress left, and their cheeks were wet with tears.

"Now what?" Cheryl finally asked afterward.

"Now, there's nothing to do but stick out our thumbs to catch a ride." Kate grinned.

A few cars passed until a local farmer driving a truck full of watermelons came to a lumbering stop. He was pleased to pick them up. As the scenery on the roadside flashed by again, Kate and Cheryl practiced their Spanish with the man, grateful for the breeze from the truck's open windows.

When they reached Guadalajara, the watermelon man needed to go to the same destination as they did and the truckdriver dropped them off at a busy corner of the multi-block fascinating market square. Kate and Cheryl thanked him profusely and got out to wander around hundreds of tiny stalls stuffed with exotic clothing and merchandise.

"I found some cool silver earrings. They're handcrafted, and see, that's a real opal in each one." Kate had to have them and rummaged around to pull some money out of her knapsack.

"Wait, we're supposed to barter with the vendor to get the best price, remember?" Cheryl spoke under her breath nearby. "I'll wait over there by the embroidered blouses."

Kate didn't feel it was fair to haggle down the price much, and she and the vendor parted both with pleasant smiles. But when Kate looked up and down the narrow aisles for Cheryl, she couldn't see her anywhere. The exotic merchandise piled high on the counters and hanging from the walls blocked her line of sight.

"I'm over here," Cheryl shouted after coming out from behind a wall of colorful ponchos.

"Whew." Kate laughed and joined her. "It'd be easy to get lost in here for days." They wandered into another section displaying plastic kitchenware and black pottery painted with bright flowers, all in a hodge-podge of disarray. After hours rummaging around for unique gifts to take home, they stumbled into a rustic food court and realized they were ravenously hungry. Each stall had a friendly cook beckoning them over to tempt them with cauldrons of soup and steaming pans of tamales, tacos, rice, and beans. From a multitude of tantalizing dishes, they chose plates of piping hot enchiladas and sat down to eat on the long wooden tables with the locals.

A nearby quaint hotel gave them a pleasant end to their day's adventure and when they headed back to San Blas the next day, they upgraded and took the first-class bus, not the second or the third.

...

"You sure found some gorgeous things in that market," Kris said, admiring Kate's silver earrings. "The bus ride sounds awful, though."

"I'll go somewhere with you, Kate," Joanne said in eagerness. "We could go north and explore another beach town."

"We could catch the combi, the local van that goes up the coast. I think there's a fishing village nearby."

"Let's pack a few things in our knapsacks and some food for lunch, in case we want to walk along the beach."

Kate and Joanne's trip in the combi was a fun way to get around, but the settlement had only two streets and could hardly be called a village. The beach wasn't good for swimming either. They discovered a hiking trail that wandered up into the countryside, so they decided to hike out into a bit of rural Mexico.

Foot traffic had worn the path down, but they didn't meet anybody else. It led through the fields and then into a forested area, where exotic flowers cascaded down from under the leafy foliage of the trees.

"Do you hear that? There must be a waterfall somewhere." Kate stopped to listen after they'd hiked a few miles that morning.

"I heard the same sound a while ago, too," Joanne said, wiping the sweat off her forehead in the heat of the day.

"That cold water is calling to us." Kate couldn't help herself, and she pressed through thick, scratchy bushes with Joanne following her. A short distance away, they came to a sparkling creek that rippled over smooth rocks and emptied into a pool of calm water.

"Come on. It'll be refreshing." Joanne looked around at the privacy of the stream. She stripped down to her underwear and splashed in to cool off.

"Hey, you can't be the only goddess in this primal scene!" Kate whispered, threw off her outer clothes and followed her in, splashing water every which way.

Thick jungle-like greenery grew up around the boulders at the edge of the pool, and the babbling water and an occasional bird trill were the only sounds they heard.

"We should fill up our water bottles. This water looks so clean." Joanne whispered, gliding gracefully across the pond.

"I'm sure it is. Kate did another mermaid dive, pleased with the cool liquid on her skin. After they dressed and packed away their water bottles, Kate led the way back to the trail, and they continued to explore the rich greenness of the area. And whenever they got too hot again, they detoured off the track and splashed around in the deep holes of the sparkling stream.

"I love those orchid flowers hanging from the trunk of the trees. I've never seen plants grow, almost in the air like that," Joanne gushed in wonder over the lush abundance of vegetation.

"And so many exotic birds around us too," Kate said, stopping to rest. "This footpath seems to go on forever, but we should start back. What time is it?"

Joanne glanced at her watch. "Oh no. It's already four o'clock, almost too late to return to the village. Doesn't the sun set around six?" Joanne asked.

"Yeah, we're so close to the equator, it'll be night soon."

"I don't think we should hike in the dark. There are too many roots to trip over, and maybe animals."

Kate stood and thought about what to do. "We haven't seen anybody on this trail yet, and we packed our ponchos; we could wrap them around us and camp out for the night."

"I'm game if you are. Let's do that."

They chose a secluded spot under a massive tree off to the side of the beaten path. Its thick limbs spread out wide, making a canopy of green leaves to block the heat of the late afternoon. The location seemed like an ideal place to hide out and camp.

"What strange seed pods. Look, they're all over." Kate pointed to the ground under the tree. Each two-inch pod looked like a dried skeleton of a pumpkin sitting in her hand.

"What kind of tree is it?"

"It beats me. Weird seeds anyway," Kate said, looking at the one she held in her hand.

"There are shiny black beans imprisoned inside like a tiny jail cell." Joanne shook the pod to make the beans in the cage rattle. The seedpods littered the entire area, and they both collected a few for souvenirs. Up in the mass of branches, they saw thousands of round green pods waiting to mature.

Kate and Joanne dragged their ponchos out of their knapsacks for bedding and took out the rest of the food they'd brought to munch on. They chattered and laughed in nervousness with the predicament they found themselves in. But just when they had stretched out to relax from their long day of hiking, men's voices came from up the trail.

Two older seasoned rancheros and a couple of muscled young cowboys on horseback shouted out to them. They rode in closer but not quite up to the tree where Kate and Joanne were camping. The men in their cowboy hats seemed agitated about something and stared at them in consternation.

"Chicas, que pasa aquí?" they demanded, controlling their prancing horses.

Kate thought they probably wanted to know what two young American girls were doing out there, miles from the village. She became concerned because the men were rough looking, and there were four of them. In broken Spanish, she explained they were only hikers enjoying the beautiful countryside. "Solamente somos viajeras en su hermoso país."

"Aquí es muy peligroso," the older man said.

Kate knew the word peligroso meant dangerous, but what the risk was, she had no idea.

"No acampen bajo el árbol," he stated, clearly upset.

Why didn't these men want them to camp under the tree? Kate wondered, getting more nervous now, waiting to see what they would do next.

The rancheros talked among themselves. Afterward, the boss man gave a gruff invitation to accompany them to their ranch for safety that night. Joanne caught the drift of the conversation, and Kate knew she felt danger in the air, too.

"Senorita," one ranchero said, gesturing for Joanne to sit behind the saddle and ride on the horse with him.

"I'm not going with them," Joanne mumbled to Kate.

"No, we won't," Kate whispered. Her intuition told her something wasn't right, but what was it? She tried to comprehend their rapid dialogue, but the language barrier was too great.

Kate shook her head to decline their invitation. They were fine where they were camped. "No gracias. Aquí estamos bien," she told them.

But the two older rancheros insisted. They gestured for Kate and Joanne to walk beside the horses if they didn't want to double up and ride.

"No, gracias. No." Kate and Cheryl waved them off with firmness, feeling almost rude. After long minutes of discussion, the rancheros peered up at the sky and shook their heads. Their horses danced with restlessness. Finally, all four clip-clopped down the trail, but the two younger men glanced back with vivid intensity.

"What shall we do?" Joanne asked, realizing how vulnerable they were as the shadows deepened under their tree.

"It's impossible to hike back in the dark. Besides, if the men were going to take advantage of us, I guess they had their chance."

Kate and Joanne had trouble getting to sleep in the warm evening, even with their flashlights beside them. The sun woke them in the morning, streamed down through the leaves in sparkling rays of light. After packing up their ponchos, they hurried off to the nearest pool in the stream to wash their hands and faces. Once more, the magical setting and the cool water refreshed them, and they set off down the trail.

Back in the village, Joanne saw a corner store, and they bought some food for breakfast. The local owner spoke English, so they chatted with him about their overnight adventure.

"What did these seed pods look like?" the shopkeeper asked.

"Here, I saved some in my knapsack," Kate said, and dug one out.

"Dios mío," he said when Kate held it out. "My God, you slept under a Manzanilla tree. That tree is the most dangerous in our country. The tiniest drop of sap on you will burn your flesh like acid."

"You're kidding." Joanne looked at Kate as they checked their exposed skin.

"No, it is true. Our people go blind if they rub their eyes after contact with the leaves. And when it rains, even water dripping from the branches can blister your skin."

"Then those local rancheros wanted to escort us away for our safety. That's what they were trying to tell us." Kate clasped her hands in awareness.

"Yes. I know these men you describe and their families. They are good people."

"That explains why they were so persistent and the reason the horses were dancing around. They wanted to get away from the tree."

She and Joanne had slept there all night under the green leaves and seedpods. What if it had rained? Yet, no harm came to them, like they'd been given some supernatural protection. She imagined the concerned rancheros going back to homes with ornate Catholic crosses hanging on the walls. Their families had probably prayed at their dinner table last night for the crazy American girls.

"Why do you let trees like the Manzanilla live in your forest?" Joanne asked.

"It is difficult to get rid of these trees. If we cut them down, those who hold the saw must use extreme caution to protect themselves from the sap. Few will volunteer to do that kind of work. Even if one tree catches on fire, it can blind an entire village by the smoke." He nodded solemnly. "Everyone here knows this danger."

Kate and Joanne stared at each other wide-eyed, imagining a horrible could-have-been scenario for themselves. Kate gave a bow of respect to the shopkeeper. "When you next see these rancheros in your village, will you please convey our gratitude to them for trying to protect us?"

"I will pass on your wishes. And señoritas, please know that the Almighty has touched your lives. Vayan con Dios!"

...

Kate and Joanne returned to San Blas and shared the exciting adventure with their other two roommates. But the very next day, Kate's life took on an entirely new direction.

"Hey, Kate, you got company," Cheryl called to her in the back of the kitchen. Kate hurried to the door and there stood her high school classmates, far from their Oregon hometown.

Chapter 17

HITCH HIKING THE HIGHWAYS

"You're here. You found me!" Kate squeezed Joey and Leah with big hugs.

"We made it, but boy, are we exhausted," Joey answered for both of them, as she looked around their tidy brick home. "We followed the instructions in the note you left at the post office and just wound our way through the streets to your door."

Leah was looking down at her feet and said nothing as a greeting. She wore a rumpled purple T-shirt and dirty jeans, which contradicted her previous classy style. Joey helped to take Leah's backpack off, but it slipped to the floor with a clunk.

"Well, come in. Mi casa es su casa." Kate welcomed them warmly. "My housemates want you to stay here, so we can all crash in my room." She gave them a cheerful tour of the place, but her friends didn't act like the same carefree girls she remembered. Kate pulled Joey aside to talk in private.

"What happened to Leah? Why is she acting like such a zombie? I'm shocked at how she looks."

"I know. Welcome to my world." Joey shrugged her shoulders. "Leah is like a child, afraid of everything, and she can't make any kind of decision, even what to wear. I have to help put her socks on."

"That's pretty serious then. How did she get this way?"

"We were at a Mexican party in this big fancy mansion with some people we met. All kinds of fancy food were spread out on long wooden tables, maybe enough for thirty people, and there was a beautiful glass punch bowl with fresh fruit floating in it."

"That sounds fantastic. I wish I'd been there," Kate said.

Joey had a faraway look as she continued to recount the events. "On the private beach, there were cushy lounge chairs set out and hammocks strung between the coconut trees. Guys with guitars were playing Latino music, and it was so much fun, you know?"

"I can imagine."

"Then Leah started acting weird. She climbed into a hammock on the beach and just stayed there. I wouldn't get out of it," Joey said, rubbing at a frown on her forehead.

"What do you mean, she stayed there?"

Joey frowned. "She was in that hammock for two whole days."

"Why the heck wouldn't she climb out of it?"

Joey gave a big sighed. "Somebody spiked the punch with a psychedelic drug, and Leah didn't know about it. She was thirsty, I guess. She must have drunk lots of it."

"That's terrible." Kate chewed on her thumbnail.

"Leah doesn't talk about her experience much, but she told me some of it the other day. All she could do was stare at the waves coming in and watch ugly monsters rise out of the water. She saw ships crashing on the rocks, people drowning, and all kinds of gruesome things."

Kate flashed back to her beautiful windowpane acid trip and the powerful spiritual truths she had experienced. She'd never forget her fear of being lost in dark timelessness, though, and that was nothing compared to the violent intensity Leah must have experienced. "No wonder she can't talk about it. Did you drink the punch?"

Joey shook her head. "No, I was drinking shots of tequila."

"We'll have to do something. I think Leah needs professional help, and not just you or me trying to support her until she gets over it."

"I think you might be right, because it's already been almost a month and she's not getting any better. But Kate, I barely have enough money to get myself home because Leah ran out of cash a long time ago." Joey's shoulders hunched over in exhaustion. Her small silver earrings tangled up in her long brown hair as she stretched her head back and forth from the stress.

"That's not good," Concern for both her friends hit Kate hard.

"I can't break through Leah's catatonic state or whatever it is. I've tried."

"It's okay, Joey. I'm here to help." Kate gave her friend's arm a squeeze and hoped she had a Higher Power to help her.

"I don't know what to do." Joey looked teary-eyed.

"I think you have to go home." Kate squared her shoulders. "I'll take over and try to get Leah to talk to me. And if that doesn't work, somehow I'll arrange for her to see a counselor." Kate didn't feel optimistic, though, only the weight of responsibility with a touch of fear thrown in. If she brought Leah back home like this, her upper-class parents would come unglued.

...

They left Leah with the other girls at the house on the day of Joey's departure. She walked with Joey up the gravel road going out of San Blas. Joey had on her tattered backpack and carried a large, handcrafted satchel full of souvenirs. She was taking home a rolled-up five-foot-long woven mat she wanted, too. Joey's worn leather sandals slid around on her feet, and grime already caked the spaces between her toes.

Yet Kate knew her vivacious friend was fearless. She would have loved to travel with her, but there was no time or money for that. They said their sad goodbyes to each other and stood there waiting. Joey stuck her thumb out, and soon a young Mexican in a pickup truck stopped to offer her a ride. She loaded all her stuff into the bed of the truck, and with a last hug and a grin, she hopped in.

Kate stood on the side of the road and evaluated her own before she made her way back to the house. Leah wasn't just depressed; it was like there was vacant space inside her head. Kate always envied Leah's soft femininity, and how she exuded love for everybody she met, yet now she was flatline in personality, with no emotion at all.

After of few days of trying to break through with Leah, Kate couldn't put their departure off any longer. She had to get her some actual counseling, but after paying rent for the extra weeks she'd waited, she didn't have enough cash to buy the two train tickets needed to bring Leah back to Oregon. They would have to hitchhike.

Kate wanted to travel with English-speaking gringos because of the state of Leah's mental health. She went out and asked around town if anyone planned to head north soon. Someone said two California guys were driving up in their van, so Kate kept inquiring until she found out what they looked like. She saw them in the plaza the next day.

John stood six feet tall and seemed older than Kate, which was a positive. He spoke adequate Spanish, too. Ken had a mop of red hair and wasn't as friendly, but they both seemed nice enough. Kate explained her situation and asked if they'd give her and Leah a ride to the border.

"Sure, we can help you. I'm fine with that," John, the tall one, said. "But we're making it a fast trip and not stopping anywhere."

His companion voiced some objections. "Our van doesn't have any back seats, so it won't be very comfortable for you."

"That would be okay." They couldn't afford to be choosy. "We'll just sit against our backpacks and sleep a lot." The guys finally agreed to take them up through Mexico, and best of all, they planned to leave the next day.

Kate said regretful goodbyes to Cheryl, Joanne, and Kris at the house to start the long trek back to Oregon when John and Ken picked them up. She and Leah spread out in the back of their van surrounded by everyone's luggage, and they headed inland. The guys took turns driving, making good time going north.

In the middle of the night, the van came to a stop on a deserted stretch of the highway. Kate and Leah woke up, rubbed the sleep from their eyes, and saw a vehicle parked sideways, blocking the road. Three swarthy men sauntered up to their van, and they carried heavy rifles at their sides.

Kate's pulse pounded. *Are they bandidos or policías Federales?* She couldn't tell. "What's happening?" she mumbled the question up to John and Ken.

"Hush…" John twisted around from the driver's seat and whispered to them. "We've been pulled over. Don't make a sound. Pretend you aren't even here."

Kate's hands grew jittery. It was all too much. She motioned to Leah to hide under the baggage and blankets they were sleeping on and gently covered Leah's mouth so she wouldn't say a word.

"Pronto, sus visas por favor!" The burly face in the dark growled at their driver. John was quick to step out of the van, and she heard two or three men speaking in curt, broken Spanish. Kate admired John's composure because the men's rudeness suggested they were bandits or corrupt local police. Maybe both.

Kate was peeking out from under the blankets only a few feet away when the driver's door of the van opened. She froze. Adrenaline rushed to her head as she watched the Mexican man paw through the compartment in the middle console.

He searched for weapons or drugs, she guessed, but only brought out a box of breath mints to examine. She wondered if John and Ken were transporting illegal drugs. There was no toleration for that in Mexico *and in the horrors of a Mexican jail cell for possession of drugs, Leah would go completely crazy.*

John became agitated and rushed forward to reach in and offer an object for inspection. "Mire señor." He held a fancy pocketknife in a leather sheath up to the Mexican, explaining the knife was an expensive quality tool and had belonged to his grandfather.

"Lo tomas. It's for you to take but let us head north and be on our way." The nasty-looking man feigned disgust with such a small bribe but ended up pocketing the knife.

"Okay, gringos, you go." He sneered at John and waved him off.

John jumped back in the truck and pulled out on the road fast before the banditos thought to search the rest of the vehicle. "Damn it. Oh shit. Are they following us?" He gritted his teeth and concentrated on driving with as much speed as possible.

"Don't think so," Ken said, letting out a big curse in the passenger seat. "Whew, but that was close. Those men weren't Federales."

"Nope, they weren't."

"Why did you give him your grandpa's pocketknife? You treasured that one."

"I didn't want them to notice the girls hiding in the back," John said. "Can you guess what those three rough men might do to them? It wouldn't have been a pretty sight."

"Oh God, that's for sure." Ken's voice was contrite. "I didn't tell you either, but I left the film container full of hashish in the glove box."

"Jeez, you did? Throw it out the window right now. You better be glad he didn't find it. If they were Federales, we'd all be in some flea-bitten jailhouse."

Leah still didn't show any emotions. Kate wanted to vomit from the residue of fear she held back, but she couldn't ask them to stop for that. If the bandits had seen her and Leah hiding in the van, they might have been raped, and all four of them murdered and tossed in sandy graves on a back road somewhere. She'd read of things like that happening before in rural Mexico.

Thank you, thank you, God. She continued to chant the refrain in her mind.

The dark night dragged on in tension as they looked ahead for other roadblocks. Finally, the sun rose, and the trip continued with no more surprises. They let out a loud cheer when at last they crossed the border into the United States.

John pulled into a rest stop off the freeway. "Ken and I are driving east to Texas at the next junction, but it should be safe enough for you to hitchhike up to Oregon now. Just be careful," John advised her.

"I hope you find help for your friend soon," Ken added quietly, while Leah was getting her backpack out of the van.

"I hope so too, but I have to convince her she needs a professional counselor," Kate said. Life was a fragile gift, and the four had bonded somehow because of the danger they faced together. They circled and held hands in an impromptu farewell, and even Leah joined them with a tiny smile.

"Thanks, John, Ken. You guys have been very kind. I won't ever forget how you protected us last night." Kate reached out and accepted the hug they each offered. Then the van pulled away, and she and Leah were alone on the shoulder of the freeway.

Leah sat down in the gravel to wait while Kate stuck out her thumb. When they caught a ride, she talked to the driver while Leah slumped back in the seat. When that ride ended, Kate led her down the streets to the next freeway on-ramp and in that manner, the trip north became a blur of strange people, fast food, and too many paunch-bellied truck drivers, suggesting more than what they wanted to give. Kate faked her confidence, and, for distraction, she pressed Leah to sing folksongs with her to entertain the drivers.

"Come on, Leah. Remember when we used to sing, 'Me and Bobby McGee?'" When her friend responded from rote memory and sang along, Kate smiled with tenderness because that's what they were, flat broke and far from home.

Things were a little different after they reached San Francisco. Kate met a hippie couple at a fast-food restaurant who invited her and Leah to sleep on the couch in their apartment for a while. That solved their accommodation problem because Leah refused to travel anymore. She didn't know what she wanted to do instead, and Kate grieved over her friend's lethargy.

"I'm going to walk down to get a few groceries. Why don't you come with me?" Kate urged Leah to take some kind of initiative.

"I want to stay here," Leah mumbled, and Kate knew she'd sit for hours on the floor in that same position.

At the same coffee shop, Kate made a new friend whose landlord was a psychologist. She called the doctor's office and explained her predicament. After telling him they hitchhiked all the way up from Mexico to seek treatment, but had no money, he agreed to meet with Leah for a few counseling appointments at his home. Leah agreed to see him, but after two sessions, the psychologist talked to Kate on the side.

"Leah will only get worse without intensive therapy."

"I can't cover the cost of that, but I want to help her get over her breakdown." Kate bit her lip.

"For that to happen, she needs to go home to her parents," the doctor said.

Kate thanked the man and sighed. Her heart ached. She had to take charge of their situation and by the next morning, she was resolved.

"I'm sorry, Leah, but I'm making the decisions for both of us from now on, and I say we're leaving." She was quick to stuff their belongings in their backpacks and grabbed Leah by the hand. Leah didn't resist her quick action and firm authority.

They walked the long blocks in silence down to the I-5 freeway ramp to resume their journey. They ate cheap food at gas stations and, with little money left, they slept in the bushes off the freeway in the dark of night.

Their very last ride dropped them off in Portland, and if a city could welcome a prodigal child, it seemed to have open arms for them. Kate allowed herself to relax for the first time in weeks. It felt good to be in familiar surroundings.

They walked to a nearby restaurant, and when Leah went to the bathroom, Kate asked the waitress if she could borrow a phonebook and use the phone. She knew Leah's older brother was a young, clean-cut business manager who lived somewhere in the city. Kate searched for his number and dialed it.

"I don't know if you remember, but I'm Leah's high school girlfriend. She's here in Portland with me."

"She's here in the city? Oh my God. Our parents will be so relieved. They haven't heard from her for months. But why isn't she calling me herself?"

"Leah overdosed on drugs," Kate spit out the words and waited. There was no other way to describe what happened to his little sister. She explained how she became involved in bringing her back to the States and she didn't minimize the seriousness of the situation at all.

In less than an hour, Leah's brother was there to pick her up. Kate was so relieved she almost cried in front of him.

"You called him?" Leah looked at her with hurt and reproach.

"I had to, Leah. Your parents and brother love you no matter what happened. Things will get better for you now." Kate tried to take her hand, but Leah didn't accept it.

Her brother stepped in to throw a protective arm around her. "Of course, we love you. Mom and Dad haven't heard from you for so long." He led her off to his car with a backward nod of thanks for Kate.

With that, Kate's rescue mission came to an end. She walked away in grief, praying her friend would recover. Kate had to pick up the pieces of her own life, and like Leah, she had no idea what that was going to look like.

Chapter 18

A HEART OF STONE

Kate visited her parent's home in Hood River the next day. It didn't give her any warm fuzzies. Her mother and father carried on the same family dysfunction, and on the television the political world seemed even more violent.

She and her brother Barry watched the national news with their father like they always did. A well-known war correspondent named Nick Ut was sharing film footage from Vietnam's combat zones that day. His camera zoomed in on a small naked child, charred black by burning napalm, blind and zigzagging down the street.

Kate's eyes riveted on the grotesque, revolting scene. She couldn't breathe, and she held back an outburst of tears. What if she lived in one of those houses? She'd be running up the street with the same terror and pain, trying to escape exploding bombs in her village. The US government was to blame, and the inhumanity was happening right there on the screen in front of her.

Kate's father uttered a long groan. "My Gawd. They're using chemical warfare on civilians now."

"Oh, for heaven's sake, turn off that news channel." Her mother's oh-so-capable hands were in the air as she marched off toward the kitchen. "They shouldn't be showing those kinds of scenes on the television," she scolded.

Kate noticed her rigid back as she left the room. Her mom always spoke out with strong convictions, and maybe her mother was right. For the first time in history, the public was able to see events on the other side of the world on their television sets, the violent and gory scenes even as they were happening.

Her father tried hard to appease his mom. "Now, dear, don't carry on like that. At least the war hasn't spread over into our country."

"No? It's happening right in the middle of the living room from that box you're all glued to."

"We have to stop the Communists, or one day they'll land their ships on our coastline.

"You call that little girl a communist?" Her mother shouted from the kitchen door as she pointed to the screen. "What's the matter with you?"

Kate's dad glanced over at her on the couch. He shook his head in exasperation. "The enemy did worse things when I was overseas," he muttered and took another long swig of his beer.

Kate knew he fought for his country, but he seldom talked about it. Now she wondered what her father had experienced for himself.

...

After visiting her family, Kate returned to Portland. She was eager to meet up again with Joey, who had found a room to rent in a large house.

After a quick hug at the door, Kate threw her tanned legs over the arm of a big leather chair in the living room, ready for a heart-to-heart talk.

"We sure had some grand adventures in Mexico, didn't we?" Joey said as she returned from the kitchen. She carried in steaming cups of coffee for them and then flopped down on the sofa.

"We did. And despite it all, we brought Leah home safe to her family." The taste of the late morning coffee was on the tip of Kate's tongue, and she savored the velvety feel. "You heard? Leah is living with her parents and seeing a psychologist."

"I'm so glad. I wish we could have helped more."

"Would you go back to Mexico again?" Kate asked.

"You bet I would. I might live down there one day."

"Well, if you ever hike into the countryside, be careful. Mexico has some scary vegetation." Kate explained how she and Joanna had camped out under the dangerous Manzanilla tree.

"Those rancheros sure were persistent. They tried hard to move us away from the poisonous sap. I bet their families prayed for us that evening because I believe we were miraculously protected."

Joey cocked her head and scoffed at Kate's summary. "Divine protection from an acid-burning tree? So, it was God Almighty who kept you safe?"

"He did. I know it. The whole population of Mexico is afraid to touch even the leaves of the tree. We slept underneath them and didn't suffer at all."

"That's a strange story, all right."

"There was something supernatural about it." Kate pressed the point.

"I think you guys were just damn lucky it didn't rain."

"Yeah. But I bet you've had experiences you couldn't explain where some power intervened to save you from something. Everyone has things like that happen, but they just call them coincidences." Kate loved to discuss bigger concepts and ideas.

Joey frowned at that and sat upright on the couch. "Well, something happened to me last week, and I thought I was a goner."

"Joey. What happened?" Kate asked.

"I was walking home after shopping, and I used the bathroom in one of those run-down gas stations on Broadway Street. When I was washing my hands, a black dude came in and backed me up against the wall. You know, to get it on with me."

"Oh, no! What did you do?"

"I refused him, of course, but then he pushed me into the corner and held a knife to my throat."

"But that's horrible!" Kate sucked in her breath. "Joey, he didn't rape you, did he?"

"He could have. He would have, but I started sobbing and his face softened. He said, 'You really don't want to do this, do you?'"

"Well, duh. Of course, you didn't." Kate gritted her teeth, imagining her friend in that predicament.

"So, I answered him, but I don't know where the words came from."

"What did you say to him?"

"I was crying and said, 'I... I'm your sister.'" Joey pantomimed the pleading look she must have given him. "But that was ridiculous cause I'm the little white girl, and he was all, you know, young black strapping muscle."

"So, he stopped?"

"He glared at me for a minute, and I was shaking like a leaf. Then he folded up his knife and put it in his pocket. He told me to give him five minutes, and he'd disappear." Joey twisted her shoulders inward to release the tension after reliving the scene.

"Oh, Joey."

"What I said was weird, right?" she asked Kate.

"No, the words you spoke were perfect. Divine Spirit came right there in that little gas station bathroom and protected you. I bet you might have even changed the guy's life with just those very words."

"Katie, you're such a Pollyanna."

Kate didn't think the description fit but she let it go. "I'm so glad he didn't hurt you."

"You know, maybe he had a little sister or something, and it made him think. He acted different after I said it."

"I think God was looking after you."

"I wish God would put a decent man in my life then." Joey grimaced with her face downcast.

Kate straightened up on the stuffed chair. "Are there any decent guys out there, I wonder?" She dragged the footstool over to plop up her feet.

"We shouldn't have to defend ourselves from guys in our own country. We're not supposed to be at war with them." Joey threw her shoulders like a female warrior.

"They always want to take more from us," Kate said. "I gave Mark everything I had, and even that wasn't enough." Kate's heart still had tight straps wrapped around it.

"You were crazy-in-love with that boy, all right."

"I'm never going to fall in love that hard again."

Joey nodded. "I know what you mean. Men like to be in control, and how do you trust any of them?"

"We don't need to submit to a man." Kate slapped the leather chair to emphasize her strong feelings. "Not if we don't want the house with the white picket fence around the yard."

"Yeah, we're modern women." Joey hammed it up by throwing her arms in the air. It was false boasting because Kate knew they both still dreamed of finding a love that would last forever.

"Life is never boring for you and me, is it?" Kate squinted at her friend with concern. They sat in silence, contemplating the years they'd known each other.

"What are you going to do now?" Joey asked.

"I guess I'll go back to school in the fall. The Psych Department offered my old secretary's job back for summer prep work, but I'll need to find a place to live in Portland."

"Hey! There's an empty upstairs bedroom for rent at the house here. We could have fun together if you move in." Joey gave Kate a tour of the run-down character home. Five bedrooms rented out to adults of various ages. Some were students, others had regular jobs, and there was always drama going on. The furnished, vacant bedroom was small, but big enough for Kate's meager belongings. Downstairs, the old-fashioned communal kitchen was functional, with two fridges and designated shelves for each resident. Everyone was on different shifts, so it seemed to work.

"How much is the rent for the room?"

"It's cheap. Hang on. I'll go knock on Marvin's door and see if he's rented it yet."

Kate stood and waited. She dug in her bag to count the cash she had.

A few minutes later, Joey returned and told her the rent amount. "If you have a deposit, you can have the room today."

"Fantastic. I'll move in on the weekend." Kate handed over half a month's rent for the deposit and she had a new home.

Each Saturday night, the house residents invited various friends over, and their parties were legendary in the neighborhood. People from all walks of life mingled in strange conversations.

Marvin, the oldest resident in the house, was a character. He bought pounds of homegrown marijuana and enlisted her and Joey to roll up joints to sell to his customers. They had to be the size of Kate's little finger, and for their efforts, Marvin always rewarded them with a few free ones to smoke. Kate was okay with the arrangement. She wasn't using hard drugs but refused to sell the weed for him. She wasn't letting any guy use her for his own agenda.

Out of the blue, just when the summer was ending, Kate received a call from Mark. Kate hadn't heard from him in over two years. His voice caressed the length of her spine and made her melt as she clutched the phone.

"I'm in the city," he said. "I got your phone number from your mother and thought I'd drop in to see you," his husky voice drawled in her ear.

Kate's mind went into a flap, but she invited him to the house that same afternoon. She was glad none of her housemates would be around and went to fix her hair. When Mark arrived, Kate answered the door in a dither, and the pulse in her neck was pounding.

"Hey, Sunshine. You're looking good. It's great to see you." His quirky smile spread over his lips, and she remembered how tender they once were on her own.

"You too, Mark," she said, suddenly shy, and just like before, the crinkling laugh lines around his eyes pulled her in with magnetism. He had matured and wore his new confidence, like his quality sports jacket.

When he hugged her, the electric sparks went off the charts between them again. Broken images of the past swirled in her brain in a kaleidoscope of emotion. She led him into the front room, where he took a seat on the couch, but she chose the armchair.

"I'm still in Corvallis, going into my fourth year of pre-med school, and it's a grind. It seems like all I do on campus is study."

Kate remembered his adoring female friends. "I bet you find time to relax on the weekends, though."

"I down a few beers, but I'm still single if you're asking," he teased with a smile.

She let that go. "Don't you pass a joint around with friends sometimes?"

"Can't. I need all the brain cells I have." He chuckled. "And you, what have you been doing with yourself?"

Kate decided on honesty. "Well, I dropped out of school last semester to hitchhike to Mexico, but I'm returning to the university this fall. And I drink wine and smoke the odd joint now and then."

"Still the wild child, I see." He said, humoring her.

Kate stared point-blank at him in defiance, but he didn't seem to notice. Her silent words were shrill inside. *You made me what I am.*

"So, are you seeing anyone?"

"Not at the moment." She composed herself and asked, "How's your family?"

Mark talked about his life, and she shared some of hers, but their conversation was uncomfortable. Kate tried hard to mesh the jaded self she had become back into the younger, dew-drenched girl she once had been, but she couldn't project that core goodness anymore. She and Mark should be relating as mature adults, but there was a chasm between parallel universes they couldn't connect.

After more stilted conversation, they ran out of things to say. They talked but didn't communicate about the things that really mattered. Mark looked awkward when he stood up to say goodbye, but he reached out to hug her again. "What do you say we get together and go out on a date sometime soon?"

A rush of emotion, almost panic, hit her hard.

"I…" She clasped her hands together. She wanted to, but was she brave enough to risk being discarded all over again? "I don't think it would work," she whispered.

"Oh." He stood for half a minute and gazed down at her. "I guess I was hoping…." He hesitated, but then he didn't finish the sentence. He chewed on his lip instead. His brow wrinkled up before he turned to go. "Well, I guess I better be on my way then."

Kate closed the door softly behind him. She sank against it, sobbing in a huddle on the floor. What did she just do? He was walking out of her life again. She ought to forgive him, but he was killing her with his casual desire to date again. "Killing me Softly with his Words," was Roberta Flack's new song and that's what was happening to her.

After the tears stopped, Kate took a walk. She found herself lost in her neighborhood, in the maze of residential streets, and she ran out of Kleenex. Kate even had to ask for directions to figure out how to get back home.

Chapter 19

THE END OF THE WAR

A new atmosphere emerged in politics over the summer after the majority of American demanded the withdrawal of troops in Vietnam. President Nixon softened his pro-hawk image by
cutting the level down by seventy thousand and Kate figured he made the political move to get re-elected. Henry Kissinger, the National Security Advisor, had been negotiating for months with the North Vietnamese generals to end the war, and it finally happened. The US signed the Paris Peace Accords on January 27, 1973 and declared the official end to the Vietnam War.

Kate stopped and purchased a good bottle of wine. When she arrived home, she grabbed two glasses from the kitchen and hurried to Joey's bedroom. "They've ended the war! No more men will be getting killed over there," Kate declared as she bounced into the room.

"I heard it too! I can't believe it's for real." Joey held up both hands in triumph, fingers in double-V peace signs.

"It's taken so long. It's almost anti-climactic. But we need to celebrate." Kate poured out two glasses of red wine with a flourish.

They clinked glasses together, and Joey grabbed her guitar. "I learned the perfect song for this, too. It's called "Last Night I Had the Strangest Dream." You have to sing it with me."

Joey spread out notebook paper with the chords and lyrics scrawled in pencil. Her fingers fit over the neck of the guitar, and she strummed out the first chord to resonate in the air. She played the melody once and then they sang the song together with sweet passion.

"Wouldn't it be beautiful if all the world governments did sign agreements to end wars forever? Everybody would celebrate in the streets." Kate played with her long hair thoughtfully.

"That would be amazing if Vietnam was the last one." Joey pursed her lips and pouted.

"It won't be." Kate said, letting out a deep sigh, almost a groan. "Like Jimi Hendrix says, 'When the power of love overcomes the love of power, the world will know peace.'"

"Those big men in the military will continue to play their little war games," Joey sneered.

"Like boys moving their plastic army guys around. They're addicted to power.

"But damn it, Kate. Look at us. Why are we attracted to strong, dominant men, then?"

"That's the crux, isn't it?"

Another housemate from down the hall stuck his head in the door at that point. Tom heard them celebrating and brought his guitar. He was an excellent player and found the chords to all the melancholy folk songs they knew.

She and Joey sang the lyrics along with him, long past the time when the bottle of wine was empty.

Tom's average looks and calm presence were the antonyms of the powerful male figure she and Joey talked about earlier. Kate found that attractive, and they spent a lot of time together after that. He had integrity and always treated her with steadfast gentleness. She sensed he'd never play around on her and that's what she wanted in a man. Sparks flew between them, and many evenings he tiptoed into her room, or she went to his down the hall.

A few months passed, and when Joey took off to go backpacking in Austria the house dynamics were changed. She and Tom weren't close to any of the other house mates who sometimes got on their nerves. "Let's get a place of our own," Kate suggested.

"Yeah, why rent two rooms? It wouldn't hurt to look." Tom said in agreement. It was only common sense, and they did get along very well.

They found a unique older apartment on the northeast side of Portland. It had a narrow balcony overlooking the park, with sunshine and gentle breezes floating in through the open windows. In the evenings, Tom played the blues and old gospel music on his guitar. He even wrote his own songs.

"Listen to this one," he said, his fingers jumping around to strike the right chords. "I think I got the lyrics except the last line doesn't sound right."

Kate suggested a few words, and they tried things out again until he liked how it sounded. Tom gave depth and spiritual meaning to the songs he wrote, and she loved trying to harmonize with his voice. Her trust in him grew, making Kate melt inside, and she hoped with all her heart their relationship would grow into something pure and lasting.

But Tom and Kate attended different schools and had separate friends. He commuted by bus outside the city for his Community College classes while she attended her classes close by at the university. Then, without warning, Tom made plans to transfer to a college in Washington State for the Spring term. He wanted to become a pastor.

Kate felt like she'd fallen off a high diving board blindfolded. Tom had his religious beliefs, but she never thought he would make it a career choice. God might be leading him, but his departure was ripping her apart.

"We're different, Kate, and I have to follow my calling," Tom explained.

Why doesn't Tom want me to transfer to another college with him? He acts as if he's ashamed of what we've shared, like it was a sin or something. But in his mind, maybe it is.

Kate couldn't make sense of what their relationship had been for him. Was it just his last affair before becoming a serious Christian? That reasoning seemed too harsh, but then, why?

Tom packed his meager belongings into one big suitcase and a duffel bag. He slung his guitar over his shoulder, preparing to leave. Kate couldn't bear to say goodbye, and in a blinding storm of tears, she left their apartment before he did. She had loved him and respected him. It was supposed to be a permanent relationship. She had given her heart away again and didn't understand why this had happened.

Kate wandered around the streets of Portland devastated by his departure for a few hours. When she returned, she stood alone in their stunning, unique apartment, one she could no longer afford. *Get over it. I don't need love right now, maybe never. I have a college degree to pursue.* Kate was firm with herself. Her heart hardened and she pushed the pain away.

...

Kate scoured the newspaper and found an ad for a shared apartment that weekend. She met with Elsa, another female student at the university and toured her apartment. It was adequate, with a study table in the bedroom, and Kate rented it on the spot. She and Elsa became friends and even traveled to their classes together. Better yet, Elsa had a large group of friends.

"Come with me tonight. I hang out with the owner of my favorite tavern on the weekends," Elsa persuaded. "It's called the Questing Beast."

"That's a weird name for a tavern," Kate said.

"Isn't it? I don't know why Alvin named it that." Elsa knew many of the regular patrons, and on Friday and Saturday nights, a couple of musicians sat on stools and belted out music in the corner.

Alvin organized a co-ed baseball team for his staff and friends when the weather warmed up, and they played against teams from the other bars in the city. After the Saturday game, everyone relaxed on lawn chairs at the edge of the field and drank beer.

Kate met Robert there. She wasn't looking for romance, but it just happened. He was in his mid-thirties, older than her, but not bad looking.

Kate thought maturity might be a good attribute to have in a partner. Free-spirited like her, Robert loved to travel and explore new places. They toured the Oregon Coast to explore the rugged shoreline on the weekends when Kate was out of classes. They drove up into the mountains to the local hot springs and hiked into an old, abandoned cabin set way back in the forest. He became her 'bestfriend with benefits,' and that was all Kate wanted from any relationship because she had locked her heart off bounds.

One Friday night, when spring term was over, Kate sipped her beer at the Questing Beast as usual and waited for Robert to arrive. She was comfortable in their casual relationship.

"Wahoo!" He rushed in and grabbed a chair. "I just got hired to crew on a fifty-foot sailing ketch and get to help sail it back to Sausalito." His grin was so big Kate thought it took years off his face.

"You're kidding." She leaned forward over the table. "Sausalito, like near San Francisco?"

"Yup. The ship is the Phoenix from Hiroshima. She's famous for making peace voyages and was brought up to Portland for the Rose Festival. They docked her right alongside the other battleships and destroyers on display at the marina."

"What do you mean by peace voyages?"

"Earle Reynolds owns the ketch, and he sailed it all over the world to protest nuclear weapons. Even with his wife and kids, he sailed into off-limit waters in the South Pacific, where nuclear bombs were to be tested. They tried to arrest the guy for it."

"That was dangerous. I wonder what drove him to take such radical actions."

"He worked for the government in Japan and studied radiation effects on the children who survived World War Two. Remember they dropped the atomic bomb on Hiroshima? That mushroom cloud incinerated the entire city."

"Seeing all those damaged children must have impacted him, then." Kate shuddered.

"It must have because a few years later, he quit his job and designed his own ship. He hired some Japanese boat-builders to build it for him, so he could sail the world to protest."

"That's amazing." Kate admired people's grandiose missions in life.

"He sailed into Vladivostok and Leningrad and even talked to the Chinese in Shanghai to challenge their nuclear testing. Our government didn't sanction any of his trips, but he went anyway."

"That's a serious effort for world peace."

Robert nodded. "Just a few years ago, he sailed to Northern Vietnam with a ton of private medical supplies. The guy has balls."

"And you get to sail on this celebrity ship? That's so cool. When do you go?" Kate's envy came out in a petulant voice. He was leaving, but she was excited for him.

"After the weekend. Hey, do you know how to cook?"

"Sure, but why." Kate learned to make family meals when her mother worked full time at the City Hall.

Robert gulped down a big swig from his mug of beer. "The captain is looking for a galley chef for the trip," he said with a mischievous smile.

"Oh, Robert." Kate clapped her hands and held them to her chin. "Do you think the captain would hire me? I once steered my brother-in-law's fishing boat out of Newport in stormy water. We were hauling in salmon so fast he didn't want to go back to shore." Kate was talking fast and couldn't contain her enthusiasm.

"Way to go. I bet that was a hoot."

"It was. The wind blew so hard I had to plant my feet at the wheel and crank it back and forth to keep the boat headed into the waves."

"So, our little Kate has experience." Robert grinned at her eagerness.

"Will you ask him if I can be one of his crew members? Please?"

"I already did," he chuckled.

...

The next day, Robert and Kate walked past all kinds of yachts and sailboats and continued down to the main marina office on the Willamette River. Inside, Robert introduced her to a serious, mild-looking man.

"Captain Dan, this here is my girlfriend, Kate," Robert announced. "She's the one I told you about for the cook you needed."

Kate exchanged a firm handshake with the young captain. She accepted Captain Dan's scrutiny and tried to think of something to say. "We saw your ship at the end of the dock. It must have been exciting to sail up the west coast."

"It's not my ship. The owner brought the Phoenix up from San Francisco, but then he had to fly home early for an emergency," Captain Dan said.

"So, he hired you to bring her back down the coast?" Robert put his hands in the pockets of his jeans and leaned on the counter.

"Yeah, Reynolds himself was too busy. He teaches Peace Studies at the University of California and has quite a reputation for being an activist."

"Did you find enough men to help sail the boat?" Robert asked.

"I got a crew, but not one of them say they can cook." Captain Dan scratched his neck.

Kate burst into the conversation. "Please, consider me. I can do it. I'm used to making enormous meals for my family." She went on and boasted about her salmon fishing experience.

"Well, here's the big question," the captain said. "Have you ever been seasick?"

"Nope. I was concentrating on steering the boat straight into the wind. We were in a school of salmon, and my brother-in-law didn't want to stop pulling them in."

Captain Dan was silent. He measured her up, and after a long pause, he nodded.

"Okay, you're on, but don't disappoint me," he stated firmly. "My crew of five guys will need heaping plates of hot food for each meal."

"That's fantastic." Kate bounced on her feet, mustering her confidence. "Thank you. I won't let you down!" She made that a solemn vow to herself.

"Can you make up a menu and give me a list of the groceries you want by Saturday? I'll pick up the supplies, and we'll plan to load up on Sunday afternoon."

"Sure. How many days will we be out at sea?" Kate asked.

"Plan for at least seven," he said.

"You got it." And with that, Kate became the sixth mate on the crew and the sole female on board. She was about to sail from Portland, Oregon, down the west coast to San Francisco. When Robert led her down the dock to his car, she was giddy and asked, "Do we get to go under the Golden Gate Bridge?"

"Hell, yes." He grinned and gave her a high-five.

...

Captain Dan met them at the marina on Sunday, his truck loaded with supplies and groceries to carry onboard. From up close, the Phoenix looked old and worn. She was a double-ended ketch, and her wooden masts stuck up like candles on a slice of cake. Rope ladders hung taut from the top of them, and the sails were rolled-up tight around the booms. Kate imagined the family and the other sailing crews who had walked on the mahogany decks years before. History was embedded in the scarred wood of each plank.

The captain gave Kate and Robert a grand tour of the ship and assigned two berths for them in the bow of the boat. "You'll have some privacy here, but I have to warn you. You might not sleep well if we get some big swells in bad weather."

"We'll make do with that," Robert said. The cramped quarters and bunk beds were not conducive for extracurricular activities, but Kate didn't care. She and Robert brought in their backpacks and left them in the tiny room. After the tour, Kate filled up the galley cupboards with the groceries she had ordered while the captain took Robert on deck and showed him what his duties would be. Afterward, they returned to check on her progress.

"There's not enough room in the fridge for all these eggs," Kate said.

"Just put them up in the cupboards and turn the cartons over every day. They'll keep for weeks that way." It was clear the captain had experienced long trips before.

"What type of stove is this?" She studied it with apprehension. One large burner suspended on spokes hung over a metal tray.

"That's an oil stove set on a Gimbal ring. No matter which way the ship pitches, the burner always stays level. We use oil in it because it's the least flammable liquid in case of accidents."

That information didn't reassure Kate, but Captain Dan continue to show her the tricky process of lighting the burner. It was doable, but black smoke billowed out each time. Kate examined the assortment of beat-up pots and pans and taped her seven-day menu inside the cabinet door. She was ready. She better be, because the crew was counting on her.

Chapter 20

A STORM ON THE OCEAN

The Phoenix rode high in the water, tethered against the seawall on the Willamette River's south side. It was not fancy, this sailing ship. She had weathered well in her age but was out of place among the other modern pleasure crafts and tugboats moored at the pier. Her age didn't bother Kate and Robert's excitement or the rest of the crew they met on the deck of the Phoenix. Gorgeous spring weather promised them a grand voyage.

Captain Dan shouted to the crew to cast off when everyone was on board. The men drew in the lines, and the Phoenix swept off into the river. Ten minutes later, their small ship passed the last huge naval destroyer still at the docks for the Rose Parade. They heard the Navy commander roar, "about-face." And all the sailors on that ship's deck turned their backs on the Phoenix as it passed by them.

"Hey, look at that. We're famous," Captain Dan cried out. It was rather humorous, because their ship seemed like a toy compared to the huge gray destroyer. The Phoenix had an anti-war reputation, and the US navy had made a point in dishonoring it.

Kate was proud to be sailing on the ship and wore a huge, excited smile as the sun shone down from a bright blue sky. She sat at the bow watching the men's actions on deck as the city seemed to flow along beside them. "How come the river became so wide all of a sudden?" She asked one member of the crew close by.

"It's because we're merging into the larger Columbia River. See the way the water changes color in that distinct line?" A faster dark belt of blue water glittered on the surface to her left, causing them to pick up speed as they turned into it and were pushed west to the ocean.

"You'll see the town of Rainier show up first on the right. Then the next port will be Astoria."

Kate watched the towns glide by, and Robert came to join her a few hours later. "We'll cross the bar and into the mouth of the Columbia pretty soon. The captain told us to get ready for some real action."

"Okay, isn't this awesome?" Kate twisted around in all directions to stare at the land they were leaving and the churning seawater ahead. Under full steam, the captain shouted quick orders as the ship plowed through the rolling swells, thrashing back and forth through the current. Seagulls squawked above them. On the final forward heave, the Phoenix broke through the surf and entered the calm water of the vast Pacific Ocean.

"Hooray!" Whistles and shouts rang out to celebrate crossing the bar. "Three cheers for our captain," Robert yelled, and then everyone was busy. First, two of the men pulled out the mainsail from a storage cabinet on deck. They hooked the canvas to lines and pulleys with various clips in preparation, but it looked like a mess to Kate, who watched from the sidelines. Captain Dan cut the engine, and the awful chugging noise stopped. For a minute, they floated in stillness with no sound except minor creaks in the ship's timbers.

An invisible curtain seemed to flutter open on the wooden stage, and Act One of the voyage began. The crew hoisted the mainsail now, and it flapped in the breeze until the men trimmed the lines taut. The beige canvas billowed outward when the sail caught the wind, forming a huge quarter moon. It snapped tight with a low-pitched whistle, making ship tremble like the wings of a condor ready for takeoff. Then they were sailing.

No sound came from the crew, or the motor, just the rustling wind in their ears. It was the most soothing sound Kate had ever heard. She hummed the gentle chords of "El Condor Pasa," which seemed to match her surroundings. Kate faced forward on her bench at the bow and threw back her head to catch the wind in her hair. She became the Prima Donna of the Pacific as their ship sailed south through the gentle swells of turquoise water.

"Hey, Kate," a crewmate tapped her shoulder. "Captain wants a late lunch soon."

She remembered she had to work for her passage, and hurried down into the galley, but she was still smiling.

...

Kate figured out how to use the gimbaled stove, except nothing prevented the black smoke from rising in outrage each time she lit the burner. The pots of stew, chili, and other hearty meals she cooked in the next few days stayed level, no matter how much the galley tilted. Kate received compliments for the dishes she served, and between meals, she went topside to watch everything happen.

Most of the time, she sat at the bow and rubbed her hand over the figurehead, carved from camphor wood. It was the mythical Phoenix, a powerful bird stretched out in free flight from the ashes of destruction. It was a fitting symbol for a peace boat from Hiroshima.

On deck, the blue sky blended in with the ocean, and as far as Kate could see, there was no land in sight. Yet, the seagulls still swooped over the water to visit them. Farther out, Kate spotted other ships, but they kept their distance. When the wind picked up, they clipped along at a good pace, but seemed hardly to move at other times. Their ship was a bubble of humanity on a private watery globe.

That day, the surface of the water became almost a mirror. Robert and a few others took turns and scrambled up the ladder to the crow's nest on the mast.

"The view's fantastic," Robert said. "You have to try it, Kate."

With the men's encouragement, Kate climbed up and clung tight to the ropes on the tiny platform. The horizon dropped off all around her as though she were at the top of the world.

Kate peered down at the smallness of their craft, with the air whistled around her. She stood still and hung on to the swaying masthead while the entire surface below her seemed to be in motion. She breathed in exhilarating power and cherished the moment.

They saw whales in the distance the next day, as big as their boat. Later, Kate spotted the school of friendly animals she had hoped to see. "Look at the porpoises. They're doing tricks for us!" Six of them performed a choreographed circus act for half an hour in the wake of the Phoenix.

Robert and Jason set out salmon fishing lines to trail behind the ship. "If we catch some fish, you have to cook them," they told her.

"Sure. You catch them and I'll cook 'em," she promised. After they reeled in a couple of Chinooks, Kate stood over the smoking gimbal stove to fry up the salmon steaks. That impressed the crew, and they celebrated, pretending to be seasoned sailors enjoying the day's catch.

Captain Dan had to sail into the marina at Newport to collect signed petitions from various Peace organizations. Reynolds, the Phoenix owner, planned to present them to the Republican National Convention to protest nuclear weapons.

"Do you want to stay on as crew members after Sausalito?" Captain Dan asked Robert and Kate. "We'll be heading down to other California ports of call, and we'll end up in San Diego."

She and Robert gave him a resounding yes, excited that they could extend their adventure.

"Guess we passed the test." Robert shared his keenness with Kate that night in their little bunks in the bow.

"Yeah, we'll get to sail almost to Mexico on the Phoenix now," Kate said with pride.

The next day, the wind picked up and made it a perfect day for sailing. Kate watched from the bow as the captain shouted new orders. "Hoist up the foresail."

The men clipped and raised it, and their second sail billowed out in the wind, making the ship double its speed.

"Let's get the jib sail up next," the captain ordered. "It's a good day for sailing in this steady wind." The crew pulled more canvas out of another storage compartment. Once they raised it on the lines, the sail extended in a bowl shape out in front of the bow. Captain Dan barked out orders to the men to trim each canvas for maximum tautness. Then they had three sails capturing the wind, and the ship skimmed over the water with accelerating speed.

Everyone worked their shifts each day in a smooth rhythm until the fifth day of the trip. At that point, the captain called a meeting in the galley for all the shipmates. He asked Kate to join them, so she edged in too. But Captain Dan appeared stern as he spread out a chart on the small table and articulated his next words with care.

"The marine VHF Weather channel just broadcasted a warning for gale-force winds off the west coast," he said. The men gathered closer to peer down at the map where he was pointing out their location.

"We're right about here, five miles out." Captain Dan had his finger at the northern California coastline, four days south of Portland.

"Should we make our way back to land?" one crewman asked. It was the first sailing experience for most of them.

"There are no close ports we can hide in; we wouldn't make it in time, anyway. We'll have to ride out the storm on the water."

"How bad is it going to be?" Robert asked.

"We'll plot a course to steer away from the worst of it, but we have to expect at least twenty-four hours of being tossed in some pretty rough weather."

"Are we going to keep the mainsail up?" Tim asked. The wind had turned blustery already.

"Not during a gale warning. The winds can get up to fifty knots. All the sails come down, and we'll take shifts around the clock."

"Are we in any real danger?" one of the other men asked.

"Well, the Phoenix has weathered a lot of rough seas, even a typhoon or two in the Indian Ocean. But she's an old lady now, so everybody follows orders exactly as I instruct them."

The crewmates nodded. "Aye, aye, Captain," and they spoke the ageless words without their usual banter.

"Those of you not working this shift, I want you to go and get some sleep. You're going to need it. This foul weather can last days before it blows over."

Kate climbed down into the galley and cooked up an enormous pot of homemade chicken soup on the smoky oil burner. She hard boiled some eggs, set out trays of sandwiches, and strapped everything down tight. She even wedged the remaining cartons of eggs inside the cabinets.

As the night turned dark, the old timbers of the ship creaked, rising, and sinking in the rolling motion of the sea. The engine clunked away in low reverberations, getting louder as the ship crested each swell. Despite the noise, Kate managed to fall asleep in their tiny quarters in the vessel's bow.

In the middle of the night, she woke up. Her heart beat fast. The wind had changed to a screeching howl like the voice of a demonic creature. Nothing was level. She was flat on her bed but tied to a teeter-totter. Each time the ship climbed to the top of a swell, Kate's head went up on the incline. After a moment of stillness, the ship slid into the next trough, and she was upside down. Seawater crashed intermittently against the four-inch outer hull close to her face. *How could the old boat hold together with such force pounding at it?* The angle of the ship's bow continued to dip and rise for what seemed like hours. Kate had no sense of balance in the blackness. She panicked.

Where's my damn flashlight? Are beads of moisture seeping through the ancient cedar planks already? Kate found the light and searched her surroundings. There were no leaks, thank God. Robert slept in exhaustion from his last working shift in the next bunk and she didn't want to wake him. The single beam of light made the low ceiling of the bow close in, turning the space into a two-man triangular coffin about to sink into the depths of a watery hell.

Sleep for her became impossible. *I have to get out of here. I've got to do something!*

She knew the skipper and the first mate had been at the wheel for close to twenty hours. They had to be exhausted, and the whole crew depended on them. Who else would bring coffee and food up to the helm to help them keep awake but the galley cook? And that was her job.

Kate gritted her teeth and climbed out of bed. She bumped along the tight hallway to the galley, bracing herself against the walls. As the ship tilted, she grabbed the countertop to keep from sliding across the floor. She struck a wooden match and lit the swinging lamp to fill the kettle with coffee and water. Then she lit the stove burner as it gyrated and balanced the kettle on the gimbaled ring. Miraculously, it still stayed level on the burner.

Kate was quick to wrap up sandwiches but pouring hot coffee into the thermos took all her concentration. Next, she heated the soup next, poured it into another thermos, and stuffed everything into a duffel bag. Slinging it over her shoulders, she lurched to the foot of the wooden ladder going up to the deck.

She looked up at the hatch door, closed tight. Kate had never seen it shut before. How was she to climb that writhing column of narrow steps and get the hatch open? And what was she going to find?

I have to do this. Captain Dan and the first mate must stay awake. With determination, Kate struggled to the top and wrenched the door ajar. The wind roared, and dark, cold seawater slapped her in the face. Waves crashed over the deck and flooded down into the stairway she had just climbed. She anchored herself against the doorframe as the ship sunk to the bottom of a trough and leveled out.

Through the stinging rain and spray, Kate looked forward and saw the next gigantic wave, a massive wall of salty liquid bearing down on them. It soared taller than the Phoenix, now only a puny boat in contrast. The top of the mast stood but halfway up that wall of water, and it was coming toward them fast.

Kate's stomach turned somersaults. She froze and watched the bow rise skyward like a gigantic underwater hand was lifting the ship. Zigzagging in slow motion, it climbed the face of the watery slope. Fear hit hard, and shook her body, for how could the captain keep the Phoenix running straight on these high seas?

From the hatch, Kate watched the two men at the helm in horror. Captain Dan's brawny arms yanked the wheel four spokes to the right, then pulled it back again as the ship surged up the rippling ramp of swirling surf. An awful truth hit her full force; *if the ship turned sideways, it was going to capsize and drown them all that night.*

At the summit of the next swell, the Phoenix held its upright position but wavered precariously in screaming wind. Then like a giant surfboard flying on a fast run out of control, it shot downward. At the bottom of the swirling black liquid, the ship paused again.

Kate moved fast and reached out as far as she could on the handrail. She shouted, "Captain Dan." She had to scream louder through the crashing rain. "Captain, Captain!"

From the cockpit doorway, the captain and first mate saw her grimacing in alarm.

"I brought hot soup." She yelled each word separately. Foam surged across the deck as Captain Dan stepped out to grab the bag. His face was haggard, his eyes wide and piercing. He shouted out a strange question against the wind with full soul contact, "Is God with us tonight?"

Captain Dan desperately needed to hear an affirmation. Kate stared into his face and then looked upward into the grayness. Yes, she sensed God out there in the wild surf. She nodded solemnly to the captain because, without divine help, they had no chance to survive. And in that precise second, they connected with something even more significant than the storm.

The captain mouthed an exaggerated silent thank you. He motioned for her to go back inside before returning to the helm.

Kate clutched the rail as the sailboat began another ascent. She climbed down and fought to shut the hatch door tight before they crested another wave. In the galley, she noticed her shaking had stopped. She should have been more terrified than ever after witnessing the storm and seeing her fear mirrored in the captain's eyes. But that wasn't true. Her fear had morphed into something else, and a strange fatalistic acceptance had taken over.

Robert was still sleeping on his narrow mattress in the bow when Kate stretched out again. Her body rose and fell like before, but the events of her life seemed to sort themselves out on a weight scale. The regrets piled up on the downside, the acts of kindness accumulated on the upside. She regretted all the sad things she had said and done, yet so grateful for the moments of beautiful memories.

It's okay. That's what life is for; to build character. Life's an incredible adventure, a voyage on the waters of humanity.

In the darkness, Kate thought of her family and a few friends. How would they feel if she never returned? She thought about Mark, wondered if he had found happiness with anyone, and what her life would have been like if they had gotten back together. Then a Sunday-school song came to mind, and it comforted her. "Little ones to him belong. They are weak, but He is strong." A serene calmness dissipated her worry. Then she curled up like a child to sleep despite the crashing water that shook the cedar timbers so close to her head.

...

The gale winds sounded less treacherous when Kate woke up, but still the boat rocked wildly. Kate stumbled to the galley to light the stove, and black smoke billowed out as usual, permeating the air. Steadying herself against the counter, she made coffee. Then she put on a pot of hearty oatmeal with nuts and raisins to bolster the crew's energy. When the exhausted men came in, they lurched back and forth to collapse in their seats, nodding to each other before they wolfed the food down in hunger.

"Do you think we're out of the worst part of the storm?" Robert asked the others.

"It's too early to tell. It might be only the eye of the storm," Captain Dan answered.

After eating the quick meal, half the men went on shift, and the rest stumbled to their bunks, desperate for sleep. Kate put together another tray of tuna sandwiches and crept back to bed herself.

The next time she woke up, everything was quiet. She hurried up on deck to find the sun sparkling across the surface of an undulating turquoise sea. A soft breeze ruffled the canvas of the mainsail, whistling pleasantly. The Phoenix sat tall on the water again, and countless seagulls screeched around the mast. Kate inhaled the salty sea air and joined Robert and the others sitting in the warmth on the deck. It was a sacred space now, and everybody sat in silence in the beautiful calmness.

"There it is," Captain Dan shouted. "Can everybody see it?" A hazy landmass appeared on the horizon, making them all whoop and cheer. The Golden Gate Bridge came into sight an hour later. Kate had traveled over it once in a car, but now they would enter the city sailing under the grand expanse in the sunny golden morning. Kate's heart soared with a sailor's pride at the end of a hazardous journey.

Once the Phoenix chugged into the Sausalito marina afterward, they inched their way to the pier, and the men scurried around to secure her lines. The ship was tired and older now, like the crew that sailed her. When Kate stepped out onto the dock, her legs wobbled like she was drunk, her balance off from the days at sea.

Captain Dan thanked them all and announced the trip to San Diego was canceled because the ship's damage had to be assessed. He gripped Kate's hand extra tight when she and Robert said their farewells, and with one last look at the Phoenix, they walked away to find accommodation on solid ground.

"Please, can I take a shower first?" Kate begged with eagerness once they had booked into a hotel room, and Robert obliged her. After seven days of cooking over the smoky soot of the oil burner stove, hot water had never felt so good. When she washed her hair, the residue ran in black rivulets down the drain. The shower wasn't only about the sweat and dirt coming off. It was spiritual, a baptism, for Kate had survived. She had faced her fear, and God had given her safe passage.

Kate cried tears of joy in that shower, feeling weightless and pure. She put on clean clothes and was changed forever.

Chapter 21

TOXIC LIFE

Portland seemed tame compared to sailing on the Phoenix. Normal life started up as if Kate had turned a record player back on. She needed to find a job again to pay for her fall college term, but Robert wouldn't buy into that mediocrity.

"Let's drive across the country this summer," he suggested.

"Wouldn't that be expensive? The hotels and the gas?" Kate asked, tempted by the idea. The travel bug had bitten her since her trip to Mexico and then San Francisco.

"We have our camping gear. And once we get to Michigan, we could stay at my parent's house for a while."

"I need to earn money for university classes, though." Kate realized he wanted employment only long enough to fund his next travel destination. Her goal was to educate herself. Still, she learned things from traveling, too, like the profound spiritual shift that happened during the storm on the ocean. "Let's take your Volkswagen because it's cheap on gas, and then we can find jobs back east," Robert said.

That made sense to Kate, and if she moved out of Elsa's place, she'd save a couple of months' rent while she was gone. They packed their meager belongings and took off two days later with Bob Dylan singing, "Like a Rolling Stone," on the radio. They crisscrossed east on minor roads, exploring the rural towns in the backbone of America. Oregon's flat wheat land jutted up against the mountain range and merged into rolling countryside. They stopped at scenic parks at night to set up a two-man tent. Their outdoor kitchen was a small camp stove and a cooler full of food. Kate would spread a cloth on the picnic table and pick a few wildflowers to put into a drinking glass. With this pattern to their days, they made it to Michigan in a little more than a week.

"Robert, it's so good to have you come to visit." His aging parents greeted them with smiles when they showed up at his family's home.

"Mom and Dad, this is my friend Kate," he said with little fanfare. They welcomed her into the house with polite smiles, but his mother showed her to a separate bedroom down the hall. Even though her son was over thirty, sleeping with a girlfriend was not acceptable.

That first week, Kate and Robert dropped off resumes to local businesses and then did a whirlwind tour of local sites and hiking trails. Robert landed a job driving a forklift at a large paint company. "Why don't you try to get a job nearby as a waitress?" he asked.

"Waitressing at a café pays so little. I want to look for something with higher wages."

The Fisher Body Shop for General Motors was hiring for their swing shift on the assembly line, and she applied for a factory position. The hours from four-thirty in the afternoon until one in the morning sounded horrible, but they paid the women the same wages as the men, plus on the late shift, she'd receive time and a half pay.

Kate was hired for the job, but Robert didn't like her schedule. "You'll be making more cars to pollute the air and selling your soul to the capitalists," he said.

She helped make cars, alright. As the vehicles rolled by, she screwed on four plastic liners to the inside of doors every two minutes. Holding a power screwdriver for hours each night was tiring, but the higher wages built up her college fund fast.

They found a funky upstairs apartment to rent together, and on the weekends, they'd visit parks and quaint little cafes and taverns to have their evening meals. But Robert was gone during the weekdays, and Kate was far from home. She often walked around the rich residential areas, imagining herself in that lifestyle, ashamed she felt that way.

The summer months flew by with interesting weekend outings until Kate had to deal with an ugly situation. She noticed tiny growths where they shouldn't be growing and made an appointment at a medical clinic. After an embarrassing doctor's examination, he informed her she had contracted a case of venereal warts. Kate cringed with mortification. "How can a girl get those? Where do they come from?"

"Not from toilet seats." The doctor declared. "They can cause cervical cancer, so we have to treat them aggressively," he said, leaning back in his chair.

It's a venereal disease, an STD! How could I have gotten them? And from Robert? Kate was so embarrassed. "How do I get rid of them?" she whispered.

The treatment plan called for burning them off with acid which is what the doctor proceeded to do that morning. It was the most degrading, excruciating thing that had ever happened to her. Afterward, he gave her a brochure to read and asked her to make a follow-up appointment if more treatment was needed. "You might want to ask your partner if he has any signs, too," the doctor suggested.

Kate confronted Robert when she was back at their place and told him about the diagnosis. He saw no sign of it on himself and feigned ignorance about the whole situation. For the next three days, Kate stayed home from work and endured the agony alone in their apartment. She had to take aspirin every few hours because it felt like her insides were on fire with third-degree burns.

"How are you feeling?" Robert asked when he came home late again for the second night.

"Not so good," she said, thinking that was definitely an understatement. "Why are you home so late?" she asked in a pitiful tone. What had he been doing while she endured hours of painful sensitivity with every move she made?

"I was working." He explained, sounding defensive.

"But how come you always get home much later than when your shift ends?"

"A few of us go out for a beer after work. You know how it is."

"No, I don't know," she said but when she thought about it, he probably came home late every evening. She worked those hours, so how would she know. Kate didn't want to accuse him, but she was the one suffering from an unaccountable STD. Distrust tasted foul in her mouth, but she swallowed it down. "Do some guys you hang out with happen to be girls?" She stepped up close to his face. "Have you been sleeping with anyone else?"

"Of course not." Robert stayed calm and casual.

"Well, the doctor didn't think I caught these things from a toilet seat." Robert wouldn't meet her eyes, but he reached out to hold her. Kate would never sleep outside their relationship. He wouldn't either, would he?

"That's stupid. You could have caught them from anywhere," he said and went to their small kitchen to make something for them to eat.

Kate had her suspicions, but no proof. But then her thoughts turned inward. *Could she have had a few for a long time and not noticed them?*

She never discovered how she came down with venereal warts, and after getting over her horrible treatment, she worried about them returning. Kate tried to rationalize it into something she could accept. A chance occurrence perhaps. At least she hadn't come down with gonorrhea or something worse.

Isn't that odd? I've tripped out on windowpane acid. I've slept under a dangerous tree that dripped acid. And now I've been treated for an STD with acid. What's the message in these coincidences? Is my life toxic or what?

...

In late August, she and Robert quit their jobs and headed back to the west coast. Robert purchased a pickup truck, which meant Kate drove her Volkswagen alone each day. Their separate vehicles matched the current distance in their relationship. Had Robert slept with someone else or were Kate's suspicions just feelings from the past playing havoc with her emotions. She had to quit thinking about it if she wanted their relationship to work.

Kate went to register at the university once they were back in Oregon, but it was too late to get the courses she wanted for her major in Psychology. She should have known to register before leaving the state.

"Why pay for classes you're not interested in taking?" Robert asked her. "Let's head south to Mexico instead. We're good travel partners."

"How can you say that? We both drove separate vehicles across the country?"

"We camped together each evening. Remember that huge orange moon shining over the lake that night and the hike along the river where we saw those fish jumping clear out of the water? We saw some beautiful things."

She might as well take another term off. Besides, she always wanted to go back to Mexico again, and it would be safer to travel with a male partner. "Would you want to drive your pickup?"

"We can travel a lot cheaper if we ditch our vehicles and hitchhike down to the border. We'll take Mexican buses and trains from there."

"You mean, 'have backpack–will travel?' That's the motto we seem to live by."

People considered them hippies, but she had traveled light that way before. They stuffed only the basics into their backpacks and started the trip the very next day. Kate was the bait. She would stand in front of Robert with her long blonde hair hanging to her shoulders and her thumb held out. He was her security as they climbed into various vehicles with strange-looking drivers.

After crossing the US border, they joined the Mexican families on the green vinyl seats of old school buses and headed south. Each night, they got off and found cheap lodging in the towns they wanted to explore. But the weather was hot that time of year, much hotter than what Kate remembered.

They found themselves in a hippie migration, a flow of tie-dyed T-shirts and patched-up jeans. Kate, too, wore her favorite pair of cutoffs, soft from washing and hanging low on her hips. She had embroidered ivy leaves and flowers up the sides to make a personal statement. Her first choice for an extended stay was San Miguel de Allende, the famous artist community high in the mountains north of Mexico City. The town was rich in local color, with many skilled artists and craftsmen. Kate wanted to stick around and get to know the other Americans who lived there. Maybe she'd take painting classes and sell pictures in the artsy shops that lining the cobbled streets.

But Robert became bored after a few days and convinced her to continue south again, but this time by train. Kate spent her time looking out the window at the interesting scenes as the countryside flew by.

Women from the villages were scrubbing their clothes on the rocks in small streams. She took pictures with her small Kodak camera of the colorful fabrics hanging on the bushes to dry.

"Look, there's a pyramid in the distance," she cried out. "Do you see it? Oh, I wish we could stop here."

"That must be the Pyramid of Teotihuacan. It's just a bunch of stone temples," he said.

Kate was determined to visit ancient ruins on the trip somehow, regardless of his lack of interest. The whole country fascinated her with cultural differences in every scene she saw. When Mexico City appeared in the smoggy distance, the countryside completely changed. Small villages now looked more like slums. The train rattled across rivers so polluted the slimy water had islands of soapsuds floating down on the current. When they reached Mexico City, it was monstrous and congested. She and Robert walked around for a couple of hours and then bought a train ticket, going east to Veracruz.

The train broke down in the middle of nowhere the next day. Kate watched from the dusty window as steam billowed out of the engine. The train crew gathered beside the engine to analyze the problem.

One of them cut down a green prickly cactus trunk with a machete. Then they used the large organic pipe to channel water from a higher spigot down into a container. That water was poured into an opened valve on the engine's other side. She didn't understand the 'why' of that operation, but their ingenuity impressed her.

After that, the train sputtered and chugged along again, down through the mountains with grainfields far below. They roared through tunnel after tunnel of the mountainous track before reaching the port town of Veracruz.

The first thing Kate did after getting off the train was to walk down the street to a beach. Then she took off her shoes to wade in the warm turquoise water, so different than what she was used to on the west coast. "I'm in the Atlantic Ocean on the other side of the North American continent," she shouted to Robert as she splashed around up to her knees. He sat on his backpack in the shade and waited for her. There was a festive air on the promenade, and as they strolled along, local guitar players serenaded the guests eating at the outdoor restaurants.

"It must be a local holiday here," Robert said. "Look, those men are dressed up as pirates. They're walking on stilts down the sidewalk." He took her hand to weave through the crowd.

Kate stopped to point at something else. "You got to be kidding. That guy is crazy. He has flames coming out from his mouth."

"They call them fire-eaters, I think. They put some kind of gas in their mouth and light it up. Can you imagine the taste of that?"

It was a fun day mingling with the crowds, and Veracruz had many European tourists. An interesting Dutch couple at a restaurant were leaving on a cargo ship the next morning and invited them to a farewell party that night. They planned to start the first Mexican restaurant in Copenhagen when they arrived home.

Kate and Robert booked into a hostel and walked to the commercial marina to board the freighter. They drank stout Holland Beer with the couple and Kate envied the common goal they had together.

Kate looked at brochures the next morning showing the ancient historical sites near Veracruz. "There's a National Park nearby, Robert. It's famous for giant Olmec heads carved out of huge basalt boulders. Let's go see them."

"Okay, I'll go see the big Olmec heads with you. See how big-headed I can be?" Robert joked. They hopped on a local bus to get there and found the statues to be almost twice the height of themselves, each weighing tons. The boulders didn't originate from the flat plain of the historical site so how were they transported there. It was the kind of mystery Kate found intriguing.

"Robert, just think how long it must have taken to carve the expression on this face out of sheer rock." Kate ran her hand over the stone lips and eyelids. "This sign says they were made around 900 BC."

"That's a hell of a long time ago," was all he said.

...

Days later, they were back at the bus station with their packs on and a map spread out, deciding where to go next. Mexico's landmass had narrowed that far south. They could continue south into the Yucatan or on a short bus ride crisscross the continent to the west coast.

"What town are you guys heading to?" a young gringo waiting at the station asked Robert.

"We're looking for a cheap place on the west coast to veg out for a while."

"You might like Puerto Escondido. We stayed in a palapa hut on the beach for two dollars a night. The huts have a sand floor and a couple of hammocks to sleep in, but it's a bargain for the price and the beautiful sunsets are thrown in for free."

They thanked the guy and bought tickets at the counter to Puerto Escondido. The trip was longer than expected, but the beach town was as lovely as the gringo said. Coconut trees edged the pristine mile-long shoreline, with the ocean shimmering in a deep blue velvet. The sun's heat penetrated Kate's skin like heat from an oven. Kate soon sported a fiery-red sunburn from walking along the beach so often. She stopped to chat with another hippie couple who had gorgeous dark tans.

"Wow. You're both so brown. What kind of expensive lotion do you use to get that color?"

"We don't use anything but a can of Crisco. We bought it from the corner store down the street."

"Vegetable shortening works as a sunscreen? But that's crazy. You don't burn at all?"

"Not since we started using it." They laughed, proud of their thrifty money sense.

Kate bought a small can of shortening that day and oiled her skin like fine leather. Her skin soon turned soft and a rich coffee color from the sun. She liked to use simple, inexpensive products, so she didn't have to support the big mega-corporations. She strung healthy tips together like pearls of wisdom.

She and Robert settled down for a few weeks in their small, thatched hut on the waterfront. In the cool mornings, Robert got up and bought seafood from the local fishermen right off the boats. Kate would barter for produce from the farmer's market, and every few days, a dairy farmer came by on horseback. He sold fresh milk dipped out of a metal canister tied to his saddle. The days rolled by in lazy contentment, and at night they watched the sky turning pink and gold as the sun sank into the ocean with a tiny after-blaze of neon green.

Kate dressed and grabbed her backpack to leave the palapa one morning. The manager of their grand accommodations greeted her on the path, but then yelled for her to stop.

"Hijo de la chingada!" Son of a bitch, he said. He took his sandal off and brushed a large creature off her backpack. A scorpion, the size of her little finger, fell to the ground, his deadly looped tail quivering, strong pinchers ready for battle. Kate let out a screech and shook herself.

"No hay problema." The landowner pounded the predatory creature on the ground until it was dead. It seemed like a problem to Kate. After that morning, she checked her clothes and her shoes methodically before she put them on. Robert didn't think it was any big deal. "The sting of a scorpion carries a lot of toxins alright, but most people don't die from it," he said. But somehow, that didn't comfort Kate at all.

...

The Mexican people went out of their way to be helpful, and Kate and Robert started hitchhiking with the locals.

The language barrier was always there, but smiles were universal. Kate discovered that a genuine smile builds bridges between all kinds of people. One driver even stopped at a restaurant and bought bowls of chili and beers for them. Of course, it was spicy hot like everything else, not like the food Kate was used to eating. She wondered if that was causing her stomach to act up with indigestion.

"Mi estómago no sentir bueno aquí." She confided in Spanish to the driver.

"He doesn't need to know that, Kate." Robert reprimanded.

The driver urged her to eat the hot, peppery food for her health. "Usted necesita comer chilies picosos para una mejor salud," he said, explaining how hot peppers kill the harmful organisms in the digestive tract.

"I guess people don't have refrigerators in rural areas, so eating spicy food must be important for Mexicans," Robert added.

"Si," the man agreed and explained that everything grew fast in the tropical climate. He pointed to a row of new fence posts in a field. Fresh green shoots were budding off each post already. "Incluso los árboles."

"So, that's why rows of trees grow on the edge of fields in your country." Kate made the connection.

"Es lo mismo en el estómago," their driver said, patting his stomach.

Kate laughed at the logic. The farther south they traveled, the hotter the climate and the food. She vowed to add a little hot sauce to everything she ate from then on. Still, the idea of acid indigestion bothered her. Was it another toxic symptom? Perhaps it wasn't her lifestyle at all. She had to consider that subject sometime soon.

Chapter 22

DEEP IN A DARK CAVE

San Cristobal de las Casas was a must-see on any tourist list of destinations, and it seemed like a different country altogether to Kate. With its picturesque red-tile roofs, the colonial architecture stood out perfectly against the lush green mountains.

"Look how the Mayan people dress. I want to wear colorful clothes like that." The traditional bright red, hand-woven tunics were unchanged for centuries, while Kate's old jeans and tattered T-shirts hung on her in sharp contrast.

"Let's go shopping in the street markets today," she suggested.

"No, you go ahead," Robert replied. "I'll find a hostel for us and maybe visit the other gringos around town. Meet me back here before dark, though."

Robert loved to sit in the outdoor cafes and drink beer with whoever was handy, so she drifted off by herself down the cobblestone streets full of handcrafted merchandise displayed by the locals on blankets on the ground.

Kate couldn't resist the simple braided bracelets made of colorful string. She bartered for a few hand-embroidered blouses in the market square and stuffed them into her backpack. She gave a couple of her worn T-shirts to a beggar-woman on the sidewalk, who smiled and held out her hands to receive them.

Robert was conversing with young gringos when Kate joined him in the plaza. They had just returned from the Lagunas de Montebello region, where fifty beautiful multicolored lakes lay in Mexico's national park near the border of Guatemala. Robert had already set the park for their next destination.

...

The local public vans used for transportation were called *collectivos,* and she and Robert waited on the street corner to catch one. Kate snapped a picture with her camera of a gnarled old grandmother in red embroidered Mayan garb, thinking nothing about it, but the woman became furious. She yelled at her with outrage in some ancient Mayan dialogue, making the sign of the cross in front of her for protection.

"What the heck is wrong with her?" Robert asked.

A young Mexican waiting with them at the corner spoke English. "Our indigenous people believe a photo taken of them will capture part of their spirit. It is forever lost and can never return to them again."

How tragic, Kate thought. "Lo siento, Señora," she approached her and apologized profusely in broken Spanish. She learned the proper etiquette for taking pictures of people in foreign countries is to ask permission before you point a camera at them.

The Lagunas de Montebello were beautiful and made her homesick for Oregon's fresh, cool air. In that hot southern landscape, Kate was surprised to find open forests of pine trees similar to those back home. It was a land of magic where each lake in the national park reflected a different shade of blue.

Kate and Robert set up their small tent at a campsite on a serene turquoise lake, but Kate was stressed out from being constantly on the road. She could feel a bladder infection coming on and she hated getting those. She was tired, and they were painful.

The campground had a tiny store in front of a local home but there was no medication on the shelves. Kate expressed her dilemma using her limited Spanish vocabulary and some comic pantomime, and the woman shopkeeper seemed to understand. She led Kate out to a nearby field and picked some lemongrass out of the shrubs. Using gestures, she instructed how to make a medicinal tea. After a dozen cups of the hot drink, Kate experienced much less pain by the next day. She picked handfuls of lemongrass for herself and spread it out on a towel to dry in the sun. Then she scrunched it up into fine bits and packed the herbal remedy into a small container for later.

Robert met four other backpackers camped in the park who were young and adventurous. They invited him and Kate to explore a vast cave north of the lakes the next day.

"When you explore caves, it's called spelunking," Robert explained.

"What a funny word," Kate chuckled. "I don't know if I want to go with you, though."

"Come on. Let's go spelunking with these guys," Robert said. "When will we ever get a chance to explore a fascinating cave like this again?" He began stuffing a day's food supply in a smaller knapsack in readiness for his next exciting challenge.

But Kate wasn't as keen and rolled the decision over in her mind. They were supposed to be equal travel partners, but why was she always doing what he wanted to do? She needed more information. "You said they're planning to go two or three kilometers down into a big hole in the ground, but they don't have a professional guide."

"One of them says he has experience. And anyway, we'll all carry flashlights."

"What if the batteries run down?"

"Kate, all the torches won't quit at the same time," Robert said in exasperation but with humor. He gave her a tight hug to encourage her.

So, despite her fears, Kate gave in. She could do this.

...

The entrance to the cave gaped open like an enormous mouth at the end of a dirt road. On one side stood a rustic hand-painted warning sign, in Spanish, of course.

"Robert, this is not a tourist site."

"So what?" He read the sign. "The cave is supposed to be mammoth, so it's called Gruta de Mamut."

Each of the four explorers brought a packed lunch, a water bottle, and a precious flashlight. The girl named Georgina gave her a grin and a thumbs up, but the other girl looked as nervous as Kate. As they entered the mouth of the cave, the trail descended ahead of them into dark gloominess. Kate looked back at the black frame around the circle of pale sky and watched the dot of light grow smaller as they walked along. Then it disappeared.

At first, the rough path led through a large cavern about fifty yards wide. Jagged rocks on the ground pointed upward, and those hanging from the ceiling jutted down like yellowish teeth in a monster. Kate learned the terms.

"Stalagmites are the ones that might grow up to the ceiling in a thousand years," Jeff said. He looked Italian with dark dreamy eyes, and Kate was glad one of them knew something about caves.

"And the stalactites are those that you hope will hang tight from the roof until you get past them," his friend Stanley finished explaining.

The group skirted around the 'stalag-mights and tights' and made their way through an area of limestone boulders protruding from the ground. As they went deeper in, silent stone statues in various earth hues confronted them, guarding the access. Jeff showed them how to play musical tones by tapping on their surfaces. Sometimes the small pathway divided and turned in various directions, but always seemed to come back together again after passing through colorful rock formations. Other times the track narrowed into shafts so small they had to hunch down to squeeze through them. It became a confusing maze of cliffs and archways.

"We should follow the larger opening, so we won't get lost when we come back," Stanley suggested. Kate grunted and hoped his plan would work. Hours passed, and the tunnel became so narrow they walked in a single file with their arms brushing both rocky sides when suddenly, the air on their skin felt cool. The trail turned sandy around the next corner, and a glistening underground stream flowed beside them. The crystal water rippled without a sound as they followed it for some distance. Then the path opened into a large room, and the stream emptied into a dark pool, mirrored on the surface. Rock statues sat on the edge to guard it like gods.

"Oh, que linda eres!" Kate described it using the Spanish words she knew. It was eerily beautiful. Their flashlight beams moved around to dance on the surface, but the light wouldn't quite penetrate the mysterious shadows in the rocky crevasses on the walls.

Georgina waded in ankle-deep, swishing her ponytail and throwing water upward to rain down on her. Kate held back, hoping it wasn't acidic like so many other things in her life had been. But soon, they were all splashing themselves with the icy spray, for the cave was hot and dead humid air pressed up against their skin.

"I bet ancient Mayan ceremonies took place right here," Kate said to the others.

"It's possible. The native people considered any underground passageway to be a sacred portal to the underworld," Jeff said.

"Maybe virgins bathed in these waters before they were sacrificed to honor the warrior chiefs." Robert had caught the mood.

"What events these walls might have witnessed throughout the centuries." Kate was in awe at the scene before her.

The six of them splashed around in the shallow pool of blackness to relieve the tension they carried, a tension they tried to disguise. "We came a far distance to see the pool, and it's a beauty. But aren't we going back now?" Rowena asked.

"No way. This cave spelunking is way too cool." The guys were all in agreement.

"Let's continue and see where the main tunnel goes, at least," Jeff said, adjusting the sweat bandana across his brow. He was the self-appointed unofficial leader of their expedition, with the previous cave experience he claimed to have.

The group continued to climb up and over great protuberances of rocky obstacles. They crawled under stone arches that opened into yet more rooms where dark shapes closed in on them. The flashlights were held tight in their hands, lights shining every which way as their shadow-shapes contorted themselves like ants on a rocky beach at night. And still, they went in deeper.

Fatigue got the best of them, and after taking a vote, they sat down on rocks in a small cavern room to devour their lunches by torchlight.

"Hey, let's eat in the dark," Stanley suggested.

"Well, we're already doing that," Robert retorted.

"Yes, but everybody shut your flashlight off. Then we'll see how dark it really is."

"No way," the girls shouted. "Our lights are the only thing that keeps the bats away."

They'd been hearing the zing of fluttering small wings near the ceiling as background noise for some time. There seemed to be hundreds of them over their heads and thousands that hung upside down on the stone walls.

"Just for a minute or so," Stanley persuaded.

When all the flashlights clicked off, the darkest feeling ever invaded the space. Blackness seemed to consume their flesh and made their bodies disappear, leaving only six semi-intelligent disembodied souls sitting in a circle in the cavern.

"Whoa…" someone whispered.

"This is so weird." Headless voices mumbled the words.

"Help me, Kate. I can't find my body." Robert joked.

Kate knew his clowning around kept the actual apprehension of the group from showing. In relief, they clicked on their flashlights again and finished eating. After repacking their bags, they resumed their expedition but now they moved closer together and stumbled forward in a line. The tunnel they followed was only seven feet high and four feet wide, but something compelled them to find where the squiggly branch ended. Kate figured it would dead-end soon, and they'd start back, but that didn't happen.

Jeff walked in front, and suddenly he halted and screamed. "Don't move. Stay where you are."

"Why? What is it?" They shouted as panicky fear crawled up their backs. Jeff stood and blocked the tunnel until they were all bunched up to face him.

"We have to turn around and go back." He said firmly. "Don't come any farther."

"But why? Why not?" They asked in unison.

"I'll show you. Shine your flashlights ahead to where our tunnel ends." There in the light of all the torches, a humongous cave opened to the size of three or four football fields at least. Kate couldn't see where it ended. The massive dome was central to a multitude of smaller tunnel entrances leading off like black, never-ending spider legs.

"Whew." Robert hissed between his teeth.

"Oh shit. Look at the size of it," Stanley said in astonishment.

"This is really getting scary, you guys." Rowena voiced their thoughts. "If we stumble out into that enormous space, we might never find our way back to this entrance we're in." Their tunnel was only one among a multitude, and an eerie chill swept over them as they gazed out into the dark expanse. Thousands of bats zinged around in the darkness of the otherworld.

"Oh my God," Kate whispered. They had come so near to a death-threatening possibility of becoming lost forever in a dark labyrinth of confusion. They all beat down their panic and, with one last look, backed around into the narrow tunnel they came from. Once again, they climbed in and out of a maze of obstructions in single file. Nobody talked much. They recognized where they ate lunch and then where they had waded around in the dark pool and continued on at even a faster pace.

Three hours later in sweat soaked T-shirts, the entrance of the cave came out of nowhere and they stumbled out. There had been no dot of welcoming light, for the sun had already set. But even that dusk was still bright for the six spelunkers, and they threw their arms around each other in liberated freedom.

Kate took in big breaths of sweet fresh air, but still, she winced. The spelunking seemed to affect her with a physical change, as if something dark had lodged itself into her lungs. Thoughts of being lost in the cave rolled around in her head and materialized into an electric awareness with a warning.

~~IF~~YOU~~TAKE~~
~~THE~~WRONG~~PATH~~IN LIFE~~

~~SOMETIMES~~
~~THE~~BIGGER~~BLACKNESS~~
~~CAN~~SWALLOW~~YOU~~ WHOLE~~

Did she think that up, or was Divine Spirit whispering words into her mind again? And if so, what did it mean for her?

Chapter 23

THE JOURNEY ALONE

Kate climbed out of the tent to another blue-sky sunny day at the campsite. Robert was up rummaging around for breakfast food, and the lake lay placid in the morning sunlight.

"Wasn't that a fantastic adventure we had yesterday? I wonder if there are any more caves around here."

"Arrgh. I didn't want to explore that cave with you in the first place," Kate groaned. She slumped over the picnic table, still wound up from the spelunking experience.

"Why'd you go then?" he asked.

"Because you wanted me to." Kate thought couples were supposed to support each other's interests.

"You didn't have to, you know." He stretched in the sunshine.

Kate didn't know what she wanted from Robert right then, maybe appreciation or understanding. The depth of their relationship as travel companions seemed shallow. She longed for genuine love from him, at least a little tenderness, but was that possible?

When they arrived in the town of Comitán, they rented a spacious room and Robert suggested they splurge on a nice restaurant meal. Afterward, Kate sent a letter off to her parents describing her recent experiences in a glowing report. She didn't mention the scary parts because they worried enough already. Then Robert agreed to head north by third-class bus to visit Palenque. It was one of the ancient and fascinating Mayan cities in the middle of the state of Chiapas. Palenque was hot and humid, and the jungle's fast-spreading vines climbed over the walls of the ruins like arms with fingers perpetually encroaching upon the massive pyramids. The largest one stood almost thirty meters high, built with square blocks of stones, some weighing over twelve tons, the sign said. *How did the Mayans haul them up to the top? She wondered. Could modern technology even do this?*

Leaving Robert to wander around, Kate climbed the steep steps to the top of the gigantic Temple of Inscriptions. The land was so flat she could see how smoke signals could be used to communicate with other nearby pyramids. A tour group stood waiting to descend inside the massive temple to see the tomb of the ancient Mayan ruler, Pacal the Great. When she joined them, the steps and twisted hallways going down were dim, lit up with only a few small electric bulbs.

Kate fought down the panic at being so far underground again. It reminded her of the darkness in the mammoth cave, but at least this group had a guide. The pathway soon emptied into a small sacred room where a long stone sarcophagus sat in the middle of the floor. She stared down at the coffin lid. Intricately carved in stone, the great warrior was thrust back into what looked like a cockpit seat in a space rocket. He even seemed to manipulate instruments with his hands and feet in the tight quarters, like a modern traveler in a spaceship. Flames shot out at the bottom of the capsule. Yet Kate read the sign saying the Mayan king ruled in the early 600s AD, so her imagination was overactive. Or was it? Perhaps earth had been visited by travelers from outer space.

Once she was outside on the park grounds again, she met up with Robert and was excited to tell him about it. "I got to see the carved lid on the king's sarcophagus, and it looked...."

But just then, a group of howler monkeys scampered out of the jungle, swarming over the exposed nearby temples.

"Come on, let's follow them." They ran after the chattering creatures, laughing at their comical antics. The monkeys led them to yet another temple, and they explored the other ancient ruins in the thick surrounding jungle all afternoon.

"Chasing those monkeys was a blast," Robert said when the day had ended. "It's a pretty cool place." She agreed, but she never mentioned seeing the famous coffin of Pacal, the Great.

...

Kate wanted more meaningful travel experiences on the return trip heading home. She and Robert tried to agree on their next destination, but he refused to consider her suggestion.

"I have no desire to go back to Mexico City again." Robert's mouth formed a hard, straight line.

"Wouldn't the Anthropological Museum there be fascinating to visit?" Kate asked, trying to persuade him. "That's what educated tourists do. They go to historical sites and museums."

"I'd rather hang out on the beach and relax with a cold beer."

"You've done that. A lot. The museum has three floors of exhibits on the Mayan civilization, and I'm interested in seeing those."

Kate had always followed Robert where he led, even going into the caves with him. So why couldn't he accompany her into Mexico City? She pleaded, but he wouldn't budge.

"Go there on your own, if you want," he said, throwing the words at her.

She wondered how safe it would be to tour the big city as a single woman. But after seeing the carved sarcophagus at Palenque, visiting that specific museum was important to her. When would she ever get the chance again? "Then maybe I will." Kate stomped off in a pout.

Robert reopened the conversation at their campsite later. "We have an open relationship, so let's not break up. Let's go our separate ways for a while and meet up later after you do your mundane tourist thing."

She thought Robert might have other reasons for wanting his space. He was always friendly to the other gringos they met and hooking up with another woman could tempt him. It surprised her when she realized she wouldn't care that much if he did.

In the end, she and Robert separated and planned to meet up again in eight days, in the town of Morelia, near Mexico City. They would rendezvous at the central park at noon because they didn't know in which hotel they'd each be staying. After all, every Mexican village had a central plaza.

Kate left in a taxi with a heavy heart and took the fast train north to Mexico City. On the southern outskirts of the metropolis, the train slowed down and chugged its way through miles of cardboard shacks. Never had Kate seen slums with such poverty. Yet even in the squalor, narrow paths meandered through the tiny huts. She realized it was actually a miniature organized community. Children dressed in rags played their games in the packed dirt, and adults went about their activities despite everything around them. What if she had been born in one of these shacks? By comparison, Kate was wealthy, free to go anywhere, even if it was on buses and trains with a pack on her back.

Then the slums changed into warehouses, then shifted into commercial areas, and she arrived at Mexico City's train station just like she had before with Robert when they had come from the north. Kate adjusted her pack and wandered out alone into the congested streets.

The sky was no longer blue but a pale gray with air pollution unbelievably bad. Her breathing grew rapid as she struggled to gain oxygen into her lungs, and tiny particles from the traffic bombarded her face in the swirling air. She ambled down the street alone in the crowd searching or an inexpensive room.

It took ten blocks of meandering before Kate saw an entrance doorway into a hotel. The desk clerk had a nametag that read Jorge. He combed his middle-aged gray hair slicked back and over to one side.

"Buenos días, señorita." Jorge looked Kate over with suspicion, as no husband was accompanying her. Kate's backpack and hippy clothes seemed to trouble him, too.

"Buenos días, señor. Tienes una habitación para unas noches?" she asked. He seemed charmed with her pleasant Spanglish and a respectful nod and smile. He showed her a bare room on the ground floor with paint peeling from the walls, but it was a welcome refuge from camping and the hectic, busy street outside. She paid for a five-day stay, and afterward, Jorge became much more helpful. Still, Kate was careful to lock the deadbolt on the door that night.

The next day, she was ready to venture out. Her Spanish had improved over the weeks in Mexico, enough to converse in the basics, anyway. She faked some confidence and asked for directions at the dusty check-in desk, hoping a taxi wouldn't be too expensive.

"Donde esta el museo arqueologico?"

"Aqui, señorita." Jorge handed over a miniature map and gave her a gracious smile. He pointed to a small symbol on the map for a subway system, a route that would take her to the museum.

Different symbols designated various tourist sites that she might want to see later. Best of all, the brochure described what was on each subway line and the site of the closest station.

"Fantastico." She'd never been in a subway before, but at least she wouldn't have to ask for directions all the time. "Muchas gracias. Ustad es muy amable, señor," she said to thank him for his kindness.

"De Nada." He said, bowing with a flourish.

For the third time in a week, Kate went underground with trepidation, down into the subway system of Mexico City. But to her delight, the train was excellent for getting around the city in just minutes. All the symbols appeared above the entrance to each car, and she scurried out when the museum symbol flashed green.

Beautiful, landscaped park grounds surrounded the Anthropological Museum and its three amazing floors of exhibits. Kate soaked up the history. She read the placards, listened to taped English explanations, and peered at strange ancient tools and pottery. Kate didn't have time to view all the displays, or the beautiful ponds and parkland, so, despite the horrible air pollution that made it hard to breathe, she returned another day. After that, Kate rode the subway all over, feeling quite cosmopolitan. She got off at different symbols to see the various attractions and strolled down the streets to window-shop the foreign merchandise.

A proper young salesman spoke some English in a shoe store, and he struck up a conversation with her. After exchanging the usual 'how-are-you' and 'where-are-you-from' comments, he offered to be her guide on a tour of the city that afternoon.

"My name is Jesus." He said, introducing himself with a charming slight bow.

Kate thought he was joking with her. "Oh, but that's the religious name for the Son of God."

"Si, but the name is common in our culture. In Spanish, it is pronounced 'Hey-sus.'"

He had such an earnest, wholesome look about him, and Kate decided it might be nice to have Jesus guide her in one of the largest cities in the world. How ironic! As a child in Sunday school, she sang about Jesus leading and protecting her. Now the physical manifestation of it was happening, and she laughed over the strange coincidence.

"Mucho gusto, Jesus," she said. It's nice to meet you. "Mi nombre es Kate."

"What is a young gringo girl doing alone in Mexico City?"

Kate told him about her excitement seeing the Anthropological Museum. He had visited it before, and the exhibits had impressed him too. After his work shift, Jesus showed her a beautiful cathedral and a fancy shopping mall nearby and then later invited her out to a cinema to see a movie that night.

"Pero, no hablo Espanol mucho," she said.

"No problema." The movie had subtitles in English so they could both understand the dialogue.

Kate enjoyed the show and afterward, he introduced her to some of his friends at a fast-food place. She got to practice her Spanish with friendly people her age in a different culture and almost wished she hadn't made plans to link up with Robert again so soon.

But after four days in Mexico City, Kate was extremely fatigued and a dull pain in her chest came on like she was coming down with the flu. She thought it might be the air pollution because the smog was still so thick it pin-pricked her skin.

Kate headed north by bus a few days earlier to rendezvous with Robert. When she reached Morelia, she found a posada to rent in the center of town. It was a drab upstairs room near the central plaza, where she planned to reunite with Robert soon.

...

Where am I? Why is it so hot? Kate's mind was hazy and confused when she woke up the next morning. She fumbled to dress and left her room to buy food, although she wasn't hungry at all. She was thirsty and bought fresh mango juice instead at a street vendor's stall. Her chest felt tight and constricted. Her high fever and dizziness made walking the streets like a bad trip on LSD, so she returned to her quarters to crash.

In the morning, she felt much worse, and her anxiety was growing. Kate realized it wasn't just the common flu because the symptoms of this foreign ailment weren't familiar at all. Yet she had to dress again and make her way to the park in case Robert showed up. She'd need somebody's help to get through whatever it was she had. She sat alone on a bench at the plaza in a daze and watched the Mexican adults chatting with their friends during their lunch hours. Lively teenagers in their school uniforms, sauntered by arm in arm, and the well-behaved children played in the shade. But there was no sign of Robert.

By mid-afternoon, she walked one step at a time back to her room before she passed out. Feverish dreams overtook her in what sleep she managed to get that night.

Daylight came again much too early. Kate had to labor to fill her lungs with air to take each breath. With sheer will, she made herself get out of bed and stagger to the plaza again, hunched over in discomfort. Her chest hurt all the way through to her back now, and each time she sucked in air, the movement doubled her up in pain.

Every time Kate saw a brown-haired gringo, her hopes soared. But she waited hour after hour and couldn't even sit up straight. Just when she wanted to give up in the late afternoon, a familiar figure came strolling toward her through the plaza. She watched him as he came up to her.

"What happened to you? You look terrible." Robert was startled at the sight of her. He didn't even give her a hug.

"I need your help…." Kate's voice wheezed. She broke down then and cried miserably, but the sobs hurt so bad she couldn't bear to even find release with tears.

"You need to be in bed, Kate," he said and supported her with an arm as they limped to her hotel room.

Robert settled her against the pillows and listened to Kate's halting description of her symptoms. Her voice came out between her gasps of breath. And when the dry racking cough happened again, it brought nothing up.

"What can I do?" His concern was touching, but she only cried silent tears of helplessness. "When did you last eat? Are you hungry?"

Kate hadn't eaten for days. "Fruit might be good." She mumbled. "No, hot spicy soup," she said, thinking it might be parasites causing the havoc in her body.

Robert purchased a quart of fresh-squeezed orange juice and a Styrofoam bowl of chicken garlic soup. He carried them back to the room and had to feed her because she had no energy and couldn't keep the spoon steady in her hand.

During the next few days, he came back and forth from his room while Kate went in and out of consciousness. She was delirious with pain and fever, and he didn't want to catch what she had. Sometimes her eyes opened for a while, and she watched the wooden fan in the ceiling go around in a blur of monotonous sound. Would she ever feel better? Her lungs felt like deflated balloons, and it took all the energy she had to make her chest rise each time she took a breath. What kind of flu bug did that? For five more days, she and Robert stayed in Morelia before she could even consider the possibility of moving on with him again. When the fever finally went down, she breathed a little better, but all she wanted was to go back home, and this time someone was taking her back.

A roadmap of North America showed a full two thousand and seven hundred miles from Mexico City to Portland, Oregon. Kate focused on counting the miles off by the hundreds. She slept whenever she could, draped over her backpack on the hard-plastic seats of the second-class buses they took. She leaned on Robert, who tried to make her comfortable, but her body slumped like a ragamuffin between each painful coughing spell.

At the California border, they hitchhiked like before, but she wasn't able to stand for long between rides. "The exhaust from the traffic hurts my chest," she complained, scrunching down into a squat from the pain.

"You'll feel better tomorrow," he always said. But that's what he'd been saying since they left Morelia. Kate didn't object. She needed him. After each night in cheap hotels, she stood in a daze with her hair flowing, her thumb held out, knowing each ride would bring her a few hundred miles farther north. When she finally saw Mount Hood in the distance, her lungs took in the Oregon mountain air like medicine.

Robert moved them into a bedroom at a friend's place on the outskirts of Portland so Kate could continue to recuperate. He fed her fruit and vegetables, and she slept for days in a proper bed.

Chapter 24

LIFE HITS BACK

"Hey Kate, my cousin is throwing a party. He wants us to stay overnight at his house. Do you feel up to it?"

Robert expected her to be social again with the return of better health. She was thankful for the way he had taken care of her. "I guess I could go if you want to," she said.

Alvin was Robert's cousin, older by six years, making him seem ancient to her. He owned the Questing Beast tavern and had organized the baseball team they once played on. But Kate was perpetually tired and didn't want to think about packing even an overnight bag again. Still, it sounded like she'd be able to crash early if the party lasted all night.

"Alvin wants you to meet his girlfriend." Eagerness played on Robert's face, an emotion she hadn't seen for a while.

"Then let's go and make some new friends," Kate said.

The party took place in a shabby older home where couples milled around, drinking, and laughing. They talked about shallow topics, but their voices had an edginess that Kate didn't quite understand.

A few joints were passed around, although others were drinking rum and Coke. Kate chose the latter to spare her lungs and drank a little more than she normally would to celebrate her return to health again.

She couldn't figure out the purpose of the gathering, as most people didn't even know each other. Later that night, she overheard the guys in conversation as they refilled their drinks in the kitchen. The men were eager for the evening to end so they could bed each other's women.

Oh, damn it. This is a partner's swap party. Kate cringed in disgust. Robert's idea of an open relationship descending to that level of free love was shocking. Right after Kate figured out what was going on, she saw Robert disappear into a bedroom with his cousin's girlfriend. Dear cousin Alvin, with pasty aging skin, then engaged her attention. She tried small talk, which worked for a while, but he was out for a bigger prize than that.

"Come on. It's the seventies. Let's get to know each other better in my study."

"I'm comfortable right here," Kate said primly. But she wasn't at all comfortable. It was in the middle of the night. Her chest still hurt, and exhaustion left her open to a bad case of self-pity. She tried to redirect his advances and keep a platonic conversation going, but she was getting frantic inside. *Where was everybody? Am I the only one at this party who doesn't feel right about what's happening? I don't even have the address of the house, so I can call a taxi.*

Her efforts at preserving the few moral standards she still had were wearing thin. Maybe she should just give up and let him have sex with her. Obviously, everybody else was having consensual sex in the house. Alvin continued to flirt and fumble around in his attempt to make love with her. Kate let him hold and kiss her, but she swore nothing else would happen, not this time with this man.

In the wee hours of the morning, he finally fell asleep on the couch in his study. Kate sat there, livid. Does *Robert value me so little he thinks he can trade me off like a piece of merchandise? What am I to him, anyway?*

She had heard of parties where the guests arrived and threw their house keys in a basket at the door. When the party ended, the men grabbed a random set to take a new woman home to sleep with her. Kate was not that type of woman. Her life may have gone off the track, but this was taking it one step too far, and that's where she drew the line. She and Robert had agreed to an open relationship, to be free to discover the things they wanted in life, but she wasn't free, just manipulated and used. She had already violated the standards she'd been brought up with, and for what? *Sex for fun? Well, it isn't fun anymore. It's degrading. Is this all there is to love?*

The next day, Kate argued with Robert about the night's activities. "Why didn't you let me know what kind of party it was before we went?" Kate demanded.

"I didn't think it would be anything organized. Alvin wanted to get together, and we were going to suggest a swap afterward."

"You knew all about it and just didn't tell me. I wouldn't have gone to the party if I had known what it was."

"Don't be like that. There are no right and wrongs anymore in our world. Everything is relative."

"I'm certain you men benefit from that."

"What harm is there if nobody gets hurt? Sex is a natural pleasure for all of us."

"Women do get hurt. I get hurt." She spit the words out with blurry eyes. "If an open relationship involves trading sexual favors with other people, I'm against it." Sex, just for fleeting pleasure, might be the new cultural norm, but it wasn't acceptable by godly standards. She was guilty of living that way, but she hadn't been proud of herself for a long time.

"How was the evening for you? Did you sleep with Alvin?" he asked.

"Robert, if you think I'm going to share juicy details about what happened, you're mistaken. How dare you try to trade me off to your cousin as if I was your property."

"Okay, okay. Maybe it wasn't such a good idea."

"You think? But obviously, you must have enjoyed Alvin's girlfriend. I saw you go off to a bedroom together without a glance at me, and what was I supposed to do?"

Robert apologized profusely for putting her into that situation and admitted it was a poor decision on his part. Kate thought about her actions. She supposed she could have left Alvin in the study and hidden in the bathroom, or interrupted Robert and demanded to be taken home. *Damn, I have to learn to be more assertive and set my own standards.*

Kate and Robert talked about their relationship and drew up new boundaries. They would remain traveling companions because neither of them was ready to rent a place together at that point. Kate didn't have the funds for the spring term at her university, and she was so mixed up she didn't know what she wanted for the future. When he suggested backpacking up in Canada for a fresh start, she agreed to try it out.

"We'll have a good time hiking in the backwoods of BC," Robert assured her.

But for Kate, having a good time didn't seem rewarding anymore. After they drove across the border and headed north to the national parks they had marked on their map, she fell into a pensive state.

"Don't you ever want to settle down and take life seriously?" she asked.

"Nah, why ruin a good thing?" he touted back. "You know like Bob Dylan sang in his song, 'It Ain't Me, Babe.'"

"I want to settle somewhere and not travel all the time. I want to grow roots and have kids someday." She wondered what it would be like to raise children you loved, who would naturally love you back.

"Sounds pretty boring to me." Robert glanced in the rearview mirror and accelerated to pass a semi-truck. "But hey, we're on another adventure right now. Let's not ruin it by getting all serious about things, okay?"

Kate didn't voice her thoughts anymore. Robert was who he was. They drove in silence while the lyrics of Bob Dylan's song rolled around in her mind.

...

British Columbia was a large province, almost a country of its own, and wildly different from the US or Mexico. Kate and Robert explored the provincial parks and stopped at trailheads to hike into stunningly beautiful sites. Then they headed up the Frazer River Canyon, staying at various campsites along the way. When they came to Williams Lake, they went west into a frontier so rural, Kate wished she had a pair of cowboy boots to put on.

Hiking into the backwoods of the Kleena Kleen Valley, they came upon a group of hippies camping together on an abandoned ranch. Guitar players strummed folk music at night around a massive campfire. Joints of good weed were passed around while the melodic tunes drifted through the pine trees in the clearing. The communal scene was mellow, yet the experience didn't satisfy Kate's hunger for spiritual depth at all. In the morning, she wanted to leave, and thankfully, Robert obliged her.

They set out on the trail after the sun had dried the dew on the grass and soon caught up to a younger couple walking back to the road. The woman wore a long paisley skirt and carried a redheaded infant in a child's backpack.

"What's her name?" Kate smiled, drawn to the perfect smallness of the beautiful child. Her longing to reach out and hold the little one surprised her.

"We call her Snow-Owl." The nickname elicited a strange pride in the man.

"That's so cute. What's her real name?" Kate asked.

"That is her real name. It's Snow-Owl."

They chatted for a few more minutes and then let the young parents pass them on the trail. The exchange puzzled Kate. *What kind of parent would call their little girl, Snow-Owl? How would that child feel about her name when she attended school? Maybe I'm not much of a hippie after all.*

Kate lagged behind so she could be on her own. She loved hiking and the sense of purity in the forest. The path skirted a high cliff, and she cut through the thick brush to look out over the edge. There below her, Kate sighted a huge bear that was fishing on the shoreline of a roaring river. Another one wobbled back and forth on the bank, searching the water with her mate, her two half-grown cubs playing in the shallow water beside her.

Kate stood on the opposite side of the river, unnoticed by the family of bears scavenging for their food. She watched spellbound as the larger bear swiped a paw into the water and slung a young salmon up onto the rocky shore to his mate. The cubs gathered around to tear into the food. Each of them had large furry humps behind their heads, and Kate realized she was looking at a family of fierce grizzly bears who could forge the river and charge up the bank at her to protect their cubs. In trepidation about her proximity, she carefully drew back without a sound. Then she hurried along the trail until she caught up to Robert.

"I was worried about you. Why were you so far behind?" Robert asked.

"Just thinking, I guess." She didn't want to tell him what she had seen. The wild family of grizzlies made a unique impression on her, but it had nothing to do with him.

The next trail they explored was off on a side road leading to a string of meadows. Wild grass spilled over the banks of a sparkling stream that zigzagged through the landscape. Colored ribbons of green grass painted the fields on both sides with raw beauty, while black ravens cawing overhead made the only noise in the wildness of the scene.

Kate and Robert followed the stream to the shore of a lake, where they spied a canoe and paddles tucked away in the brush. There was no other sign of human life, except the path they were on.

"Come on, let's use it for the afternoon," Robert said, pulling out the paddles.

"Promise me we'll return the canoe here later?" Kate was not going to steal it or leave it where the owner couldn't find it.

Robert rolled his eyes. "Of course, we have to come back to the truck anyway."

The lake mirrored the blue sky, and Kate soaked up the rhythm of their paddles splashing in the water. There was such peace in that isolated spot. Robert set the far shore as their objective until he spotted an old log building, and they glided the canoe over to it. The homestead had a huge untended garden growing profusely on the south side of the cabin. Robert beached the canoe, and they got out to explore the grounds. Kate looked around for residents and listened for the sound of a vehicle, but the place looked abandoned.

"Let's grab some free food. Look how big the spinach leaves are." Robert walked over and bent down, plucking leaves out of the rich dark loam.

"Robert, wait. This garden belongs to whoever lives here," Kate cautioned, "the same person who probably owns the canoe we're using.

"Well, they're not living here now."

"Maybe not, but they'll come back. We'd be stealing."

"We'll be long gone by the time they get back, and it's not like they're going to charge us with theft." He continued to pull out a bunch of large carrots before returning to the canoe.

Kate steamed up the fresh vegetables on their camp stove that night while Robert pitched the gray tent on the edge of a pristine natural meadow. Their two-man tent established a tiny island of civilization in a vast empty wilderness. A spotted loon serenaded them on the lake until dark, and with the sounds of a lonely breeze in the background, they slept well.

At first dawn, Kate unzipped the nylon door of the tent. She lifted the flap to see a white mist rising above the lake. A gentle breeze stirred the poplar trees, making the leaves shimmer in silver and green. Just before she stepped out, Kate froze in the door of the tent.

Crossing the upper end of their meadow was a giant, majestic cat. *It must be a cougar. A big one, almost three feet in height. Thank God the breeze isn't blowing my scent that way.*

The cougar's paws spread wide, massaging the earth with each step after a nighttime prowl. Probably, she had just quenched her thirst on the shore of the lake. Her long tail swayed back and forth in rhythm as her body moved in perfect alignment. She paused with her nose in the air to sense signs of danger. Then the huge cougar padded on, unaware she had an audience.

Kate didn't breathe, but her eyes followed every movement of the wild, magnificent creature. She thought the cougar had to be female with such exquisite gracefulness, and she tried to soak that feline feminine power into her own body. Goosebumps made her shiver, and if Kate had fur, each hair would have been electrified and standing straight up in the morning sun.

Then the tawny-colored cougar sauntered off into the forest, queen of her natural habitat. Kate watched until the cat disappeared. She let out her breath slowly and made a monumental decision for a new life. *I will live like that; proud, regal, self-reliant. I'll be true to who I am, like this wild cougar in the north country of Canada, pure and without deceit.*

But could she be that powerful and feminine? Could she build a life for herself that she could be proud of?

Chapter 25

HOMECOMING BLUES

Kate had a long time to think while Robert drove south to the border, and down the I-5 freeway back to Oregon. They didn't talk much. The scenery blurred like a kaleidoscope of patterns as she looked out the window. Her life was like that, derailed, off track, with no meaningful purpose. She figured out how to live her own in life, yet she didn't have a good enough reason to live it.

Robert put in a cassette tape by Simon & Garfunkel playing "The Sound of Silence," and the lyrics drifted out from the car speakers, hitting her on a personal level. It was about the political decay nobody dared to talk about in the country, but the words also resonated with the detachment she currently had with Robert.

Kate broke the silence after the song ended from her side of the front seat. "I'm not happy, Robert."

"Yeah, the world is a mess, isn't it?" He assumed she wanted to discuss the song.

"No, I mean with us. Being together, traveling. It isn't fun anymore for me." She rolled down the window of his pickup a few inches to inhale the fresh air.

"What do you mean? We had good times backpacking in BC, didn't we?" He glanced out the window at the coastal mountains south of Seattle.

Kate had discovered exquisite beauty in nature, even the smallest flower nestled in the low-lying groundcover. She found joy in the grandeur of the tall pines that swayed in the wind, those dancing giants bridging the earth to the sky. But could she learn how to grow roots strong enough to support her spirit? Perhaps in the Canadian wilderness, she would find a reason for living because that's what she didn't have. She had no purpose.

Hippies believed one could live life the way they wanted because everything was okay to do if you didn't hurt anybody else. That philosophy meant that each day, you focused on having fun. The next day, you came up with something else to do that would be fun. She had lived like that for a while, but even fun just wasn't fun anymore. It was a meaningless existence. *I think I've been hoodwinked. There's something wrong with my generation.*

"Robert, I need different things in life than you. I want a husband, children, and a small rural house somewhere. I don't want to be just a convenient travel partner for you."

"Jeez, don't get all prissy on me. We agreed to have an open relationship and enjoy whatever comes along."

Kate didn't even respond. She was tired of being tied to Robert. They weren't married, and he never planned on having kids. He didn't even want her exclusively, did he? Besides, when she had children, she'd want the father to be a man other people looked up to, a guy she could respect. But wasn't that ironic? She didn't even respect herself anymore.

That's where I need to start, to figure out how to be proud of myself again. Like that cougar walking strong and confident in the wilderness. That's the way I want to be.

She spoke her truth to Robert. "I don't enjoy the relationship we have anymore," she whispered, but he had no answer for that.

They sat again in silence as the miles whizzed by. Kate looked over at Mount Adams, the snow-capped mountain east of them. She remembered the simple joy of picking huckleberries up there years ago with her family. Her melancholy thoughts of childhood gelled together and rose to the top. *I'm homesick. I need to go back home to find my roots and again.*

Kate's childhood wasn't that pleasant. The distance she felt with Robert reminded her of how broken her parent's broken relationship had become and one specific night came to mind.

She had been sleeping on the top bunk in the small bedroom she shared with her younger brother when her parent's angry words came from the kitchen and woke her up. The sounds of scuffling frightened her. When a plate got broken, she cringed. Then Kate heard her father stomp out of the house to the garage, where he always went to do his serious drinking. In the quiet, she listened to her mother crying in their small front living room.

Maybe Spirit had talked to her even back then. She had heard strong words that kept repeating.

~~GO~~AND~~HELP~~HER~~

Katie didn't know how she could do anything. She always felt helpless when the arguments between her parents happened, and this time, it sounded terrible. But she climbed out of bed as silently as possible and filled the kettle with water in the kitchen. When it was hot, she made a cup of tea and brought it in on tiptoe. On the couch, her mother burst into fresh tears and scolded her.

"You shouldn't be awake to see your parents fighting," her mother said through her sobbing.

Kate sat down and cuddled against her, trying to compensate for her father's staggering drunkenness again. Now years later, it was still a poignant memory. Many times, her father had treated her mom with disrespect. Kate had always thought her father's trouble was trying to live up to her mother's high standards. Her parents had irreconcilable differences, and that was what she had with Robert.

When she and Robert got back to Portland, their breakup wasn't harsh, just the soft closing of a door. She packed her meager belongings into her car, and they gave each other one last hug. Kate drove off alone, up the Columbia Gorge to her hometown of Hood River.

...

Kate was free and weightless. She wanted to revisit everything, but her home wasn't the same place anymore. Her parents had separated, so there wasn't an actual house to come back to. Her mom worked for the city and had moved into a smart older condo. Her father was still employed by a building contractor but lived in a rundown townhouse. Kate stopped by to visit him first.

"Katie, look at you. You're all grown up." He stood up slowly to work out the stiffness in his legs, and his arthritis was painful for Kate to watch.

"How are you, Dad?" She asked giving him a hug before they drew up chairs at the kitchen table.

"Oh, I'm getting by. Did you come to see how the old folks were before you fly off to your next roost?"

"No," she chuckled. "I thought I'd settle down and try to find myself a job here."

"Ah, Katie, girl. I sure would like that." A rueful smile spread across his face. "Say, I have a second bedroom if you want to stay here until you're settled."

"You sure you wouldn't mind? I could help buy groceries and cook the meals."

"It'd be nice to have the company. I'm tired of my cooking, anyway." He laughed at himself. "Why don't you bring in your suitcases from that little blue Volkswagen I see parked out there?"

Why not? If I stay here, maybe I can make my father's life a little more enjoyable. Perhaps this is part of my purpose for coming home. But Kate knew it was not the only reason. She needed time to figure out how she had managed to mess up her life so badly. Three failed love affairs, countless other men, a college dropout, no career and currently, she didn't even have a job. She brushed those thoughts away and got her backpack and suitcases out of the car, determined to enjoy a good long visit with her dad.

Once, when she was in the third grade, she had to stay home from school sick with a fever for a week. Her father came home after work and sat on the side of her bed. He brushed the hair off her feverish forehead and said words so sweet she'd never forgotten them.

"Ah, I wish I was sick instead of you, Katie. If I could change places, I'd do it in a split second."

"You would, Dad? You'd do it in a second?"

"Yup. You'd be outside playing again, and I'd be lying flat in this bed with your fever."

Later that night in the kitchen, Kate shared that specific memory with her father, but he couldn't recall the incident at all. They laughed about how sweet it was, and he caught her up with the news about the family. A sentimental quietness settled in, but it was tranquil in a weird sort of way.

Kate visited her mom the next day and apologized for all the worry she had caused her by hitchhiking so far from home.

"So, you're actually going to live here for a while. I wish you could stay with me, but I only have a one-bedroom apartment. I'm afraid your father's place might be dreary with all his drinking," she said.

"I'll be fine, Mom. Maybe Dad needs the company, but I promise to visit you often." After that, Kate picked up the pieces of her old life and settled down. She went shopping for groceries and clothes to wear for a job interview. She dug through boxes she had stored to find her resume so she could search for employment again.

"I made tuna patties, brown rice, and a big salad for you, Dad." Kate had the supper meals ready when he came home tired from work. She enjoyed their time together.

"I don't think my old body knows what to do with all this healthy stuff you're feeding me," he said, reaching for his fork.

After supper, they sat around the kitchen table and drank beer together. That evening, Kate told him about her grand travel adventures in Mexico and her experiences backpacking in Canada, a censored version of them, anyway. "But Dad, there are things I'm ashamed to tell you about."

He smiled with compassion and patted her hand. "Some people just have to carry those memories inside of them, Katie. I've traveled some too, served as a communications expert stringing telegraph lines in the South Pacific. That was back during the Second World War."

"Wow, the South Pacific is supposed to be a beautiful part of the world."

"The island we were on was a fine-looking place, all right, but I had a crew of men to look after. We supplied the communication system for the front-line squadrons."

"Is that where your welding helmet came from, the one with the ferocious face painted on it?"

"Yeah." He sported a small grin and looked off into the distance.

"What island were you stationed on?"

"We were in the New Hebrides. Plenty of exotic vegetation to hide in, and fierce tribes of headhunters way up in the hills."

"That's primitive, all right. It must have been exciting, though."

"At first, it was, but then I came down with malaria. They sent me home to the States to recover. After quite a few weeks, I got better but then received new orders to return to the front again."

Kate winced. "Oh, no."

"By that time, the fighting was pretty intense. My crew and I... well, they caught us between the front lines and the base camp." He stopped talking and tilted his beer up to drain it.

"It must have been hard being sent back into the war zone."

"I want to show you something." Her father went to his bedroom and brought out a canvas bag. It was stuffed full of seashells and coins he had kept. She'd never seen shells like these, and the details on the coins were fascinating. "But in the war, did you have to kill anybody?" she asked.

His reminiscing stopped. He put his collection back into the leather bag. "We've talked long enough, Katie," he said.

She couldn't let the subject drop. "If you were my age and drafted today, would you go?"

"A bunch of damn pot-lickers, those war generals. All they do is plan maneuvers on blackboards in their safe little underground bunkers."

Kate sensed what her father didn't share, things in his service for his country he'd never been able to talk about. And maybe he needed to tell somebody.

"How bad was it over there, Dad?" she whispered and touched his arm.

Her father's whole countenance hardened. His eyes bore into hers in anguish, working his jaw to spit out the words. "I lost them all, my whole damn crew." His face crumbled, and tears squinted up his eyes. Hunched over the table, he jerked back and forth with a loss of control.

Kate sat still. She didn't know what to say. Images of horror fluttered across her mind, a telepathic transfer in vivid, harsh detail.

Her father struggled to lock his emotions away again. After a minute, Kate stood up to get two more beers and handed him one. Now she understood why he drank.

...

On other evenings, Kate visited her mother after supper. She loved the time they spent together talking about life experiences and romance, relating to each other as two adult women. After Kate's prodding, her mother shared her private horrors of war.

"My first husband, Paul, went off to fight when they bombed Pearl Harbor. He was killed in action in the Okinawa Islands."

"Were you deeply in love with him, Mom?"

"Yes, very much so." She smiled as secret memories danced in her head. "We had rented an apartment on the sunny hills above Santa Barbara, California. But when Paul enlisted, I took your sister Sherry back east to Nebraska to live with his parents while he was overseas. She was only a toddler then, but she liked the farm."

"Did you see him after that?"

"No, they shipped him off, and that was the last time we saw each other."

"That must have been terrible for you."

"It was awful, and I didn't know Paul's parents at all. Months went by like that, and then one morning, I was nauseous, dreadfully so, which surprised me because it came on so fast. We had no indoor plumbing in those days, you know, so I hurried to the outhouse to be sick. I was in there for hours with cramps so bad I couldn't stand up. I kept vomiting until bile was the only thing left in my stomach."

"But what made you so sick, Mom?"

"I didn't know what it was until the next day. Someone in uniform came with the telegram, and Paul had died at that exact time. I had known it, you see. I experienced it, just as it was happening."

Kate let her mother's sorrow soak in. "What a strange experience, Mom. Your depth of love must have connected you across all that distance."

"Something like that." She waved her hand in front of her. "I don't know. I still can't explain it even now."

They sat together in silence until the memories had time to fade again. Even though the story was about Sherry's father and not her own, Kate got choked up with emotion.

"Oh, your father was handsome in his khaki uniform too, when I met him," her mother reassured her. "Of course, that was a few years later."

Kate left her mother's house in a contemplative mood. She knew her father's alcoholism had caused her mom to shed many tears since then. She was a strong woman because of her faith. Kate knew her own values, a kind of hit-and-miss Christianity, had been passed on to her from her mother.

Kate's father had also introduced her to something sacred, though he rarely went to church. He found his spirituality in nature. He'd often take the family camping on the weekends in the summer at Lost Lake. She loved those family times, playing cards on the picnic table, hiking around the lake, and fishing with her dad. Kate's mind went back in time, trying to put together the pieces of her life.

"Pssst, Katie." Her father used to whisper, waking her up before everybody else.

Without a word, she'd wiggle out of her sleeping bag to join him outside the old canvas tent. He'd grab the tackle box, and they'd sneak down to the lakeshore to start up the small horsepower motor on his red-striped aluminum boat.

She remembered one special day when the sun peaked over the skyline, and the water lay as flat and still as a mirror. Mist rose off the surface, creating an ephemeral glow of shimmering beauty as they motored out into the middle of the lake. At the south end, snow-capped Mount Hood stood white in the morning light. It was another world, one of exquisite perfection.

"Fishy, fishy in the brook, come and bite upon my hook." Kate would sing softly once the fishing lines were in the water. When she and her father talked in the boat, it was always in whispers so the fish wouldn't hear.

"Is God real, Dad?" she asked that morning.

"I guess you will have to decide that for yourself, Katie."

"I think he's in these sunbeams coming down through the clouds. Could that be God?" She wanted to hear about his beliefs and compare them to her Sunday school lessons.

"It might be him, all right. Something big had to create all this beauty." His face softened as he looked at her.

"I think he's dancing in the sparkles on the water right here with us this very moment," Kate had said.

The drone of the boat motor lulled her into a sleepy harmony as they waited for action on their rods.

They used a fishing lure called a wedding band. That and a worm on the hook were all they needed to catch the half-dozen rainbow trout they brought back to camp. Her father set the cast-iron skillet over the campfire grill and fried the fish up in butter. Oh, what a breakfast they had when the rest of the family woke up to the sizzling aroma.

...

Kate came back to the present and pulled into her dad's driveway. She loved her father, flaws and all, because of those unforgettable memories. He loved her despite being the prodigal daughter who hadn't amounted to much. A smile spread out on Kate's face as she realized the enduring quality of love. Then, a lightning bolt of truth came to her.

~~PERFECTION~~IS~~NOT~~REQUIRED~~
~~TO~~BE~~LOVED~~

Kate didn't have to be perfect for God to love her, either. She was deeply loved.

Chapter 26

FREE THINKING

Her savings were getting low, and Kate needed a job. She went and asked all the local businesses for secretary or receptionist work but had no success. She did find a job at the local Bar & Grill, and although the wages weren't anything to brag about, and was flung into a social setting.

The restaurant had regular customers who stopped by like clockwork. A guy named Nathan came in each Wednesday and Friday night and monopolized her time when she went to his table. Nathan was interesting, yet not her type. But she didn't want men in her life again so soon, anyway.

"Come out with me, and I'll show you the valley from high in the sky tomorrow," he said.

"From the sky? What do you mean from the sky?"

"I'm a pilot. I own a Cessna plane out at the airport."

"Cool. That's part of your job?"

"I spray fruit trees in the orchards and give private charter trips when I can get them. Have you ever been flying before?"

"Once in a jet plane," she said.

"I'll take you up tomorrow if you're not working. Meet me out at the airstrip, say eleven o'clock?"

"Wow. That sounds awesome, Nathan."

And it was awesome. The noise in the cockpit when the plane lifted off the ground gave Kate a rush of adrenaline. She looked down over a miniature land of checkered orchards and hayfields, all interconnected by ribbons of pavement.

"Fantastic, isn't it?" Nathan asked. He beamed at her enthusiasm as he swooped around like a bird, floating on the currents of wind.

Kate nodded vigorously, grateful for the experience. They dated a few times after that, but Kate wasn't giving away free sex anymore even for airplane rides. One day at work, she overheard one of Nathan's friends talking to him at his table. "When is your wife finished with her overseas assignment?"

Nathan had been showering her with attention, so the deception hurt. "What gives with that?" she asked him later.

"Don't worry. My marriage is almost over anyway," Nathan said.

"Well, look me up when it is," Kate told him and backed away from the friendship.

Kate enjoyed her job. Her co-workers bantered and teased each other as they scurried around serving people at the tables. Behind the bar, a built-in cooler stored the beer and wine. Her male co-workers had decorated the inside of the door with Playboy pictures of pin-up beauties wearing almost nothing. Each time Kate reached for a case of beer, she had to face stunning young women in their tiny bikinis. She complained one day to her boss about it.

"Thomas, isn't this a bit over the top? I don't enjoy looking at women's naked bodies plastered all over the door each time I open it."

"It's harmless. The boys are just having fun," he said, coaxing her to accept the situation. Then the guys she worked with started complaining.

"You're spoiling it for us, Kate. Don't be such a prude."

Kate knew she wasn't a prude, and she understood how to have fun at the workplace, which made her buy a Playgirl magazine. She thumbed through the good-looking males in their speedos and cut out a few of her favorites. With some scotch tape, she added them to the back of the door.

"What the hell is this?" Tim, one of her co-workers, yelled out the first time he opened the cooler. He acted like she had committed a crime or something.

"How can we compete with muscles like these dudes?" Another one asked in chagrin. They didn't see the irony of their comments at all. Afterward, the boss made them take down all the pictures. Tim and the other guys groaned, exaggerating their sorrow. But from then on, Kate had earned their respect. *Lesson learned,* she said to herself. *Being strong and assertive feels good.*

"Hey Kate, after we close this joint, do you want to go over to the Valley View with us? They have great country music and a wood floor you can slide on."

The tavern was the staff's after-hours hangout. A younger crowd sat around the scarred wooden tables talking, and drinking beer, when they weren't dancing to the sets of country-rock music. The place was a social studies class in itself.

The shell-shocked vets looked serious, while the long-haired country boys were loud and rowdy. Kate preferred the latter. The long-haired crowd thought for themselves and questioned politics with intelligence. The abuse of presidential power in the Watergate scandal remained a hot item in the news. It seemed President Nixon was re-elected by stealing documents and wiretapping phones. Nixon denied any cover-up, but the scandal made Americans start to question the leadership in Washington, DC.

"How can you be patriotic about a country that hides things from its own people?" Tim asked, rubbing the length of his beard. He always stirred up the conversation with bold questions.

"What are you talking about?" Neil wore a tattered jean jacket and poured another beer for himself from the pitcher they shared at the table.

"It's like the news coverage of President Kennedy's assassination." Tim shook his head in disgust.

Kate held her glass up for a refill and dared to express her anti-establishment point of view. "Yeah, but that was ten years ago, and despite that, nobody knows what actually happened."

"According to the Warren Commission, Lee Harvey Oswald shot the president," Neil said. He took pride in being levelheaded.

"And Oswald acted on his own? Come on." Tim fired up their discussion with more details. "Why was he shot by Jack Ruby then, before he even went to trial?"

"And where did this guy Ruby come from?" Kate asked.

"It's government propaganda, and we're all supposed to accept it," Tim insisted.

Across the table, a red-bearded guy spoke up with a deep voice. "If all that was true, why did the government need to seal the evidence for fifty years? For public security? Good grief. That will be in 2017."

Neil sipped from his beer mug. "They said the government will release the records if it won't harm the FBI and the CIA's reputation."

Marianne, the quiet girl in their group, asked a question. "Do you think one of the political parties was involved somehow in JFK's assassination?"

"That's absurd," Neil said.

"No, it's horrible, but it might be true." Tim grimaced.

"Common sense tells me you don't have to seal up records if it was just one crazy person who shot the president." Kate tried to use logic.

"If they keep government records secret, they're not acting in the public's interest. Do the politicians think we're so stupid?" The red-headed guy was getting riled.

A clean-cut young man from a nearby table overheard their conversation. He scowled and shouted over to them. "You guys don't know crap."

"And you do, huh?" Tim and the men at their table stood up to his challenge.

"Hush. Let him be." Kate and Marianne urged them to sit down and lower their voices out of respect.

"Poor bugger, he can't admit he fought the Viet Cong for nothing," Tim said.

Thankfully, the DJ started playing music again, and the crowd spilled out onto the dance floor. That possible altercation was over.

Kate didn't dance with the others but noticed one lone guy sitting by himself at another table. He held her gaze too long and looked her up and down. So, she did the same thing, with exaggeration. He couldn't help but laugh. With a raised eyebrow and a nod, he invited her to dance with him.

Kate had fun flirting and dancing with him for the rest of the night. Mario worked on a bridge construction crew for the State Highway Department. He walked her out to her car after the place closed down and asked for her phone number. Mario's gentle, exploratory kiss made her breathless.

Kate waited a week, remembering the magnetic pull she had felt, and hoped it might be the start of something serious. When Mario called her, he admitted his crew was moving to their next job location soon, but he still wanted to see her once more. But what was the point? Tired of short-term relationships, Kate made up an excuse, but it made her think. *Would I have jumped into bed with him if he had hung around? What are my boundaries now?*

...

Kate's co-workers got together at the tavern the next weekend, and when Tim brought up a new topic, the discussion continued.

"What about the assassination of Martin Luther King? Even the whites liked that black guy."

"He preached non-violence for the civil rights movement in the South." Kate explained to Marianne, who sat beside her. King had been shot before she graduated from high school.

"Yes, but a fugitive from the Missouri penitentiary killed him," Tim added.

"Of course, and he undertook this on his own too, I suppose?" Kate asked sarcastically.

"They claim he confessed to the crime, but withdrew his guilty plea three days later," Tim explained.

"How did the guy get out of jail to shoot King in the first place?" Neil scratched his beard as he asked the question.

"He somehow managed to escape out of a federal prison. They shot him when he was on the run, the day after." Tim had the facts. "Even Hoover, head of the FBI, didn't support that story. And get this. They classified those documents under national security until 2027."

"That's a long time for the truth to come out. Let's hope the public gets smarter by then." Their political discussion was depressing, so somebody changed the topic. Soon after, everybody got up to dance.

...

Kate made a pot of coffee for herself the next morning, thinking about the conversation. She was sure anti-government views were being aired out in the obscurity of country taverns all over. Surely, she wasn't the only American who struggled with their patriotism since the Vietnam War. The industrial-military complex made such huge profits by manufacturing war machines, they had to be creating wars all over to make profits. Would it ever stop?

Draft doggers might seem unpatriotic to some people, but damn it, they had valid reasons for their exodus.

Kate had discovered how much her parents had suffered because of war. Her mother was widowed just when her first marriage began. Her father was forced to kill other men and had to watch his entire crew get massacred. Tragic memories had shaped their lives dramatically.

Now that she was an adult, Kate liked her parents and could hardly wait to start her own family. She craved a simple life without political hypocrisy and meaningless pursuits of pleasure. Like that family of grizzly bears fishing on the river, at least they had each other. She thought of Mark and what could have, no, what should have been. He was on her mind a lot while she was living in her hometown, and the loss was still painful. Kate wished she could start over with a clean slate.

I could immigrate to Canada. My sister Anna moved there, and Shari and her husband left and settled in Alaska. I can head north too. As soon as Kate formed that thought, her sixth sense told her that's what she was supposed to do. It was *The Invitation* extended to her all over again, but this time, it came with a strong urgent need.

Kate visited the library and found the address for the Canadian Consulate in Seattle. At a solid oak table, as the sun streamed through the array of small-paned windows, she wrote to request an application. She would escape the shallowness of her own existence by immigrating to Canada. It was the exit door into a different future, and Kate was determined to open it.

Chapter 27

THE UPBEAT OF HOPE

"Kate, come see my new place," Joey said over the phone. She was back home from her travels in Europe and had bought an old house trailer to live in, parked on a piece of vacant property her dad owned. Joey heated the trailer with a small pot-bellied stove and had a truckload of dry logs dropped off in the yard. She planned to cut them up for firewood with a borrowed chainsaw.

"Sure, and I'll help you cut up the wood. I might be doing that in Canada soon." Kate already shared her plans to move to Canada.

The air was crisp that day, so Kate threw on a jean jacket. She and Joey both wore hiking boots, and they tied their long hair back with red handkerchiefs. "Who needs a man around anyway?" Kate said with bluster.

Joey figured out how to pull the starter cord on the chainsaw, and it roared to life. She held the weight with both hands and hovered over a log. "Hold this sucker still for me," she said.

"Okay, but make sure you spread your legs in case the saw blade kicks back at you." Kate had seen her father use a chainsaw before.

"That's funny. You, telling me to spread my legs, Katie." She started laughing so hard she had to rest the saw on the ground for a minute or two.

Kate wrestled the log into place as Joey moved down the length, sawing off short blocks. Fine sawdust flew up in her face each time the blade bit into the wood, but she trusted Joey and closed her eyes.

"Whew. Damn, this is hard work." Kate took off her jacket.

"Nah. It's '*fricken*' hard work." They chuckled, proud of their strength and competence. Then Joey revved up the chainsaw again and hovered it over the next log in a cloud of exhaust.

At the end of the job, they snapped open cold beers and looked at the blocks of wood strewn over the grass like tinker toys.

"Why don't you move in with me?" Joey invited. "You can use the second little bedroom, and we'll split the cost of groceries like we used to do."

"You sure? I'm kind of tired of my father's drinking all the time." She would still visit him every few days.

"Sure, the room is empty anyway."

Kate accepted the offer. She got along well with Joey, although sometimes they had different opinions about things. They made meals together when their work schedules coincided and read or listened to music while sitting in the two comfy chairs in the front room. Kate often played Leonard Cohen's music, especially his rendition of "Hallelujah." They both loved singing the glorious song.

...

Joey held a Frommer's travel guide in her hand one night and shared details on the exotic destinations she wanted to visit next. Kate was reading from a Good News Bible she'd found in a second-hand store. She had connected to Spirit many times in her life since she saw the strange aura around the young woman coming out of the Salvation Army Store in Portland. She invitation she'd been given was still a mystery, the meaning of that spiritual encounter had remained elusive. And if there was some far-advanced celestial being talking to her, Kate wanted to know who it was.

She wasn't buying into any religious denomination just yet. She figured if God was real, he existed outside of any corporate church. He had to be bigger than that, bigger than any one religion. All great products came with a user manual and maybe the Bible was the instruction book for her life. She needed to know if Christianity had any powerful benefits before she signed up.

Kate highlighted the verses that jumped out at her with colored pencils, coloring the golden rule a bright yellow because it was a fundamental law for humanity. Besides, it was only fair and logical to treat others the way you wanted to be treated. It would be fantastic if everybody lived by this rule. What would governments look like then?

Kate used the red pencil on all the verses that talked about loving God. Like the one that said to love God "with all your heart, your soul and your mind." That's how she had loved Mark. She knew how to love like that.

Joey teased her about what she was reading. "Better watch out, Katie. You're going to become one of those Bible thumpers."

"Thump, thump, thump." Kate gave an angelic smile and held the book up close to her heart. She wanted to explain to her friend the spiritual insight she was discovering.

"Why do you have your nose in that book all the time?" Joey asked.

"I'm learning things. Here, listen to this verse. 'It is impossible for God to lie... we may be greatly encouraged.'"

"That's crazy," Joey said. "Everybody tells lies, at least little white ones. Even the gods in the galaxies probably lie to each other."

"I try not to lie," Kate said.

Joey's brow formed creases. "What makes you think your God can't lie?"

"Well, when God said, 'let there be light then there was light.' He spoke it into being. If he's the Creator, words out of his mouth have to manifest what he says into existence."

"Ah, so that's how he did it," Joey nodded sagely, "with his mouth."

"Yes, see, it's cool. God can't lie, not just because this book says he can't, but because whatever he says, that's what actually gets created."

"Whoa, that's deep. But I hope he watches his words then, or we're all in big trouble." She smirked at Kate.

The fact that God wasn't able to do anything but tell the truth appealed to Kate. Maybe she could trust a Creator with that kind of integrity.

...

The next time Kate and Joey were home together from their jobs, they cooked a delicious meal together. Afterward, Kate took out her colored pencils and the Bible again. Her persistence intrigued Joey, and she wouldn't let the subject drop.

"If you're going to get all religious, Katie, what about the guy with the pitchfork? The devil?" She whispered the last two words in a sinister snarl.

"You mean Satan. He already tried to make me afraid of him when I was a kid in pigtails."

"Okay. You got me interested in this story," Joey said, scrunching down into her chair.

"We lived down a country lane, and in the summer, the highway brush cutter mowed the grass on the side of the road. All the neighbor kids would gather up the fresh-cut grass to build forts."

Joey giggled. "Oh, Katie. I can see you doing that."

"I was carrying a big armload tickling my nose one day when something moved inside the bundle. A wriggling tail of a brown scaly snake was inches from my face."

"Oh. Yuck." Joey squirmed.

"What's worse, the snake had no head. The grasscutter had chopped it off. But the tail of the creature was still writhing in my arms. So, I screamed, dropped the hay, and ran home."

"It had no head? You couldn't find it?"

"Joey, I didn't look for it."

"That's every kid's nightmare," Joey exclaimed.

"Well, my no-nonsense mother made little of it. She said, 'It's only a dead garter snake, Katie. Just the muscles are twitching.'"

"But what's that got to do with you meeting Satan?"

"Satan was the snake in the Garden of Eden," Kate explained. "He was the one that tempted Adam and Eve. I learned about it in Sunday school."

"I've heard the tale. Excuse the pun," Joey's eyebrows lifted in delight. "So...."

"So, God told them the rules, but Satan tempted them, and they ate the forbidden fruit, anyway. That was the reason they were kicked out of paradise."

"And you held little-snaky Satan in your arms." Joey pointed and wiggled her finger in Kate's face making them both break down into belly laughter.

Despite the humor shared with Joey, Kate had been convinced God had cut off the head of the snake to protect her. That was the kind of faith she had as a child. She wondered what would happen if she asked for God's help now?

...

Each day, Kate checked the mail for a package from the Canadian Consulate. Finally, a large manila envelope arrived. She ripped it open, but the ten-page application appeared formidable. In addition, they wanted professional references, a full medical checkup with x-rays, and proof of a clean criminal record.

Kate hunched over the kitchen table to read the instructions. Qualifying for immigration worked on a point system, so she tallied up points for being young, and for having some college education and secretarial training. They even gave points for her single status. But if she got a job offer from someone in Canada, she'd earn big points for that.

Her sister Anna lived in Kamloops, BC, an eight-hour drive from the Washington State border. She called Anna on the phone to ask if she knew of any local businesses wanting to hire clerical help. Anna told her to send up resumes, and she would check around.

Kate met with her high school counselor next. Mrs. Larson was delighted to hear from her and gave her a glowing reference letter. Her next stop was the police station to request a criminal record check, thankful she had never even gotten a parking ticket. Then made a doctor's appointment for a physical exam.

...

Kate was ten minutes late for her doctor's appointment, and the nurse who greeted her did not look impressed.

"I'm sorry," Kate apologized, out of breath when she saw the doctor. "I'd like a physical exam, and this form sent to the Canadian consulate. I'm planning to emigrate to British Columbia."

A handsome older man, Dr. Jamison had distinguished gray hair around his ears. He completed the physical exam and asked a bunch of questions. "Why do you choose to leave Oregon? What's so special up there?"

"I just want to." Kate didn't explain it further.

The doctor filled out the personal reference form and handed it back to her. After the exam, she went off to the lab for blood tests and X-rays to be taken. Dr. Jamison promised to send her medical report separately to the consulate when the results came back.

Meanwhile, a small business owner in Kamloops read her resume and agreed to give her a secretary position once she had moved up there. Anna was excited, and so was Kate. So, with professional references and an offer of employment, Kate sent off the application. Then she waited. Four weeks later, she received a response from the Consulate in Seattle, scheduling an appointment time for a personal interview. Kate twirled around twice with the letter in hand, overwhelmed with expectations.

...

Stella was a new co-worker at the Bar & Grill, and Kate shared her exciting plans for immigrating to Canada. "But I have to pass a personal interview first with the consulate in Seattle."

"My brother's friend travels up to Seattle every week as a salesman. If you want, I can ask if you can catch a ride with him."

"That would be awesome. Thanks."

"But what's wrong with staying here in the valley? I'll miss you at work if you leave."

Kate threw up her hands. "I'm fed up with our government. First, it was the Vietnam War, and now this Watergate scandal goes on and on."

"I don't get into the political stuff," Stella said in her soft voice. "I want to find a good man and raise a couple of kids."

Kate thought that was easier said than done. "The men I've met are not the kind to settle down. Or they're married and haven't separated yet. But *'oh... they plan to do it soon,'* they say."

"What about the cute guy who took you to Lost Lake for that picnic?" Stella asked. "I thought you were serious about him."

"No, he couldn't even light a fire to roast the hot dogs. I had to do it."

Stella laughed at that because they were both country girls who could kill their own mice.

Stella's offer to help came through. Her brother's friend, Frank, was an auto parts salesman who drove up to Seattle once a week. Frank was easy to talk to on the six-hour day trip, and Kate enjoyed the luxury of his car. He insisted on taking her out to dinner at the fancy hotel restaurant that evening. Afterward, they strolled to a nearby nightclub with a live rock band.

"We dance well together," Frank whispered in her ear, as his arms pulled her in close. He brushed her neck with his lips. "We could be good at other things tonight, too."

"I don't think that's going to happen, Frank." She tilted her head at him with a soft smile. "But thanks for distracting me from being nervous about my interview tomorrow."

"I might change your mind before the night's over." He flirted with determination.

Kate felt sophisticated with Frank, and if she didn't have plans to move north, his self-assurance would have interested her. She wondered what kind of lover he would be. But then Kate's conscience took over, and for the first time, she considered how God might look at her actions. It wasn't right and even if it turned out to be fun, it wouldn't give her any lasting joy. She would go to bed alone in her room.

The next morning, Kate dressed carefully for her interview, not too prissy, but not in her casual hippy style. The warm demeanor of the consulate official and the soft-spoken dialogue between them calmed her nerves. Her written job offer impressed him, too. *If this is how Canadian government officials conduct themselves, I'll enjoy being an immigrant up there.* When the interview ended, Kate asked for feedback using a new brand of charisma. She radiated openness. "Thanks for your kindness, sir. Can you tell me what my chances are for immigration? Because I *do* want to live in Canada."

His mouth almost turned upward. "You'll hear from our office after we process all the paperwork," he said.

Kate skipped out of the consulate, and she couldn't help but grin. *That went well. I asked God for help, and it sure feels like he gave it to me!*

Chapter 28

A FORK IN THE ROAD

Kate came home elated after her interview with the Canadian Consulate. Joey jumped out of the chair with her Cheshire cat grin when she entered the trailer. "So, how'd it go?" She asked.

"I think it was okay." Kate described the interview, but her girlfriend was more interested in what happened at the hotel with Frank, and she wanted more than Kate's abbreviated version.

"I didn't sleep with him if that's what you want to know."

"But you had fun going out to a fancy dinner and dancing afterward?"

Kate frowned. "It was fun, but when we drove back to Hood River, he didn't seem that interested in me."

"Because you didn't put out for him."

"But that's sad, isn't it?" Kate asked.

"That's the way men are." Joey was always pragmatic. Kate was a deep thinker, trying to make sense out of things.

"Sure, he wanted me that night. Guys show love so they can have sex. We give in to sex so we can feel loved. It's crazy."

"Do we have to analyze it?" Joey asked. "Most of the time, sex feels good." Joey held her hand behind her head in a provocative pose. "Thank the Lord for the pill. And the science that finally gave women a contraceptive."

"We're liberated women, all right," Kate said. She was thankful to go on the pill after her miscarriage.

"We can choose to have sex with no strings attached, just like the men do." Joey danced around the room provocatively.

Kate grinned at her antics but became thoughtful. Free love hadn't given her back anything in return. All she got out of it was shame and regret, but they didn't always agree on philosophy. Joey was in awe of Kate's spiritual side, and Kate loved her friend's *joie de vivre* approach to life. They had mutual respect, and they learned from each other.

"If you're a Christian, doesn't that mean you can't have sex before you're married? You've already had lots of sex, so how's that going to work?"

"Jesus says he forgives me if I'm sorry for what I've done."

"Oh, that's a relief then." The sarcasm came out sweet from Joey.

Kate gave her an exasperated look. "The best sex I've had was with Mark. Our passion was beautiful and innocent, and I loved him for that."

"He did a number on you, didn't he?" Joey murmured.

"I guess he did." Kate had played the role of the rejected lover for years. Did she have intimate relations with other men to seek revenge and get even? Because she finally understood.

Giving out sex did not get you loved. Casual sex gave you regret in the long run, and sometimes it even gave you dreadful diseases.

"Most guys only want to satisfy their physical needs," Joey concluded.

"I agree. But if men knew the beauty of sharing intimate pleasures with a woman they cherished, they'd approach it differently."

"Perhaps we're not supposed to give in so easily then," Joey admitted.

"Maybe we're supposed to restrain their advances, so love can grow deep enough to satisfy our own. Lust and love are worlds apart." Kate wondered if abstaining from sex before marriage had some merit.

"Restrain their advances? Yeah, well, sometimes that's pretty damn hard to do," Joey said. She stood up and went to the kitchen and started preparing supper, and that ended their discussion of men.

Kate sat for a while, thinking her values had shifted in subtle ways. Spirit was now a shadow shape, following her right into the consciousness of her daily life. It was communicating strange new ideas to her through the words she was reading.

She picked up the paperback Bible from the table beside her to continue her studies. In the middle of the page, she found a clear-cut passage saying something so outrageous, it was hard to grasp. It read, "If you believe, you will receive whatever you ask for in prayer."

That sounded like a magical formula for protection and blessings. It was like another one she had read, the one about throwing a mountain into the sea.

Kate flipped back to find she had already colored those words in green. "Whatever you ask for in prayer, believe that you have received it, and it will be yours."

Didn't those two verses say the same thing? The trick to getting your prayer answered was to wholeheartedly believe you would receive it! That was the basis of positive thinking, and manifesting things you wanted. Could it really be so simple? Then it dawned on her, and in regret, she crumbled. *Is that what happened when I prayed for a miscarriage? If that's true, I'm responsible for the way I think. I have to be careful in how I think.*

...

Kate had an opportunity to test out her latest discovery in a simple experiment. The old trailer she and Joey lived in had a list of maintenance problems. When the bathroom toilet leaked in the back, Joey placed a coffee can on the floor to catch the leak. She couldn't figure out how to repair the rusted valve, and neither could Kate.

"Let's pray about it and see if God will fix it." Kate laughed at her own satire, but she was half-serious. Joey raised her hands then with solemn exaggeration.

"Dear Lord, reign down your power and heal our toilet," Joey said. They doubled up in the hilarity of the irreverent request.

But Kate put in heartfelt fervency because she knew her friend couldn't afford to call a plumber. "God, please make a miracle happen. We might be 'sinner-girls', but you say you love us anyway, so we're asking," she said the words with sincerity.

It wasn't a sacred prayer but in a week the toilet didn't leak anymore, and Joey threw the can away. Kate had tested the promise she'd read in the Bible, 'to ask and receive,' and it had worked!

"This is our first miracle," Kate said, but Joey wasn't buying it.

"It's just a coincidence. The seal shifted somehow and tightened it again."

Kate just smiled at her, but inside, her hunger for spiritual empowerment continued to grow.

Two weeks later, something ominous threatened to destroy all of Kate's tenuous faith. The receptionist at her doctor's office called, asking Kate to come in for a review of her lab test. "Dr. Jamison has an opening tomorrow. Can we schedule an appointment for you at two o'clock?"

"No thanks. Will you ask the doctor to mail the forms to the Canadian Consulate in Seattle?"

"I'm afraid he insisted you come in to discuss the results."

Kate thought it was an extra way to charge her more money for another appointment. Yet when she sat down in the examining room with the doctor the next day, his face was grave. He came right to the point.

"Unfortunately, your chest x-ray showed a dark round shadow in the left lung."

Kate froze. *Oh, my God! It sounds like lung cancer or something.* She reigned in her panic and tried to focus.

"We don't know exactly what it is, but it's about the size of a penny. We need to investigate to make sure it's not active and spreading."

"That can't be right. I'm fine. I just needed a simple physical exam."

"Yes, I've filled the forms out, for the most part." He spoke with care in a calm tone. "However, when I see a chest x-ray like this in a woman your age, I have some concerns."

Kate shifted herself in the chair and forced herself to breathe slower.

"First, let's figure out what the shadow might represent by getting a history on you." He held his clipboard and pen ready. "Now, have you been exposed to TB?"

"Do you mean tuberculosis? Nobody gets TB anymore, do they?"

"It's still a serious disease and could cause a spot to show up on an x-ray. Did you have your immunization shots in grade school?"

"Of course."

"Have you suffered any severe chest infections or breathing problems in the last year or two?"

"I came down with a bad flu a few times," Kate admitted. "But you're scaring me now." She thought of the cigarettes and marijuana joint she had inhaled. Surely, her wild lifestyle wouldn't catch up with her so soon.

"Could it be cancer?" she asked. *There, I said the c-word.* Kate's hands fidgeted with the release of the question.

"Let's not jump to conclusions before I gather all the information." He peered down at his notes and continued. "Have you ever been diagnosed with pneumonia?"

"I had laryngitis once."

"Or Sarcoidosis?" he said. "It's known as Lofgren's syndrome."

"I've never heard of it, so I guess not."

"Have you owned a parrot or any kind of bird for a pet? Perhaps you raised chickens and had to clean out an old chicken coop?"

"No. How would that have anything to do with my lungs?" The questions confused her.

"Birds can sometimes carry spores for Histoplasmosis, a rare lung disease. It can cause a fungus to grow in the lungs, but it's not common in our area."

Whew, I'm glad I don't have a parrot.

"Unless perhaps you've been in contact with bats and their droppings."

"Oh…" It hit her then. The long day in the dark cave in southern Mexico. The huge swarms of bats whizzing above their heads. They had sat on the rocky floor, right in the flying mammals' subway system. Where the heck did their excrement land if not on the slimy rocks where they had eaten their sandwiches? Kate had been exposed to thousands of bats and their guano.

In a flash, she remembered the severe sickness she endured for weeks, holed up in the tiny, rented room in the town of Morelia. And what excruciating pain she experienced just to breathe air in and out of her lungs. Her illness hadn't been the flu. Fungus had caused it and could still be growing inside of her.

"I was exploring, spelunking in caves in Mexico." The words describing the experience tumbled out while Kate's heart thudded with the ramifications. The doctor paused over his notes.

"And so, we may have found the cause." He looked up at her.

"You're saying the spot is a living fungus?" Kate imagined tiny clusters of brown mushrooms in a pink forest of lung tissue.

"We'll run some tests for various diseases, but it seems the most probable cause."

"But you said there's only a shadowy spot on the one lung."

"Yes, and if it's still growing, that fungus may decide to invade the whole lung. You have a serious condition here, Kate." He sounded almost fascinated with the uncommon ailment he was getting the opportunity to diagnose.

"If it is this histoplasmosis thing, how do we treat it?" Kate inquired.

The doctor chose his words carefully. "Sometimes, the treatment plan takes weeks. It can be almost worse than the disease itself because of possible serious side effects from the medication we must use to treat it. In unusual cases, it may require hospitalization to help the patient through the worst of it."

"But...no." she objected. "My health is fine. And that spelunking adventure happened almost five months ago."

"First, let me run more tests to determine if this is what you have." He wrote a new prescription for more blood work to be done at the lab.

"Are you sure it was *my* x-ray you looked at?" Kate had to ask the question.

"I'm sure," he said, looking at her kindly.

"Will it look bad on my medical record for emigrating to Canada?"

The doctor cleared his throat. He tidied up his notes and leaned toward her. "If it's active histoplasmosis, you won't be going anywhere for some time, Kate, because you'll need aggressive treatment."

She sank back in her chair in silence while tears clouded her blue eyes. She tried to blink them away, but they swam through her lower lashes.

Doctor Jamison continued. "We have a slight possibility your outbreak may already be arrested. If that's the case, your body has created this sack-like capsule we see on the x-ray to contain the fungus in order to protect the rest of the lung."

"That would be the good news, then?"

"Yes, but even so, the protective sack has the potential to break open and grow again if you come down with pneumonia or a bad secondary lung infection."

"But I'm planning to immigrate to Canada." Her tone was emphatic and stubborn.

He stopped her and said, "You, my girl, may have a serious disease that will demand a lifetime of monitoring. I'm not an expert on the Canadian policy for health standards in their immigration program, but I'd be surprised if this didn't raise some red flags for them up there."

Chapter 29

WAITING FOR NEWS

Kate's head reeled with her doctor's prediction, yet she had to return to work right after the appointment. Her co-workers at the Bar & Grill were complaining about their petty problems as usual, but Kate didn't have the patience to listen to them. Her hopes for moving north appeared unlikely, and there was nothing to look forward to.

A week later, the tests came back with a confirmed diagnosis. They read positive for histoplasmosis and that threatened to shatter her. *This is too much. Even my health status says I'm not good enough for somebody. How can I endure a treatment worse than when I was sick in Mexico and could barely breathe?*

Dr. Jamison scheduled four additional x-rays to view the spot from different angles and then would consult with the lung specialists in Portland to decide on a treatment plan. Kate tolerated another two weeks of waiting until the professionals arrived at a consensus.

At her follow-up appointment, she was on the edge of her seat, trying to read Dr. Jamison's expression as centered into the room.

He gave her good news! Her body had arrested the histoplasmosis and the fungus was no longer growing. The shadow in her lungs was the crystallized scar tissue around the offensive spot. "You're a lucky girl," the doctor said.

"I guess I am." Kate grinned. But was it luck, or did God take care of the problem for her? She was free of the fungus. She didn't need harsh treatment for the disease. But the doctor continued by cautioning her.

"The spot will always show up on an x-ray, and there's a possibility it could break open under any acute respiratory infection you may have in the future. You'll need to take extra care of yourself and schedule regular check-ups."

"I'll try to do that," Kate said, realizing that was the bad news.

"And you might have to rethink that decision of yours to emigrate to Canada. The US isn't such a terrible place to live in." He tapped the paperwork on top of her file.

"Could you still send the report to the Canadian Consulate, please?"

"Yes, I'll do that." He nodded with resignation. "But I still can't see how their immigration system could approve your health condition."

...

Back at Joey's trailer, Kate told her about the diagnosis and how it might disqualify her from immigration. "I knew I shouldn't have gone into that cave. I guess there are consequences in life for every choice we make."

"You wanted to move up to Canada so bad. Perhaps they'll let you in, anyway."

"The doctor didn't think so. It feels like nobody wants me. You know?"

"I feel like that a lot, too," Joey said.

"I was sure God would bless my plans."

Joey frowned. "Perhaps you can't trust him, either."

What good was having faith then? The black spot on her lungs matched the dark hole in her heart. She carried a fungus that could start to feed on her lung tissue at any time in her life. That was a fact she had to accept.

Joey tried to cheer her up by turning on some rock music as they made their evening meal, but even her silliness could not ease the loss Kate felt.

...

Grey blistery rain settled in as Kate continued to work as a barmaid. She visited her mother some nights and slurped a beer or two with her father on other evenings, but indecision about her future still troubled her.

To think things over one morning, she hiked down the path to the panorama view overlooking the Columbia River. It was the same place that tempted her to step off into the fog after Mark dumped her. She perched on a mat of dead yellow grass at the edge to look at the view.

The sky was the color of a robin's egg, forming a convex canopy across the massive river, and Kate watched the water flow down the gorge. She imagined it free-flowing all the way to the ocean as she hummed the words to the "Ballad of Easy Rider."

She had been a wild child but running free didn't fulfill her anymore. Maybe it never did. She hadn't accomplished the things she wanted in her life, and somewhere along the way, she had thrown out her self-respect, too. *Oh yeah, I've been free, all right.*

"You're a smart and attractive young woman," she recalled her mother saying one time. "You can be whatever you want to be. You could marry a lawyer or a banker and live in one of those wealthy suburbs in Portland."

"Maybe, Mom." She answered back. "Then I'd play cards with the society ladies and serve those fancy triangular sandwiches with the crust cut off. We'd discuss fashion trends and gossip about our prominent husbands behind each other's back."

No, that was not what Kate wanted. That life was way too bourgeois for her. She wasn't about to marry a rich man to live that way, and even with a university degree, she'd end up with a high-stress, nine-to-five job and become part of the establishment she hated. By traveling so much already, a mundane life was not going to satisfy her anymore.

Kate looked north across the Columbia River as the breeze up the gorge tossed her hair in disarray. She didn't jump off the cliff three years ago in a dramatic suicide. She'd chosen to play the game, but so far it seemed like she was losing at it. *God, I've sure screwed things up. If life is a stupid game to play, then damn it, where are the instructions?*

...

The next day, Kate dangled her legs off the rough planks of Joey's weathered front deck and looked out over the new grass shoots in the meadows. Golden sunlight in the late afternoon promised the warmth of an early spring.

"Don't you want more in life than to settle down in our hometown?" she asked Joey who sat in a lounge chair on the deck.

"Who said I'm settling down?" Joey scrunched up her eyebrows. "Just because I live in a trailer on my dad's property doesn't mean I'm going to stay here forever." She tossed her head back in mock resentment.

"If Canada doesn't clear me for immigration, I guess I'll go back to Portland State and finish a degree in social work. Do they offer a bachelor's degree in Political Integrity? Or Enlightenment 101?"

"Sign me up for that. I'm in."

Kate sighed. "I've always wanted some deep purpose in life, but I don't know what that would be."

"Well, golly, Miss Molly. You're dwelling on some deep thoughts this afternoon."

Kate smiled but thought of the simplicity and purity she had found in the northern wilderness. "I wanted to leave the States because of all the assassinations and the Vietnam War. America's corporate greed is all so ethically wrong."

Joey got up and stretched, making light of the conversation. "Yes, we're puppets who dance to the powers of the establishment." Her body moved in graceful ballet movements across the deck.

"I don't want to be anybody's puppet. Leaving the US in protest is my way of being patriotic."

"What you and I need is a glass of wine." Joey sauntered off to pour the drinks.

The sun sank close to the horizon, and the meadow air grew thick around them. Joey came back with two full glasses and strummed a few chords on her guitar. "You seem weary, Kate, so this one's for you." Joey learned a new song from her Simon and Garfunkel album called "Bridge Over Troubled Waters." She sang the lyrics like a lullaby, dragging out the last verse.

Kate blended her voice to harmonize with Joey's. Their passionate voices drifted out into the golden glow of the sunset like a hymn. After the last chord, Joey set aside the guitar with a Mona Lisa smile on her face.

"I'll miss you if you move north."

"I doubt if the Canadian Consulate will let me in with my medical status." Kate shrugged and plucked off an early dandelion flower by the step she sat on. She threw the blossom up in the air and caught it with her other hand.

"I think I'm supposed to leave, but where's my destiny?" Kate asked.

"I heard 'you can't really know where you're going until you know where you've been,'" Joey said. She continued to strum her guitar, and the haunting chords echoed around them as the sun disappeared down behind the tree line. Crickets chirped in the stillness as the girls finished sipping their wine.

Chapter 30

DOWN MEMORY LANE

Kate drove up the valley to find her roots because if she wouldn't be allowed to immigrate, she needed another plan. The road was familiar going up the westside, but she wasn't ready to see her childhood home. She passed the turnoff and then took the right fork leading up into the flats, where strawberry fields and orchards lay like a checkered tablecloth.

Crisscrossing through the country lanes, Kate found the fields she picked berries in as a child. When she stopped the car and turned off the engine, a time warp happened, and she was right in the middle of all those green rows again. Closing her eyes, she let the memories come to her.

...

Shimmers of heat electrified the air as she sat in the vast field in the hot dirt. All the young kids wore straw hats and their father's old shirts. The supervisor commanded her post with diligence in the shade of the distant farm shack. All the berry pickers were bent over the rows like small alien machines spaced out over the undulating stripes of green.

Katie had a good row that day. She pawed through the crispy foliage, picking the bright red strawberries from each green-leafed plant. Her stained, sticky fingers filled each box faster and faster. Could she beat her sister Anna to the shack that morning? Sure enough, four years older than her, Anna pranced down a nearby row with her punch card ready to tally up another flat of berries.

"How many flats have you picked?" Katie yelled across the field. She never had as much as Anna but always picked more than her younger brother. Poor kid. Barry often sat in the shade and ate salt from a shaker to ward off the heatstroke that overcame him.

The days stretched long and hot, but she wasn't reprimanded for throwing berries like other kids. Their loose shirts got pasted with splats of red mush. Kate liked the warm juicy flesh of the strawberries too much. She was a berry connoisseur, choosing perfectly aged specimens. She didn't choose the darker red ones because the flavor was already flat and not the orange ones because the sugar still needed to build up in ripeness, but she devoured the solid, firm, fire-engine-red ones. They were spotted with tiny white polka-dot seeds on the surface and a circle of paleness at the stem. She never tired of popping one of those into her mouth.

Her mom drove their car to pick up Kate and her sibling in the afternoons. But sometimes if she couldn't come, they had to trudge cross-country down over the hill for a mile and take the shortcut home on the railroad tracks. The hard work gave her cash of her own to buy school clothes and movie tickets, and she dreamed of the day she'd go away and have grand adventures.

Kate's memory faded as she realized her childhood *dream had already materialized in her many travel destinations. Maybe she understood what she had wanted even then.*

On the way back to town, Kate turned left at the dip and went down the gravel road to cross the train tracks. There sat the old family home, but it had shrunk to the size of a dollhouse. She played on that emerald-green lawn, but barely remembered the majestic oak tree that now shaded the whole yard. Memories came up so real, Kate had to swallow them. An almost forgotten incident happened right there on the lawn. She had sat alone in the sun for the longest time and picked tiny blue flowers out of the grass. Her mother called them Forget-me-nots, and the delicate blue blossoms grew in abundance. Kate identified with the name of the miniature flowers because she was too young for her older sisters to play with her.

She plucked a small daisy nearby and played the flower game, pulling off the petals one by one. 'He loves me. He loves me not.' When she came to the last tiny petal, it ended at 'He loves me.' But who was it that loved her?

The sun's heat warmed her little shoulders like an invisible presence wrapped around her. And then somebody else's thoughts bounced into her head.

~~I~~LOVE~~YOU~~MY~~CHILD~~

She looked around. Nobody was there, yet she remembered her thin arms reaching upward and being hugged by an imaginary, wonderful friend.

...

Wow. How could I have forgotten that? The shimmering girl outside the Salvation Army and the invitation she received wasn't the first time she had heard words in Spirit form. It began as a child. Kate climbed out of her car then, to see the playhouse her father had built in the backyard. It was currently being used as a tool shed, and the old lilac bush beside it was overgrown. Her friend Belinda lived at the end of the road, and Kate strolled down to their old house next. Belinda had been a pretty child with straight brown hair and a dark complexion, so different from her pale head and freckles.

Belinda's big brother Duffy was scary, though. Once, he grabbed her little brother Barry around the neck.

"I'm going to cut your ears off," Duffy said, holding a pocketknife against Barry's head.

"Let him go," Kate yelled as loud as she could.

"Ah, I wasn't using the sharp edge of the knife," Duffy laughed, throwing Barry to the side. Something was wrong with Duffy, but Kate didn't know what it was.

Kenny was the other boy in the neighborhood and lived in the house across the street from them. He was five years older, and acne mottled his face. When she and Belinda were thirteen, he followed them down some trails into the woods and said nasty things to them. They ran off fast to go home. Kate couldn't stand him, and she didn't think Belinda liked him, either.

Later that summer, Belinda came over to say she wasn't allowed to hang out with her anymore. Kate didn't understand why and went to talk to her mom about it.

"What does *engaged* mean, Mom? Belinda and Kenny are going together, and she says her mother is making them get engaged."

"Oh, that woman. Doesn't she realize her daughter is still a child? It's better if you and Belinda aren't friends anymore, Katie."

Kate saw little of her friend that year, even though she lived just down the road. When fall came, Belinda didn't even go back to school. ... Kate found out what happened years later. Belinda had gotten pregnant at thirteen, and her parents made her marry Kenny. She had the child while she'd been locked up in her own house. Kate couldn't help but compare their paths in life. *She too had gotten pregnant and had a miscarriage when her childhood girlfriend was already a mother.*

Kate put those sad memories aside and followed a nearby path she knew well. It edged along the field and went into a forest dappled in shadows. Streams of sunlight broke through the branches, and she remembered not to let her legs touch the poison oak on the straight stretch. When she got to the creek, she sat on a big rock and peered down through the surface of the water. Verdant green moss covered the smooth stones with a pungent aroma. She used to hunt for crawdads, big ones, and make the creatures hold twigs in their claws before she set them free.

She walked down to the river next and wondered if it had altered its course again because time was always changing things. One year it jumped its banks and carved a new channel, leaving a wonderful sandy beach to play on.

Her father would often take them hiking down another trail to visit a pine tree that 'grew pennies.' They'd find the coins stuck under the brown bark every time, although they were hard to see. The big pine produced a few nickels and dimes when they became older. Kate's heart warmed at the thought of her dad's efforts to create the magic for them.

She found the bank where the tree had stood, but after a decade she couldn't really tell which was the Penny Tree. So, she crashed up through the bush to walk back along the railroad tracks. She and her brother used to put coins on the tracks, and after the train ran over them, they were pressed into shiny metal medallions. Her father showed them how to file the edges smooth, drill a hole, and string the coin on a piece of leather to make a necklace.

Kate balanced herself to walk back on the railroad tracks and found it still easy to do. How she wished her life hadn't been derailed and she was still on track with that. She came to the large green pond where they used to pole a raft through the water. Orange-bellied salamanders still wiggled through the dark, slimy liquid. She remembered she watched hundreds of polliwogs mature and turn into frogs every spring. As she drove away in her car, Kate treasured the honest simplicity in nature. *If only the pattern of her life could be so simple.*

...

Kate she was grounded solid when she returned to work the next day. She knew what she wanted. She wanted a life in the country somewhere.

334

Her new job at the Legion Club was bar tending in the downstairs women's lounge and gave her bigger tips. The gender designation irked her, but the women who came in enjoyed their private space. They sat on the bar stools and told Kate about their secret troubled lives. She would commiserate with them while she mixed their drinks, but counseling as a bartender for the rest of her life was something she definitely didn't want to do.

Kate sold her old Volkswagen bug after saving enough money to purchase a dependable vehicle again. She scoured the want ads in the local paper and saw a yellow Ford half-ton truck for sale. Her dad helped her check it out before she bought it. The pickup had a tricky stick shift, but the wooden canopy on the back would be perfect for packing her things when she moved.

Kate parked her yellow pickup in her girlfriend's driveway with pride. "Hey Joey, did you pick up the mail today?" Kate asked.

"No, I forgot," she shouted from the kitchen.

"Okay. I'll walk down to get it." Joey had a good setup; she didn't pay fees or rent for the trailer, so she saved lots of money. Maybe it wouldn't be so bad to get a place of her own right here in the valley. Mount Hood's white peak seemed to stare at her back as Kate walked to the oval metal box, perched on a post and leaning slightly. She tugged open the tin door, and then she saw it.

A letter from the Canadian Consulate sat waiting for her.

Chapter 31

INWARD EXPLORATION

Kate held up the letter from the Consulate, scared to break the seal. Her stomach did a flip-flop as she took a full breath. That one piece of paper could change everything.

Okay, God. My future is in your hands. I will trust you, whatever the outcome. Kate ripped open the envelope which tore off the end of the inside paper too. She shook the letter out and held the pieces together to scan the fine print. Despite her medical report, Kate would have her landed immigrant status when she crossed the border. Canada had accepted her. This girl was going north!

...

"I hear you're leaving us soon," a senior employee at the Legion said to Kate, trying to be friendly. "Let me buy you a farewell drink."

The Legion had an after-hours party for the staff every Saturday night, which built closeness among the employees. Kate was the youngest, but the old-timers were supportive, even after she had given her notice.

"Let's celebrate for young Kate. To her new life up in the cold Canadian north." Drinks flew liberally while they dreamed up future scenarios for her. Someone tried to give instructions on building igloos, and another man told her how to drive a dogsled.

"You need to say, 'Mush, mush, little doggies,'" Shane said. He was one of the younger men on the staff who loved to tease her.

"I'm not moving that far north." Kate laughed at their humorous comments going back and forth. After midnight she realized she'd had enough to drink, so she found the keys to her pickup and said her last goodbyes.

"You okay to go?" Shane had showered her with attention all night, and now he threw an arm around her shoulders. "Can I take you home?"

"I think I'll be okay but thank you," she said.

Shane laughed at her. "You might want to wait for a little until you sober up. Let's walk up to my house in the fresh air, and I'll show you a view of the river."

Kate knew what he wanted because of similar pickup lines, but maybe he was just concerned about her. She needed the fresh air, anyway.

They strolled through the deserted streets in the wee hours of the morning with intoxicated hilarity. However, the view from Shane's living room gave only a peek of the river, and his efforts at seducing her became almost forceful. A year ago, she would have taken his desire as a complement, but now she picked up her purse and walked out.

Twenty minutes later, Kate was back on the street where she had parked her vehicle. She was still tipsy, but it was only a short drive from home on the back streets.

She climbed in and slowly backed up a couple of feet. Then she inched forward, trying to find her way out of the tight parallel-parking spot. Her inebriated efforts were compounded by the sticky gearshift compared to the automatic transmission she had always driven.

"Miss," said a police officer, shining his flashlight in her face.

Kate rolled down the window.

"Are you having trouble with your vehicle?"

Kate's head whirled; her hands trembled. "I'm okay. I just bought my truck, officer. I'm not used to driving it."

"You've attempted to get out of that parking spot for a good ten minutes, so perhaps you've had a little too much to drink. Please step out of the vehicle."

Kate slid out of her truck, but her feet were unsteady when she landed. She did a quick dance step to stand up beside him.

"Now, do you see the white line in the middle of the road? If you can walk straight down that line, then you're fine, but if you have any trouble, we're going to take you down to headquarters for a Breathalyzer test."

Kate decided to humor him and took up the challenge. She stepped out on the tightrope, and it seemed like five feet of space dropped off on either side. After a few teetering steps, she stumbled off the line.

The policeman was kind, still he bundled her into the rear of the cop car and drove her to the station. Once there, another officer made Kate blow through the Breathalyzer apparatus and booked her for Driving Under the Influence.

She was permitted one phone call, and in her hazy state, she pondered which number to dial. She needed family.

My brother is in college. He can't come. My father has already received a few DUIs. He'd be familiar with it, that's for sure.

But Kate wanted her mom. That surprised her because her mother would be so disappointed, but she rang her up, anyway.

"Katie, do you know what time it is? How could you get yourself into this state? What were you thinking?"

"That's the problem, Mom. I wasn't thinking," she slurred. Her mom came down to the police station to rescue her anyway, but once they were in the car, she continued to berate her.

"They're going to print your name in the paper under legal notices, and what will people think? What am I going to say when my co-workers hear about it at City Hall?"

Kate didn't have an answer for that. When she woke up late the next day, she still felt drunk. Her mother had left for work, so Kate shuffled out of bed and got dressed. She needed to walk it off and get some oxygen into her system, so she headed down to the riverbank of the Columbia. She found a smooth, hard rock at the water's edge and sat down, disgusted with herself.

What have I done? I've been so stupid. Stupid. She struggled to remember why they gave her so much to drink at the Legion's staff party. No, it was Shane who brought her the drinks.

She usually ordered a beer, not those fancy mixed ones. Did he try to get her drunk, so she'd go home with him? Probably, but that didn't excuse her. She had consumed them and drove home when she knew better. Kate hunched over the slab of rock in her misery. She was still hungover and had no energy even to hold herself upright.

Oh God, I'm such a mess. What am I doing with my life? She studied the movement of the rolling river and saw her last few years glide by. Shane was like so many others. Mark had overwhelmed her in sweet romance, and then he ditched her. Robert didn't want to be tied down. All the guys she had dated and slept with afterward were just short Ferris-wheel rides of feeling loved. What kind of sex went with that?

Kate sat and cried hard in the warm morning sun. She'd been a straight-A student in high school yet only managed two years of university. She should be a professional in respectable employment, not a barmaid in a dead-end job. Now she had to go to court for a DUI. No wonder her mother was ashamed of her. I'm *just a drunk like my father. What if I lose my license too?*

The pounding in Kate's head wouldn't let up. It ached from sobbing, but she couldn't stop, and no one was around, anyway. She was glad she was moving away.

She jerked upright when she remembered one specific question on the immigration form she had filled out. It asked, 'have you ever been charged and convicted?'

If the court sends a record of my DUI to the Canadian Consulate, they'll see it when I stop at the border to get my landed immigrant papers. They'll assume I've lied on my application

Kate melted into an unlovable blob of despair and closed her eyes to block the sun. After she couldn't cry anymore, her heaving breath became the pulse of the rocky beach she sat on. There in the middle of that wretchedness, Spirit caressed the rough edges of her shattered being and words shimmering into her heart.

~~CHILD~~OF~~MINE~~
~~ENTER~~MY~~KINGDOM~~

Great, she thought. Another invitation. How am I supposed to do that? Wait until I die to see if I go to heaven? The breeze blew her strands of long hair away from her wet, messy face. Kate gazed up at the clouds stretching across the wide expanse of the gorge and noticed their movement, an inversion of living energy swirling above the calm flow of the Columbia River.

Nature compelled life to move on, and she would have to move on too, like the water in the river flowing to the sea. The moisture was reabsorbed there, went into the atmosphere, and formed clouds. Air currents blew the clouds back inland over the mountains, where they hung out ladened with heaviness. Then they would rumble and release their rain on the land below where, once again, streams would form and trickle down to the river to flow back to the sea.

Kate envied the natural laws because their patterns had a purpose. Mother Nature governed herself with physical rules that made sense.

Even animals followed the rules, pre-programmed by instinct. Birds flew south for the winter, and bears hid out and hibernated. Nature was pure, simple, and beautiful. Words whispered back to her gently, and there was so much love attached to them.

~~PUT~~MY LAWS~~
~~INTO~~YOUR~~HEART~~
~~TO~~ENTER~~MY~~KINGDOM~~

The subliminal command ran across her mind and echoed down the corridors. But she didn't know how ancient religious laws could pertain to the bigger modern world? Her generation believed everything was relative to the cultural situation in which you were born. There were no absolute rights or wrongs for humanity. It was only wrong if you hurt somebody else while you were doing it. And wasn't love supposed to cover the whole thing, anyway?

But why do I feel so rotten about myself, then? What immutable laws have I broken? Kate sat there for a while longer, contemplating her question, but it was left unanswered.

Kate's crying ravaged her face by the time she walked back. Even her mother stopped herself from chastising her anymore that night. She just shook her head and offered her a place to stay in town since the court had impounded her truck.

...

Joey came over to see her a few days later to cheer her up. "Come on. You need some fun. Let's sneak into the heated pool at the Holiday Inn to swim like we used to do."

Kate agreed, and she and Joey put their bright bikinis on and chose classy clothes to wear on top. The gated pool was empty that early in the season, so they walked in like they were young professionals on holiday.

"Ah, this is a good life." Joey stretched out in the sun and handed her a magazine. But Kate needed to talk about her humiliating drunk-driving incident. Joey giggled when Kate told her the officer had made her walk down the white line.

"But you told me you were a pro at walking on those rails when you were a kid. Maybe they strung up a trapeze tightrope just for you."

"It looked like it. I couldn't keep my balance. Then I had to ride in the back of the police car to the station and blow into a Breathalyzer."

"Good grief. Did you get thrown in the drunk tank?" Joey no longer found the experience quite so funny.

"No, they gave me the one phone call, though."

"Why didn't you ring me?"

"I was drunk. I didn't even phone my father, and he would have understood. I called my mother."

"Your mother? Gosh, I guess that didn't go over very well."

"No, I'm a disgrace to her. I have to appear in court for a DUI and might lose my license plus a big part of my savings. What's worse, they probably won't let me immigrate when I try to go through the border. They'll think I lied about having a conviction."

"Oh, that sucks." Joey knew how much Kate wanted to migrate to Canada.

At that point, a heavy-set older man in a white shirt came through the gate into the pool area and asked them for their room number. Joey tried to flirt with the guy, thinking he must be the hotel manager, but the distraction didn't seem to work.

"We're in room 101," Kate said.

"No, you are not because we have no room with that number." He answered in exasperation, putting his hands on his hips and glaring at them. "Do you think it would be right for everybody to walk in off the street and use our pool for free?"

"Well, no." Kate stammered, embarrassed. Joey hastened to gather up their towels and bags.

"If it's wrong for everyone to do it, what makes it right for you? Why do you young women think you're so special? Get out of here."

"Jeez, we're going." Joey pulled on Kate's arm, and they walked out fast to the car.

...

Afterward, Kate spent a lot of time considering what the hotel manager had said. His words were profound, and she had to share her insight.

"He was right, Joey. Rules are good for society."

"What do you mean?"

"Well, what would happen if everybody thought it was okay to run red lights? It would cause havoc on the highways. The same principle could apply to a universal standard for humanity."

"I don't get it." Joey rubbed her forehead, struggling to see where Kate was going with the conversation.

Kate tried to summarize the principle. "If a specific action causes harm to society when everyone does it, then that same action is wrong for even one person to do it. It could be a natural law, you know. Maybe there are universal morals that define right and wrong."

"But Kate, who are we going to trust to draw up these laws? If each country defines morality, then who has the authority to oversee the world's governments?"

Kate was stumped by that question. "There must be absolutes. Doesn't our human species value similar things, like kindness, honesty, beauty?"

"Oh, Katie, it's about you and God again, huh? I could follow universal laws if they're not government ordained, or man-made church expectations for their private Sunday social club."

"Yes, God has to be bigger than that, big enough for all countries and religions." Kate visualized a world with those values, a peaceful paradise. "I could follow a God like that."

"Me too, if there were real personal benefits for us."

"I think they're called *blessings*." Kate said to tease her.

Later, Kate realized how much she had already benefited. She'd been saved from storms, and caves, and diseases. She had loved and it had filled her heart even if it hadn't been reciprocated. She knew the Golden Rule; to treat others the way you wanted to be treated. *Love is giving joy to others, isn't it? Love is good, and I can hold on to that simple truth.*

Dear God, I want to live by your standards. Make me the woman you want me to be. But if you'll help me move north, I think it would be a lot easier....

Chapter 32

LED BY SPIRIT

Kate went to the bank to deposit her last paycheck into her savings account. She took pride in her savings, knowing she could start a new life wherever she ended up. But when she left the building, Mark was in front of her, right there in the parking lot. He looked the same, except the angles of his face were sharper.

"Kate? It's you. You're living here in Hood River now?" Mark asked, his eyes filling with pleasure.

"It's me." Kate laughed at his excitement and her smile grew wide. "I've been living here for a while."

"I heard you were traveling all over the place." Mark cocked his head to one side, and she remembered his less than perfect hearing had prevented him from getting drafted overseas.

"I've been traveled some. How about you? Did you finish your pre-med studies?" Kate found it easy to chat with him.

"I graduated with a university degree but had to move back home for the summer to help manage my father's business."

Kate remembered visiting him in the small dusty gas station, saturated with the smell of oil.

"Hey, do you want to go for lunch?" Mark flashed his lopsided sensual grin at her. "It's fate that we've run into each other."

"Sure, I could use an old friend right now," Kate said.

"What happened, Sunshine? You don't seem so happy."

"Do you want to hear the good news or the bad?"

"I want them both," he laughed. "It's been a long time." They sat down at a nearby restaurant, and he shared news about his family and the jobs he'd taken to finance his education.

Kate told him about her traveling adventures, how she had gone east to Michigan, south almost to Guatemala, and then north to BC. She explained how sick she'd been when she caught histoplasmosis from bats in the Mexican caves, and about receiving her immigration papers to move to Canada.

"You want to move out of the country? But why?" He reached across the table to stroke her hand. "I'm thinking we might want to fan the embers, you know?"

His gentle touch undid her. The solid wall around her heart began to crack, fractured by his presence. She blurted the words out, hating how vulnerable her voice sounded. "But you left me." There was a moment of silence. "Kate, we were both so young," he whispered. "I thought it was for the best."

"Well, I'm not the same girl you knew." Emotion threatened to overwhelm her, but Kate swallowed it back. If only she could wipe away the years she had spent seeking revenge against him. "Besides, I have to be in court tomorrow, and I don't know what the outcome will be."

"What happened? Why do you have to go to court?" he asked with concern.

"I got a DUI."

"Oh. Well, perhaps you *have* changed from my innocent little sunshine girl." His mocking was softhearted. "You're just as pretty, though. Why did the cops think you had been drinking?"

"…I couldn't walk the white line." Kate forced a smile with chagrin and faced him head-on.

His lips curved at her admission. "I guess you have to plead guilty then, princess." Their eyes penetrated each other and got tangled up like they used to.

"Are you going before the judge alone? Would you like me to go with you?"

"You would do that?"

"I would. I'll sit right beside you in the courtroom."

"It would be nice to have you there," Kate said, and the rest of the lunch flew by fast in warmth and respect.

They met on the courthouse steps the next day before the hearing. Kate's nerves were wound up tight, but Mark's presence comforted her as they waited in the assigned courtroom. She fidgeted in the chair until they called her name from the docket.

The judge listed the date and location of the offense and then read the charge. "Driving under the influence of a 0.15% blood alcohol level. Do you plead guilty or not guilty?"

Mark raised his eyebrows at her and whispered. "You *were* drunk."

Kate stood up and gave a straightforward answer. "I plead guilty, Your Honor." The judge fined her a hefty sum for a first conviction and suspended her license for three weeks. Her pickup truck was impounded for that same time, and she'd have to pay to release it from the compound yard.

"That's it then. Come on." Mark murmured and steered her out of the courthouse. "Your sentencing could have been a lot worse, Kate. They're cracking down on drunk drivers and giving even stiffer penalties."

Kate let out a sigh of relief. It was over. "That fine is a lot of hard-earned money for me, though."

"It's a lot, I know."

"What's worse, I might not be able to immigrate to Canada. They'll see the DUI conviction when I get to the border."

"You sure have your heart set on moving north, don't you?"

Kate stood on the steps outside the courthouse. She gazed across the Columbia River to the northern mountains in the next state. "It's a beautiful virgin wilderness up there. It helped to change me when I was there. I think it's my destiny." She didn't tell Mark about how it was all wrapped up in her growing connection to God.

Mark watched her closely as they walked aimlessly along the sidewalk in silence. A shadow of sorrow crossed his face as he exhaled. "I still care deeply about you, Kate."

"I feel the same about you." She eyed him with honesty and bit her lower lip.

At last, he spoke. "Your DUI conviction has to be registered and filed here before it's available to send to the Canadian border. The whole bureaucratic process takes time."

"That's true. You mean I could leave right away before the court forwards the paperwork."

"Yeah. Something like that."

"But what if I can't get there in time and still get turned down at the border?" Kate was thinking this through.

"Maybe you can ask at the courthouse when your record is sent to the border officials."

"I could ask that. I might have time to cross the border before Canada gets any official documents if they can tell me. Oh, Mark, I'm excited again." Kate reached out to give him a spontaneous hug like she had done so often before. "I want to see you happy, Kate," he said, hugging her back. "I'll always be here if you need help, no matter where you are."

In that instant, the hard shell around her heart shattered into a million billion pieces. Kate absolved him for what she thought was a betrayal all that time ago. It had taken years to process the loss of his love, and yet now his eyes were filled with adoration.

"That's the nicest thing anybody has ever said to me," she said as they strolled along. Her heart still ached over what might have been. But even if there was a possibility of rekindling the relationship, the timing was all wrong. After a while, she and Mark headed back to where he had parked his vehicle. Neither of them was eager to say goodbye and didn't know how to say it. In bittersweetness, he kissed her on the forehead.

"Call me in a few days when you find things out. Take care of yourself, Sunshine." He got into his pickup then and drove away.

Kate told herself she was okay, but she wasn't really. Mark had swept back into her life like a tidal wave. But even if he'd been kind, he hadn't asked her out on an actual date. With conflicted emotion, her mind swirled madly. *We still care, but we can't recapture the past. We aren't those same young teenagers anymore.*

Kate thought about how powerful and romantic first love could be. In its finest, purest form, love was what she'd been searching for all her life. Could God's love for her be that strong, too?

...

When Kate returned to the courthouse, the clerk didn't understand what information she was requesting, and he called over the department supervisor. Kate had to ask her question all over again.

"When will a convicted DUI charge be made public?" she whispered at the counter desk.

The professional woman peered back at her and lowered her voice. "It's a matter of public record, dear, as soon as the judge decrees it."

Despite her embarrassment, Kate gave the woman the specific details of her concerns. The ramifications were crucial to her plans. "I'm moving to Canada soon and my landed immigrant papers will be at the border. When will the Canadian officials receive notification of my DUI conviction?"

"That might be a problem. We send reports outside the local county by registered mail on the first of each month. How soon do you plan to leave?"

Kate clenched her teeth. Her court hearing had been on April seventh, and her license was suspended for twenty-one days. "I guess I'll be leaving at the end of the month, the day after I get my license back."

The supervisor pursed her lips and nodded. Kate thanked the lady for her help and skipped down the steps of the courthouse. There was barely a window to make it work, but it was possible.

...

For the last time, Kate and Joey hung out on her back deck and complained about men and politics again. Washington, DC, had erupted in a frenzy of backbiting and abusive power in the Watergate scandal, and Nixon was facing impeachment for concealing illegal activities in his re-election campaign. She and Joey vowed they'd never surrender to the establishment and promised to stay in touch no matter what.

"Hey, there's one last song we have to sing, the one by Mary Hopkin," Joey said. She played the chords on her guitar, and they sang "Those Were the Days," with passion. It was the perfect song for their last evening together.

...

Kate chose not to see Mark again. She telephoned to thank him for his suggestion and explained what she had found out at the courthouse.

He wanted to get together before she left, but Kate put him off, knowing what distance did to relationships. She hoped he'd find happiness, even if it wasn't going to be with her.

Kate spent extra time in the evenings with her father, who seemed more depressed than usual. When she told him about receiving her immigration papers to cross the border, he stood up, shuffled around, and muttered to himself. "The world's going to hell in a hand-basket. It used to be kids would stay in their hometown and take care of their old people."

Her father's despair saddened Kate. Yet he was there to get her vehicle out of the compound yard. He helped to load a small chest of drawers filled up with her meager belongings into the back of the canopy. She added a backpack, a sleeping bag, and a foam mattress to sleep on. Then she gave her father a warm hug and promised to write.

Kate drove over to her mother's apartment to spend her last night. She and her mom had an uplifting heart-to-heart visit after supper, yet she also felt guilty about leaving her mother. Kate was the fourth child to move away, and she knew both her mother and father must be feeling abandoned.

She didn't sleep well that last night in the dark. Her mind wandered around in a labyrinth of second thoughts on the radical decision she had made. *God, if you're real, please show me a sign of your presence.*

Kate lay awake for hours, conflicted with an odd mixture of eagerness and remorse. Her life was on the brink of a radical change las though she was compelled to journey north, almost like she was needed up there. And just as she was drifting off to sleep, a vision of a face flashed in front of her.

She studied it, thinking at first it resembled Mark. But no, the piercing blue eyes probed with intensity. The face had a square jaw, a unique nose ending broader than it should, and glints of gold gilded his hair.

Perhaps it was a man from her future. If this was his appearance, she couldn't wait to meet him. She stirred awake and etched the vivid details in her mind to hold them there.

He looks like he already knows me. Maybe I'm seeing Spirit in the shape of an angel, or even Jesus himself. There's no judgment in his eyes. Sternness, yes, but with such unflappable gentleness and protection there. She had been saved from a caustic *Manzanilla* tree in Mexico and a gale storm on the open seas. She had no lasting effect from that STD in Michigan or the Histoplasmosis from the Mexican caves. She hadn't overdosed on drugs with LSD. She had had loved and lost... and lived to love again. All the while, God had protected her and downloaded encouraging words. It was time she whispered her heart-thoughts back to him.

Dear God, thank you for not giving up on me after all the stupid choices I made and for this fresh start in a new country. Thanks for helping me understand why Mark left and for his long-lasting friendship. Please, give him a good life. Help my mother to enjoy her job and her friends. Help my father stop drinking and find a way to escape the anguish of his past. Take care of my young brother Barry too, because he needs you.

Afterward, something warm and precious gushed into her heart, and a blissful sleep carried her away on a soft breeze.

...

The big departure day had arrived. Kate hugged her mom goodbye, climbed into her pickup, and drove down the street to the highway. Before Portland, she exited onto the I-5 and drove three more hours north on the freeway. But then fatigue from the emotional farewells and lack of sleep caught up with her, and she pulled off the highway to rest her eyes.

Kate bunched up her pillow and stretched out across the front seat. Then she slumped down out of sight and fell into the exhausted nap she needed.

But suddenly, something went horribly wrong! Kate was suffocating. Struggling to wake up, she found herself in the gravel on the side of the freeway. Cars went swishing by, roaring madly. She was claustrophobic, her body hot, sweaty, and she was blind! *Did I have an accident? Where the hell am I?*

The loud sounds of the traffic deafened her ears, and Kate's panic skyrocketed. Her heart pounded in drumbeats. *My neck...I can't move it. Am I paralyzed?*

She tried to scream but couldn't even do that. Then someone whispered close to her ear.

~~BE~~STILL~~AND~~KNOW~~
~~I~~AM~~HERE~~

The sound stayed beside her, and Kate inhaled slowly. She still couldn't see, but her legs would move. She oriented herself by stretching to the left, away from the sound of the traffic.

Yikes! Her left foot dangled over a drop-off, and Kate heard pebbles fall. She froze, not knowing how far down the stones would go. Had she almost fallen off a cliff?

Cars whizzed by fast, and fearing she'd be run over, she willed herself to stay calm. Then, in total contradiction to what was happening, someone spoke to her again.

~~DO~~NOT~~BE~~AFRAID~~

I'm being rescued! Kate struggled to regain consciousness and tried hard to open her oh-so-heavy eyelids, but they seemed glued together. At last, with extreme effort, they flew apart. And she was awake.

Reality hit hard. Kate was still lying in the front seat of her pickup with both windows rolled up. The cab was hotter than hell, and her head throbbed. She guessed the kink in her neck came from being squished up against the door. Once she cranked the window down, she gasped for fresh air. She gulped it in and understood exactly what the vision had meant. Kate had been blind and reckless on the road of life. At the very precipice of adulthood, she had almost gone over the edge. The oncoming noisy flow of immorality had tried to swallow her up whole, but she *had* been rescued.

Spirit had spoken to her on the front lawn as a child. It had called to her as a teenager. Those mystical words had always exuded love and now Kate cried out with conviction. *I love you back, God. I accept your invitation. I want your Spirit to lead me!*

With a blissful smile and now fully awake, Kate got out of her vehicle to stretch. She walked around her yellow truck and extended her arms up into the afternoon sun. She spied spring flowers peeking their heads out from the new grass bordering the freeway with Mount Baker standing out against a periwinkle blue sky. The splendor of the physical world pulsated in living energy, bursting into her awareness with exquisite joy. She was back on track, off on a new adventure, and not alone in the world at all.

Kate found her jug of water in the cab and swallowed large gulps until she was satisfied. Finally, she put the key into the ignition, started the truck again, and eased back into the frantic traffic on the four-lane freeway. She drove through the busy city of Seattle, and when she approached the Canadian border a couple hours later, her past had faded into the hazy distance.

...

Kate parked her truck outside the Canadian Border and Services Agency and showed her ID at the front counter. After stating her business, the clerk led her to a room where an immigration officer waited. He opened the file with her name and took out a legal document in duplicate. He read it carefully, signed it, stamped on the date, and handed a copy back to her.

"Welcome to Canada," he said with a formal smile and a handshake.

Kate was twenty-three. She had a pink copy of her Canadian Immigration Certificate beside her on the seat of her truck. She drove past the famous white Peace Arch and continued north. But that wasn't the end of anything.

It was just the beginning.

...

THE SPIRIT QUEST SERIES continues in the next
poignant novel from

Jane Catherine Rozek

PURITY FOUND
Book Two of The Spirit Quest Series

Kate chooses to
immigrate to Canada
and she's time-warped
into bittersweet
challenges in the
backwoods of BC.

Her desire for Spirit
and purity are met in
ways she'd never
imagined.
Then she's confronted
with Dave, an older
mountain man, the

very face she has recently seen in a vision. A different
kind of romance starts to blossom, but it will require
all the faith she has to travel her destined and
turbulent path…

Dear Friends,

I'm so glad to share my life story with you. I hope it encourages all those troubled by memories. Choosing the right path in life at any age is the foundation to happiness, and when that aligns with what God wants for us, it becomes magical!

For those of you interested in the musical classics of the 1960s and 70s mentioned in some of the chapters, they are listed in the addendum in the last pages of this book for you to find on YouTube. Also, there are historical notes, and the key scriptures that began to form my different perspective on faith.

I sit alone in front of my computer screen and so when I receive emails, comments, or messages through social media, I get excited! An honest Goodreads or Amazon review makes me really satisfied and helps future readers to find my books. I treasure your feedback!

Please, connect with me on my Facebook page at: **www.facebook.com/JaneCatherineRozek.net**

Or better yet, join my ever-growing tribe at: **www.JaneCatherineRozek.com** for giveaways and updates on my next book in the series.

You can get involved and learn more about me on my **Heart-Thoughts Blog** and see stunning travel photos from all over the world on our **Grand Adventures Blog**.

We're all given a ticket to play the glorious game of life on this beautiful planet. May we each find the courage and gusto to play it well.

Virtual hugs to everyone, in Spirit and Love,
Jane Catherine

ALSO BY
Jane Catherine Rozek

WHAT CURRENT READERS ARE SAYING:

*I can in all faith proclaim this as a good book. I have
been waiting for it most of
my life and admire the
author's ability to read
between the lines of man's
words and define God's
message...to bring the
good news from a different
approach from the one
most of us seem to have
trouble with, organized
religion.*

*To read about spirituality
from such a fresh and
uplifting voice leaves me smiling and thinking that
perhaps there is hope for humanity as we see it today.*
--Maria Trautman, author of best selling, *After All*

*The author has presented an entirely new way of
thinking about life, spirituality, religion, and what it
means to be a human being. I read every word of this
book, and it is truly unique. I hope The Celestial
Proposal gains many more readers, because this book
deserves attention.*
**--Thom Lemmons, author of Blameless and Jabez,
coauthor of the King's Ransom**

You use excellent analogies to get your point across ...and paint lovely word pictures. In fact, several times in your book, I wanted to stop and paint the scene you described. Not only are you a talented, gifted writer, but you have done your research!

I admire the study, work, and deep contemplation that you have put into your book...your boldness to tackle a whole new approach to Scripture. You've many more books in you, I suspect.

--Patricia Johnson-Laster, author of *Free to be Me, Free to be God's Child,* and *All I'm Created to Be*

This exciting take on Christianity presented a kind of spirituality I never knew existed, helping me to step past "department store religion" and into a very personal and super-natural journey...

The author revealed the purpose of life as an ongoing quest toward spiritual maturity. But this book did not stop there. It taught me to reprogram my mind so I can clear the things that block the manifesting of what I want. Before reading this, I was simply going through the Christian motions and I felt small, powerless and insignificant. I had no idea that God was holding out such a tremendous proposal to me.

--Rebekah Antkow, Editor, Books of Life Publishing

There is a spice in your writing style that I envy. A fresh look at an old truth wrapped in a seeker sensitive package guaranteed to pull people off the fence out of apathy!! Great work.

--David McGrinn, author of *God, Why was I Born Gay*

In today's society we tragically discredit religion, myself included. I really feel like this is the modern-day transformation religion needs to continue to grow & thrive. What a gift you've given the world.
--Adriana Chrisman

I loved this book! For many years I have tried so hard to understand religion, but I often found myself questioning concepts. This book opened my mind to new possibilities of how it all really can be true...This book is a beautiful blend of traditional religion (including many quotes from the Bible) and New Age proposals of what may be out there for us.
--Cheryl Meier

AUTHOR'S BIO

Jane Catherine Rozek is an adventurous romantic.
She loves the wilderness, spiritual deep-thinking, and
cuddly bear hugs. Her
current project, The
Spirit Quest Series, is
based on true stories
from her earlier
challenging lifestyle
from Oregon to
Mexico and to Canada.

She's the Canadian
non-fiction author of
The Celestial
Proposal: Our
Invitation to Join the
God Kind. She writes for spiritually hungry people as
an independent Christian trailblazer.

Her home now is in beautiful Kelowna, BC, and she
still travels to distant parts of the world with her
laptop in hand, for *grand adventures!*

ADDENDUM

CHAPTER ONE
"The Look of Love" by Dusty Springfield in 1967

CHAPTER TWO
"The House of the Rising Sun" by The Animals

Lincoln, Abraham, Gettysburg Address, 1863.**https://en.wikipedia.org/wiki/United_States_Declaration_of_Independence.**
King Jr., Martin Luther, American Rhetoric, Online Speech Bank. **https://www.americanrhetoric.com/speeches/mlkihaveadream.htm.**

CHAPTER THREE
"I Think We're Alone Now" by Tommy James and The Shondells

Martin Luther King Jr., "Beyond Vietnam -- A Time to Break Silence," Delivered April 4, 1967, Riverside Church, New York City; American Rhetoric, Online Speech Bank. **https://www.americanrhetoric.com/speeches/mlkatimetobreaksilence.htm.** Also: Martin Luther King, Jr., AZQuotes.com. Retrieved January 07, 2019. **https://www.azquotes.com/quote/377525.**

Martin Luther King, Jr., AZQuotes.com. Retrieved January 07, 2019. **https://www.azquotes.com/quote/358340.**

A 2021 letter written by ex-undercover NYPD policeman, Raymond Wood, alleges his department and the FBI covered up details of the assassination of Malcolm X.
https://www.aljazeera.com/news/2021/2/21/ex-new-york-policeman-implicates-nypd-and-fbi-in-malcolm-x-murder

"Fever" by Peggy Lee in 1959
https://youtu.be/JGb5IweiYG8.

CHAPTER FOUR
"The First Time Ever I Saw Your Face," written by Ewan McColl. Gordon Lightfoot sang it on his first album, "Lightfoot." Two years later, Roberta Flack sang it with so much passion her rendition became the number one hit in1972.

CHAPTER SIX
"What are we Fighting For?" By Country Joe and the Fish

CHAPTER SEVEN
"If You Could Read My Mind" by Gordon Lightfoot

CHAPTER EIGHT
"Let's keep Dancing," originally produced by Mark Daniels, sung by Peggy Lee in 1969

CHAPTER NINE
"Kent State Shooting," Editors at History.com.
https://www.history.com/topics/kent-state-shooting.

"Ohio" by Crosby, Stills, Nash, and Young, released 1970, ten days after the shooting of the Kent State students.

CHAPTER TEN
Yevtushenko, Yevgeny, 'The Hoods.' Red Cats, City Lights Books, English version 1962, p. 22-26. Written in 1960. Yevtushenko, a courageous political Soviet Russian poet, passed away in 2017. Permission for the use of this poem was given to the author on Nov. 19, 2021, by his widow Maria Novikova through correspondence with Zhenya Yevtushenko, son of Yevgeny Yevtushenko.

CHAPTER ELEVEN
"Lucy in the Sky with Diamonds" by The Beatles in 1967

'Only a free and unrestrained press can effectively expose deception in government.' Justice Black's closing statement in the Supreme Court's decision to uphold the First Amendment when the New York Times was brave enough to challenge the US government. New York Times Co. v. The United States, 403 U.S. 713, 1971. **https://en.wikipedia.org/wiki/New_York_Times_Co._v._United_States.**

CHAPTER TWELVE
"We Shall Overcome" recorded by Joan Baez in 1965. It's attributed to a hymn by Charles Albert Tindley in 1905 and developed into a protest song by Pete Seeger and Zilphia Horton in 1947.

CHAPTER THIRTEEN
"Stairway to Heaven" by Led Zeppelin

CHAPTER FOURTEEN
"Mexico" by James Taylor

CHAPTER FIFTEEN
"Ivory and Ebony" was written in 1982

CHAPTER SEVENTEEN
"Me and Bobby McGee" written by Kris Kristofferson, sung by Canadian Gordon Lightfoot. Recorded by Janis Joplin (a few days before her heroin drug overdose), October 1970.

CHAPTER EIGHTEEN
"Killing Me Softly with his Song" written by Charles Fox and Norman Gimbal, sung by Roberta Flack

CHAPTER NINETEEN
"Last Night I Had the Strangest Dream" written by Ed McCurdy,1950. Played by Joan Baez, by Pete Seeger and many others.

The Phoenix of Hiroshima.
https://en.wikipedia.org/wiki/Phoenix of Hiroshima.
"Why Restore the Phoenix?"
https://phoenixofhiroshima.org/2017/09/06/why-restore-the-phoenix-2/

CHAPTER TWENTY
"El Condor Pasa" by Simon & Garfunkel in 1970.

"Jesus Loves Me" Top Praise and Worship Songs 2018. An original poem by Ann Bartlett Warner, 1860. William Bradbury set it to music in 1862.

CHAPTER TWENTY-ONE
"Like a Rolling Stone" by Bob Dylan in 1965

CHAPTER TWENTY-FOUR
"It Ain't Me Babe" by Bob Dylan in 1964

CHAPTER TWENTY-FIVE
"The Sound of Silence" by Simon of Simon and Garfunkel in 1966

CHAPTER TWENTY-SEVEN
"Hallelujah," written by Leonard Cohen, sung by Jeff Buckley
Hebrews 6:17-18 NIV Bible

CHAPTER TWENTY-EIGHT
Mathew 21:22 NIV Bible
Mark 11:22–24 NIV Bible
"Ballad of Easy Rider" by the Byrds in 1969

CHAPTER TWENTY-NINE
Angelou, Maya, AZQuotes,
"Bridge Over Troubled Waters" by Simon and Garfunkel in 1969

CHAPTER THIRTY-TWO
"Those Were the Days" by Mary Hopkin in 1968. The original song "Dorogoidlinnoyu" (1900–1948) is credited to Gene Raskin.

Made in the USA
Columbia, SC
03 July 2022